Beyond Nova

by

Prudence MacLeod

Book three of the Nova Series
Second Edition

I0549655

Abandoned Secrets

All governments keep secrets, dread secrets. Secrets they do not want the general populace to know. Out at the very tip of the galaxy lies a secret, a secret well kept and then abandoned. Out beyond Nova lies Exile; where failures are buried deep.

GORDA SLOWLY STRUGGLED out of the downed ship; Zartah close behind him. "Was that exciting enough for you, Zartah?" he asked as he helped haul his friend from the smoking ruin of what was once a small fighter ship. They clambered away looking for cover, but the ship didn't explode.

Zartah put his back against a boulder and sank slowly to the ground. "That was a wild ride all right, Gorda. Any idea what hit us?"

"None, but I'm willing to bet it wasn't any random natural occurrence. We were shot down by an energy beam of some sort."

"Oh yeah, indeed we were shot down. What say we leg it out of here before whoever sent us the welcome comes looking for this ship."

"Agreed, my friend. Let's go." They headed into the forest, climbing steadily up the steep ridge. Zartah, knowing he was crashing and that he'd been shot down, had managed to steer the wounded ship into some difficult terrain. The idea was to slow down the enemy as much as possible while making an escape.

His comm unit crackled, sputtered, and then a voice came through. "Micha to Zartah, come in Zartah."

"Zartah here, Boss."

"Status?"

"We're alive and in relatively good shape, but the ship's lost."

1

"Extraction?"

"No, Boss, we're here, we might as well continue the mission. We were shot down though; I don't think we should leave that ship for an enemy to find and scavenge."

"Agreed. You clear?"

"Well clear, Boss."

"Zartah, report in every twelve hours, ship's time. You miss a report we'll come in. Call if you need anything."

"Understood, Boss. Zartah out." A moment later they heard the scream of an incoming shell. The remains of their poor battered ship were obliterated in the blast.

As the echo of the explosion faded, Gorda looked at Zartah and grinned. "Well, First Man, we have an entire planet to search for a single person. Where should we start?"

"Well, somebody shot us down, let's start by asking them."

"That sounds like a sensible plan to me. They'll surely come to investigate the blast; we could ask them then," chuckled Gorda.

They headed back towards the site of their less than elegant landing and found a vantage point where they could see the area and debris from their doomed ship. "Gorda, my old friend, how do we keep getting into these messes anyway?"

"It's all your fault, you keep asking for excitement."

"I guess I do at that," grinned Zartah. "Who could have guessed the day Lady Marla showed up that it would turn out like this."

———◦———

THE ARRIVAL OF THE Viceroy's flagship bearing Lady Marla, High Priestess of the Temple of Borealis and all the Borelian Free Alliance, had generated a lot of excitement on Nova Prime. The new colony was thriving and with two powerful witches, as well as the dreaded Nova Crew, to defend them, slavers and raiders had stayed well away. However, the sudden unexpected arrival of the High Priestess herself meant something big was up.

Edie straightened up and eased the kinks from her back. They had just finished setting the last of the seedlings and she was smiling with delight. She might be a hardened warrior, but at heart Edie was still a farmer's mate. She blushed softly as she noticed Micha smiling at her, the love clear in his eyes. "Edie, you're so beautiful; I love watching you work the fields."

"You like looking at my backside, and you're not leaving me here alone. Forget it, Micha."

"What are you talking about, my lover?" Micha would try, but he already knew better. Lady Marla's arrival could only mean trouble. Trouble she would need a mercenary crew to solve. Edie knew it too. She'd stand at his side no matter what danger it put her in.

"You know very well that was Lady Marla's shuttle that landed. The Viceroy brought her himself. That means trouble, and trouble means a job for the crew. You call them in while I go clean up."

"Yes, Boss," he grinned.

"Yes I am, and don't you forget it," she replied tartly. She laughed as she marched away towards their small cottage, putting some extra sway in her stride for his benefit.

Micha watched her go for a moment, a warm smile on his young face, then pulled his communicator from his pocket and clipped it on his shoulder. "Micha to Crew, ready and man the ships just in case."

"Already on it, Boss," came Zartah's voice.

Micha grinned and headed for the cottage. He reached for the comm again then let his arm fall away. The farmer he wanted was already walking towards him. "Looks like you might be heading out," called the young fellow. "Does this mean I'll get no rest this season?"

"We've got it planted for you, Abel; what more do you want?"

"Well I guess I can watch it grow for you." He stopped as he reached Micha and became serious. "I'll keep the farm for you, Micha. Just remember to come back to it before harvest."

"I'm hoping I won't have to leave at all, but I've got a bad feeling about this. Thanks, Abel." Just then his comm squawked:

"Micha, we need you at the temple."

"On my way, Lessa."

———— ◈ ————

MICHA WAS MET AT THE temple steps by Lady Arlessa herself. "This can't be good," he thought to himself as she turned and led him into the building. They arrived at her office to find Brenna, Viceroy Lortax, and Lady Marla waiting with Lady Norlene. "So, where am I going and am I likely to come back?"

"That's what we love best about you, Micha," laughed Brenna. "Straight to the point."

"I'll lay it out for you, Micha," said Lady Marla. "Viceroy Lortax was going through some of his predecessor's files and made a terrible discovery. Do you know of, or have you ever heard of, Exile?"

"I know the meaning of the word, Lady, but I assume that's not what you mean."

"Correct. Exile is a planetary system out beyond the Galactic Rim. It is three systems beyond Nova."

"Lady there are only two systems beyond Nova."

"There is another, even farther out, Micha. Apparently, the old CEO of RIM Inc. used it to exile his political enemies. When O'Loran took over he continued the practice for a time. The former Viceroy was in charge of maintaining the prison, a task which he ignored for the most part. He simply dumped the prisoners there and forgot about them."

Micha just nodded and waited for her to continue. "When I made the sacrifice, my younger brother objected. As soon as the inhibitor was placed on my head he disappeared."

"He was sent to Exile?"

"We believe so, Micha," said Lortax.

"Do you have reason to believe he is still alive?"

"None," sighed Marla. "I only have hope."

"You want me to find him?"

"If possible," said Lortax. "Micha, he's Nara Clan; we're bound to help him. He's committed no crime against the Clans."

"How will I identify him?"

"This is our best guess of how he would look now, Micha," said Marla as she passed a vid screen to him. "He was still a boy when he was taken. His name is Kathan of Borealis Three, Nara Clan."

"Lessa?"

"I'll be ready to travel in a flash, Micha, if you decide to take the job."

"I'll pay your standard fee, Micha," declared Marla.

"I can't make any promises, Lady. I can only promise to do my best."

"Understood. Thank you, Micha. I know you were looking forward to a full season on the farm. I owe you one."

"It is always good to have the High Priestess owe you a favor," he grinned as he reached for his comm. "Zartah."

"Here, Boss. One ship or two?"

"One ship, but I want our Arcalian fighters on board."

"Understood."

Micha thought for a moment then went to his comm again. "Siemon Darks."

"Here, Boss."

You and your men will stay here with Lady Norlene to keep an eye on Nova."

"Understood."

"All right, Lady Norlene, should I leave Gorda here in command of the cyborgs?"

"I've warned you before about teasing an old witch, young Micha," she grinned, shaking a threatening finger at him. "Get out of here and get to work."

"Yes Ma'am," he smiled as he rose to his feet. Lessa and Brenna had already vanished.

Norlene reached out and gently laid a hand on Micha's arm. He turned to see the concern in her eyes. "Bring him back in one piece, Micha."

"Understood." He nodded as he gently patted the hand on his arm.

Micha made his way to the ship. It was the prototype intruder class Rathbone had acquired from the emperor. She had been renamed the Defender. "We set?"

"Set, Boss," replied Zartah.

"Take her up, Gorda. Standard orbit then we'll plan the mission before heading out. Put her on auto, then join us in the mess. This part always makes me hungry." He walked off the bridge, grinning at the laughter that followed him. He felt the ship rise beneath his feet then smooth out. A short while later the crew was gathered in the mess hall. Jip, as usual, was making the rounds, looking for snacks. Edie reached down to scratch behind a floppy ear.

"All here, Boss," grinned Zartah. "What have we got? There's not a lot of call for mercenaries these days."

Micha laid it out for them. He was a bit surprised that even Zartah's usual exuberance was dampened. "That's the mission, Crew. Options? Opinions?"

"Turn down the job, Boss," said Gorda quietly.

"Second that," agreed Zartah.

Micha was actually startled at the reluctance of his two most senior warriors. He sighed deeply and leaned back in his seat. "Can't boys. The man's Nara Clan and the Chieftain says go. Talk to me, Gorda."

"Just a few things I heard while in prison as a boy, Boss. I heard a man screaming in terror as he was dragged away. I asked one of the guards about it. He said the guy was being sent to Exile. He said it's a place out beyond the edge of the galaxy; a lone star system drifting away. He said nobody comes back from Exile. All the guards used to beg for the chance to go on that trip. It takes weeks and then they retire on Elliston with full pay for life. The thing is, even the guards who take that trip are never heard from again."

"Zartah?"

"I heard much the same thing. Point is, Boss, that system is drifting away and it's pretty far out there. Anything goes wrong, we might never get back. I'll confess that idea makes me a bit nervous."

Micha nodded but didn't say a word for a moment. Finally he spoke again. "Rathbone, tell me nothing will go wrong with the ship."

"Nothing will go wrong with the ship, Boss," chuckled the big cyborg. "I've brought spare parts for every vital system."

"Keira, are we fully armed?" She smiled and nodded.

"Provisions, Jorge?"

"As much food and water as we can carry, Micha. We could feed a full crew for months."

"All right, Lessa, we're ready to go, now tell us what you didn't want to tell me before we lifted off."

"Micha, are you suggesting I would withhold information vital to the mission of my crew?"

"Ena, is Lessa holding back?"

"Yes she is, Micha," grinned Ena.

"All right, I'll talk," sighed Lessa as she reached for Brenna's hand. "I have another reason for wanting to accept this job. In the years I was running from the old Viceroy I ended up in many strange places and learned some very unusual things. I learned of a planet where the failed genetic experiments of a secret Company lab were disposed of.

"The company had been experimenting for generations trying to breed super soldiers. They failed. The malformed mutants they created were shipped out in secret and dumped on a lonely planet far from the hub worlds."

"Exile," sighed Murtah.

"Yes," said Lessa. "Exile. Political prisoners were dumped there as well. Actually, I found there are two planets there. Wealthy prisoners were sent to one, the rest to Exile. I assume the wealthy got the more tolerable prison."

"So you want to see this for yourself, to see if there is anything you can do to help those unfortunate mutants."

"Yes, if any of them have survived. Perhaps I can heal some of them, or... I don't know, Micha, but I feel compelled to try."

Micha was silent for a moment. Edie squeezed his shoulder, knowing how he hated to put his friends in danger, but knowing he would anyway. "Anything further?" he asked at length.

"Ah, hells," sighed Zartah as he rose to his feet. "Let's do it. It should be exciting."

There was a round of laughter at that and Micha grinned with pride. His crew might have a few reservations about the job, but they wouldn't hold back. "Any questions?" asked Micha.

"Can I fly the first leg, Boss," grinned Jorge. "I always wanted to fly a ship this size."

"All right, Jorge, you're up. Set course for FarStar. We'll be able to get our bearings from there."

The crew filed out to their respective stations. Jorge grinning like a kid in a candy store, headed to the pilot's chair. "FarStar," muttered Micha. "First we fly out to the very tip, the last star on the galactic arm, and then we go out to deep space looking for a ghost planet, a rumor."

"It could be worse," smiled Edie, as she linked her arm through his. "Oh?"

"Zartah could get bored."

"Yep, that would be worse," he chuckled, as he settled into the captain's chair.

Two weeks later they reached FarStar, a small star with six planets, none inhabitable. There was a marker satellite beaming a constant warning to go back. Lessa leaned over Jorge's shoulder and tapped in the heading. It was straight out from the galaxy. He set the course and the ship turned into the new heading, but didn't move.

"Nothing out there on sensors, Boss," said Murtah as he stared at the screen before him.

"Lessa?"

"That's the heading Lortax gave me, Micha."

"Jorge, one half speed for one day then full stop and hold. If we don't see anything then we go back."

"Aye, Captain," sighed Jorge as he engaged the engines.

No one spoke, if fact they hardly breathed as the minutes slowly ticked by with nothing appearing on the screens. Eventually they succumbed to the boredom and went to rest. It was mid-day the next when Jorge brought the ship to a full stop.

Micha was in the Captain's chair again. "Murtah?"

"Nothing there, Micha," he replied as he gazed at the sensor screen.

"Behind us? Still see FarStar?"

"Very clear."

"All right, Jorge, half speed, one more day." Micha rose and headed for the mess. Waiting always made him hungry.

"Aye, Boss. One more day, half speed."

Another day of silent tension passed then Jorge stopped the ship again. "Murtah?"

"Yes. There's a star out there, but just barely visible on sensors."

"FarStar?"

"Still there, but barely detectable."

"Jorge, continue on heading, three quarter speed."

"Aye, Boss. Three quarter speed." Murtah flicked the image up onto the large screen and they all watched as the lonely star slowly grew in the view. The next day they arrived.

There were ten planets around the dwarf star, but most were just rocks without atmosphere. Three seemed like possibles.

"Well, I'll be damned; there is something out here after all," muttered Micha. "Anything on sensors, Murtah?"

"There's life on two of the planets, Boss. Looks like they were terraformed at one time."

"Which one, Lessa?"

"I don't know, Micha."

"All right crew, I guess we'll have to look them over. Rathbone, you and Keira take a small fighter and check out the nearest planet. "We'll drop scouts off at the next one and come back to pick you up."

"On our way," signaled Keira. They hurried away and soon a small fighter ship dropped out into space.

"Ship's away, Boss."

"All right, Jorge. Move us over to the next one. Zartah, you and Gorda want to go down for a look?"

"Oh yes, indeed. Come on, Gorda, this'll be exciting."

"Oh, wonderful," groused Gorda as he winked at Micha.

"I've still got a bad feeling about this," sighed Micha as the small fighter ship dropped out of the belly of the Defender. He watched the screen as the craft descended into the atmosphere. A few moments later he heard the call on comms.

"We're under fire! Dammit, we've been hit. I'm losing control. We're going in hot! Hang on, Gorda."

"Zartah, Zartah, come in." There was nothing but static on comms.

Having a Look Around

Miriam was torn. Her father's teaching demanded she investigate and look for survivors, but her instincts said run far away; the Insiders would be coming, Hunters with hellhounds. That was an awfully big explosion and even if there were survivors, they would only reject her. She sighed deeply, then stomped her foot in annoyance. Her father's teachings had won out.

Sweeping up her favorite spear, she set out in the general direction of the explosion. Traveling swiftly but silently, she made her way past the encampment of the Outliers. A short while later she paused and waited quietly for three Muties to pass. They knew she was there and they knew her. They nodded their appreciation of her respect and continued on their way. Miriam ran onwards.

It was late in the day when she sensed the Insiders. They were near. She tested the breeze and caught two different scents. There were indeed survivors. Had they been captured yet she wondered? Miriam decided to find out. If she could warn them in time perhaps she would be able to thwart the Insiders for a change. She grinned with delight at that prospect.

Slipping around downwind, Miriam soon located the two survivors. They were hidden well back from the blast site, watching the Insiders approach. She slipped in behind them and put the stone tip of her spear at the throat of the closest one. He didn't move; he didn't even flinch.

ZARTAH HEARD A SOFT noise behind them. Without the witch's enhancements he could not have heard it at all. He met Gorda's eyes and saw that Gorda was aware of their company as well. Neither man moved, but Zartah was able to watch the small woman sneak up on them by using the reflection in his blaster. He was completely still as she put the spear to his neck.

"Relax, Woman," he said softly, "we're friendly."

Startled, she froze, but swiftly regained her composure. How had he known she was there? Putting her finger to her lips for silence, she gestured for them to follow her away. Zartah shook his head and gave her his best smile. "We're looking for a friend. We need to ask those folks if they've seen him."

Again, she cautioned silence. She pointed to the oncoming Insiders then pointed to Zartah and made a slashing motion across her throat. She slipped silently back into the trees, gesturing for them to follow her. Zartah looked at Gorda who just shrugged. It was the First Man's decision. Zartah grinned and followed the strange little woman. There was something about her that instantly intrigued him.

Suddenly there was a long wailing cry from behind them. Miriam leaped ahead and ran through the forest as fast as she dared. She was somewhat startled to find both men keeping the pace. She found the wide trail and raced away. They ran easily with her, much to her surprise. What manner of men were these who could keep up with her, a Mutie?

With the sounds of pursuit getting closer, Miriam veered off the trail and headed straight to a high rock face. The hellhounds couldn't climb and neither could the horses. Unfortunately, on the rock face they would be vulnerable to the arrows. The hounds were too close anyway, there was no time to climb; Miriam turned to fight, placing herself between the two men and the charging beasts.

The maddened hounds leaped at her, their jaws slavering, sharp fangs reaching for her, but suddenly the two men were between her and the hounds. Their weapons fired with hissing noises and the hounds were hurled away to lie unconscious on the ground. The two riders charged in, loosing arrows, but the strangers moved with blinding speed, batting aside the deadly missiles.

The riders dropped the bows and whipped out long bladed weapons as they bore down on the two men. Again Miriam was amazed as the men avoided the weapons and hauled the riders from their mounts. The riders gained their feet and attacked with the blades, but they had never faced opponents like these before. In mere moments one rider was dead and the other was held helpless.

"Easy, Gorda, mine's dead. I want to ask that one about our friend." Zartah pulled a small vid screen from his pocket and showed it to the man. There was no sign of understanding as Zartah asked if this face was familiar. The man simply tried to bite him and kick at him. Zartah sighed and put away the screen. He nodded and Gorda gave a hard twist of his arm. There was a cracking sound and the man in his arms went limp.

Suddenly Miriam's arm snapped forward and her spear whistled past Zartah's head, barely missing him. Startled, he turned to her, and then turned to see where she was looking. There lay one of the hellhounds, her spear sticking completely through its body. The other two beasts were awake and attacking now, but Zartah dispatched them with his strange weapon. He nudged the one she'd killed with his foot then pulled out the spear. He cleaned it on the animal's hide then passed it back to her with a smile and a wink.

Miriam turned away, blushing. She was tingling inside at this giant's approval and didn't like it. He was teasing the ugly Mutie, and it hurt more than she would like to admit to herself. She snarled and led them back onto the wide trail and away from the scene of the carnage. Miriam was angry with herself for the delight she had experienced at his smile and wink of approval.

Puzzled by her response, Zartah followed, but left her to her own thoughts. He knew better than to badger an angry woman with questions. Perhaps when she had cooled off he would ask what he had done to offend her. This small girl had been ready to sell her life to give them time to climb the rock face. That was an act of extreme courage and he wanted to know more about her.

Darkness began to fall, and she stopped near a small stream. The two men still seemed at ease, but Miriam was tired. They'd camp here, then proceed when it became light. She would take them to the Outers, then they would no longer be her responsibility. The nearness of the big man was giving her strange feelings and she needed to get away.

Miriam was startled when he offered to share his food. Humans didn't share with Muties. He insisted so she tasted the strange bar he had given her. It was chewy, but sweet and she liked it. She was chewing thoughtfully and watching as he talked to the thing on his shoulder and it talked back. That must be what Father had described as a comm unit.

"Zartah to Defender, come in Defender."

"Defender here, Zartah," replied a woman's voice.

"Nothing of interest to report; I'll check in again at daybreak."

"Understood. Defender out!"

Miriam had her finger to her lips again to shush him, but he was looking at the sky. She was startled to see fear in his eyes.

"Gorda."

"I know, Zartah, no stars. It gives me the creeps too."

"I'll take first watch," said Zartah, as he tore his gaze away from the empty sky. Gorda nodded then lay back against a tree and closed his eyes.

The big man turned to Miriam and his eyes were warm and friendly once again, his ready smile hinting at mischief. He tossed her another food bar then gestured to Gorda. "Get some rest, girl. You've earned it. I'll take first watch."

Miriam was startled and unsure. He would watch? He would protect her sleep? They had defended her against the hounds, but could she trust? Maybe they didn't know she was a Mutie; they were newly arrived after all. She was so very tired, she decided to chance it. Curling up a respectful distance from Gorda, she went to sleep.

Miriam awakened to bird song and the scent of the big man strong in her nose. She was warm, covered in something, and her head was pillowed on something hard that moved. She could feel the blood pulsing through that which pillowed her head. It was the big man's leg, and his heavy jacket covered her like a blanket.

It was daylight; she had slept the night away while the men watched. Humans had watched while a Mutie slept; more, they had warmed her. What manner of humans were these? Her reverie was broken as he shifted his weight then spoke softly. "Awake, beautiful lady?"

She looked up to see his warm smile and laughing eyes. A thrill ran through her even as the sting of his words pierced her heart. She leaped to her feet and thrust his jacket at him them stormed away to relieve herself.

"You are definitely losing your touch," chuckled Gorda.

"Shut up, Gorda," sighed Zartah as he reached for his comm unit. "Zartah to Defender."

"Micha here."

"We've acquired a local guide and are proceeding with the search."

"Understood. Good luck. Micha out."

Miriam returned just as Zartah slipped into the woods to relieve himself. She was fussing impatiently when he returned. Zartah gazed at her completely besotted. She was no taller than Brenna, but she carried considerably more muscle. Her skin was pale, almost white but covered with freckles; he'd never seen anyone like her before. Even Arlessa's skin wasn't this pale.

He gazed at her with lust in his eyes as he took in her perfect proportions, small breasts, tight waist, and full hips. She had a perfect mouth and blue green eyes; Zartah would have sold himself into slavery just to see her smile at him. "I'm ready to go, pretty lady," he said, giving her his best smile.

Miriam blushed furiously under that gaze and angrily turned away. It wasn't just. He made her feel strange, empty and full at the same time, but he kept insulting her. Tears ran down her face as she turned away and ran. After a few moments she stopped running; they had not followed.

Why hadn't they followed? Had something happened to them? A sarag? No, she's smelled or heard no predators. Perhaps the big man was tiring of the game and just wanted to be rid of her. That thought hurt more than Miriam could have imagined. She turned back cautiously.

"You going after her?" asked Gorda.

"I'm hoping she'll come back. Gorda, I know we have a mission and we need to get going on that..."

"But this girl has you all turned around and upside down," laughed Gorda. "The mighty Zartah has been brought low at last, and by a slip of a girl who won't talk to him."

"Kind of sad isn't it?" sighed Zartah. "My old Granny had a touch of the witch sight in her. She once told me I'd meet a boy/man at the temple and follow him for the rest of my life. I laughed at her. Then she told me I'd meet a strange woman on a world that doesn't exist, and she'd be my mate. Danged if I don't think she was right again."

"Maybe she was right, but you're talking to the man who has fallen for the Black Witch of legend, a woman out of the past, lost in time. I'll see your sad and raise you one."

"We're a fine pair, we are, Gorda," laughed Zartah. "What am I going to do? The woman sets my blood on fire, and I can't think straight. Worse, every time I open my mouth, she gets mad and runs away. I just wish I knew why."

"I run because you say insulting and hurtful things," said a sweet lilting voice. Zartah turned to see her standing a safe distance away. "I see you are shocked that the Mutie can speak. Yes, I am a fully trained animal, I can speak and everything." Once again she turned and fled.

Miriam didn't get far this time. Zartah overtook her easily and caught her arm. She turned and fought. She fought with all her skills, landing blows that would have felled a normal human. The big man ignored her blows. He caught her hands and turned her around. She tried kicking at him, but he fell backwards, landing hard with her atop him.

He had her arms and legs pinned and held her as she struggled. When she finally lay still, he relaxed his arms slightly. His grip was no longer restraining her, it was holding her gently. Miriam sensed the change and squirmed onto her stomach so she could see his face. There were tears in his eyes. His arms tightened around her slightly as he spoke softly. "Girl, please talk to me and listen. Will you do that for me?"

"I will listen," she whispered. The nearness of him was overwhelming her senses and her body felt like it was on fire.

"Girl, I'm new to your world. There are many things I don't know, and I need your help to understand. I also need you to hear, and believe me, when I say I will never do or say anything to deliberately hurt you; not ever. Do you understand?"

Miriam gazed into his eyes and felt the truth of his words. "I believe you."

He gently held her face in his huge hands and smiled. "You are a beautiful woman, beautiful beyond words." She stiffened, but he held her until she met his gaze. "I mean that."

"Those are words humans use to tease and mock the Mutie females. They say these things with disgust and derision in their voices, sneers on their lips," she said, not making eye contact. Again he touched her face and gently pulled her gaze back to his.

"I say these things to you so you will understand how my eyes see you." Her cheek burned under his touch and her body was responding to him in that pleasurable way. Miriam blushed furiously then shrieked as he easily rose to his feet with her still in his arms.

Zartah stood her on a boulder so she was at eye level with him. "Tell me your name."

"I'm Miriam," she replied, still blushing and in no hurry at all to move away from him. He was still holding her gently and she liked that more than she should.

"Miriam, I'm Zartah of Nova, Nara Clan, and first man of Nova Crew." Her eyes widened as he spoke. He had given her his full name, his clan, and his position in life. He had treated her as a full human. "Miriam, explain Mutie to me. What does it mean, and how does that affect you?"

"I'm a Mutie," she replied, her eyes downcast. She tried to escape again, but he held her gently.

"Please go on."

"Mutie, mutant, not born of human, made in a laboratory, or born of a Mutie; that's its meaning. My mother was made in a lab. She was made from ancient DNA from a pre-human subspecies and human DNA mix. She was smarter than they thought, and she escaped. My father loved her, and she bore me, a Mutie. I was young when the Insiders came and she was killed.

"Father protected me until he was taken by the Insiders. Since then I have done what I can to protect the humans even though they despise me. I know I can't have a mate because I would make a Mutie baby, and I don't want this life for anyone."

"I can promise you will not have a mutated baby."

"How can you make a promise like that?"

"There is a witch of great and terrible power who is also the greatest healer in the galaxy. She's a friend, and if I ask her to make sure my mate's baby is healthy and whole, I'm certain she'll do so."

"Are you so sure... your mate? What are you saying? You want to mate with me?"

"May the gods help me, yes I do," he chuckled. "Miriam, I've never met your equal. If you accept me I swear I'll do all in my power to protect you, to love you, and to make your life better. I swear I will always be respectful of you, and gentle with you. Will you accept me?"

She gazed into his eyes for a long moment. He was sincere and she wanted desperately for what he said to be true. Could she trust him? He had already proven himself willing and able to defend her, he spoke to her as an equal, and he had been gentle with her even when she was trying to hurt him to escape. Miriam was desperate for any chance for a better life. What this man offered was so much more, but dare she trust?

"You make me feel strange inside," she said at last. "Father said it would be so when I found my true mate. I will be your mate for as long as you keep that promise."

"Then you're mine forever," he breathed into her hair as he hugged her tightly. Tentatively, she returned the hug.

Suddenly Gorda came pounding along the trail. "Save it for later family, we've got incoming."

A New Life

"Who, where?"

"Riders like yesterday. Too many."

Zartah spun back to Miriam. "Lead us to a safe place."

She was gone like a shot from a bow, Gorda and her new mate close behind. She led them from the trail into the dense forest. It was hard going for the two big men, but it would be impossible for the riders. Only the hellhounds could follow. Miriam could hear them baying as they found the trail.

She and her companions burst from the forest into an open area with a waterfall. Miriam didn't hesitate, but leaped into the fast moving stream and pushed her way through the heavy cascade. There was a cave behind, and light filtered down from above to cast an eerie glow to the deep cavern. She hurried along, both men close behind her.

They rounded a turn in the cave and found a much brighter room. heavy vines hanging down from an opening high above. Without hesitation Miriam scrambled up and out of the cave. She spun to see if they could follow and was surprised to see them climbing hand over hand until they hauled themselves out beside her.

"We're safe here for now," she said, as she cast her gaze all round to be sure they were alone.

"So did you two kiss and make up?" asked Gorda.

"We were getting there," chuckled Zartah, "but then you came alone and broke the mood. Miriam, this man is Gorda of Nova crew, Nara Clan. He's my best friend and has been for many years. Gorda, this woman is my mate, Miriam of the Forest and now of Nara Clan."

Miriam gave a small gasp; he had named her his mate and a member of his clan. All Father's teachings said she must aid and protect her clan, but the clan would do the same for her. If it was true then both these men were bound to protect her. Her world had suddenly changed.

"What is it, Miriam?" asked Zartah as he noticed the thoughtful look on her face.

"Father said you would come. He said this world would see a change when you got here. He looked to the sky for you every day, but no one came. From all Father told me, I was expecting more people."

"Your father said who would come?" asked Gorda.

"The warriors of Nara Clan."

"Your father was Nara Clan?" exclaimed Zartah. "Did he look anything like this man?"

Miriam looked at the face, but she did not recognize it. She shook her head. "No, this man was not father."

"Ah well, it was too much to hope for," sighed Zartah.

"We should be moving," said Miriam. "You asked for a place of safety, but no such thing exists here, just temporary respites. Even now I can hear the hounds searching the winds for our scent. It won't take them long to find us."

"Gorda, what do you think? Is it time for a new approach?"

"I'd say so. We're getting nowhere fast this way."

"Miriam, we need to get a lot more information about this world, will you help us?"

"Of course I will. Zartah, you're my mate by your own choice, you can ask me whatever you want. First we should find a better place to hide. I can hear the hounds searching this side of the river now. The Riders won't be far behind."

"Lead on, fair lady," he grinned. She trotted away through the forest with the two men close behind.

They hadn't gone far when they came to a place where the trail widened and intersected with another. There were three creatures headed towards them. Miriam stopped and lowered her head. The creature in front nodded to her and she growled in her throat, made a grasping motion with her hand, and then pointed behind her group. The strangers nodded and picked up their pace. Once they had passed Miriam led the men along the path.

"What happened back there?" asked Zartah as he trotted along beside her. "What were those things?"

"Those *things* were Muties," she replied, as she picked up the pace.

Zartah easily matched speed with her. "I apologize, Miriam. I chose my words poorly. Can I try again?" She just looked at him and nodded. He took her arm and gently pulled her to a stop facing him. "Who were those people we just encountered?" he asked gently.

"They're Muties," she replied, avoiding his eyes. "Father taught me to show them respect even thought everyone else reviles and abuses them. We respectfully let them pass rather than chase them from the path. I warned them of the hounds and hunters. They'll distract them for us.

"You're from beyond the skies, Zartah, and wise in the ways of your people. However, the ways of Exile are very different. Come, we should hurry."

She led them on through a maze of trails that she seemed to know well. The day was wearing on when they stopped to eat. Miriam was chewing thoughtfully on a protein bar when Zartah spoke again. "Miriam, where are you taking us?"

She looked at him and smiled then moved closer. She had accepted him as mate, and she knew what all that meant. She just hoped he would be gentle with her as her father had been with her mother. Miriam had seen too many men who were not gentle, but she'd managed to avoid them.

"Zartah, you asked me to take you to a safe place. There is none; safety can best be achieved by constant movement and avoiding the humans as well as the hunters and hounds. You're trying to find your friend. I thought to take you to as many human camps as possible to see if anyone knows him."

"That's good thinking, girl," smiled Gorda.

"Ship to Zartah," squawked his comm unit.

"Zartah here, Boss."

"Report."

"We spent the day escaping from enemies. Boss, I'm thinking we need to come back to the ship and make some plans. We're about out of supplies and I want to introduce Miriam to the family."

"Who is Miriam, Zartah?" came a woman's voice.

"Miriam is my bonded mate, Lady Arlessa."

"Dammit, Zartah, I sent you down there to find a man, not to chase girls." There was warmth and laughter in that voice and Miriam smiled to hear it.

"Sorry, Boss, but I couldn't help myself."

Suddenly the voice went hard and cold again. "Hold." There were a few moments silence then it returned. "Zartah, can you hold through the night?"

"Not a problem, Boss."

"Do it. Micha out."

"All right, Miriam my love, find us a place to snuggle down for the night."

"Do you wish to speak with other humans first? There's enough daylight left to reach their camp. They will keep you safe for the night and I'll be nearby to watch."

"Miriam, wherever I rest tonight, you'll be in my arms, is that clear?" The gentleness of his voice and his boyish smile took the edge from his words.

"Understood, my mate," she blushed softly. "We'll be safe enough near their camp. Come."

Miriam led them first to a stream, then along a well-worn path to a cavern with a fire burning at its mouth. Several ragged humans were gathered around that fire. They leaped to their feet and grabbed crude weapons as strangers approached.

"Stop right there," demanded one young man as he stepped toward them. "I see the Mutie has brought you here, but we don't need or want you. Get away and take that thing with you." Zartah's fist sent him flying back to land with a thud near the fire where he laid twitching and groaning as he nursed his jaw.

"Who commands here?" demanded Zartah.

"I'm leader here," said an elderly man as he approached cautiously.

"Inform your people that this woman is Miriam of Nara Clan, hand mate to Zartah of Nova Crew, Nara Clan. She is to be treated respectfully or I will not be happy, understood?"

"They get the message, Borelian," chuckled the old fellow. "You're carrying weapons. That tells me you weren't brought her as prisoners but came of your own will. Nevertheless, you were shot down and the charge in your blasters won't last forever. Mating with the M..., Miriam, was wise. She can keep you alive and out of the hands of the hunters.

"Since you came this far out on your own you must've come with a purpose. Perhaps we can help you in exchange for a ride back to civilization. You didn't get here in that small ship; you've got something a lot bigger up there or I don't know the Borelians."

"We have a ship, but it'll be up to the boss if we take passengers or not."

"Fair enough; why have you come?"

"We're looking for Kathan of Borealis Three. He was only a boy when he was sent here. We think he would look like this now."

Gorda passed over the tablet with the picture on it. The man shook his head then passed it around. One old woman stared at it for a long time then spoke hesitantly. "I can't be certain, but there was a boy here for a while a long time ago. It could have been him. He said his name was Kat. I remember he had a bad head injury. The hunters got him, and he was taken slave."

"Where would they take him?" asked Zartah.

"To the compound," replied the old leader. "They keep slaves, mutant slaves, trade them with other compounds as well as off-world."

"Off-world?"

"There is another planet where wealthy exiles have managed to set up great palaces. They own the compounds here. They gather slaves to work their fields."

"What shot us down?"

"Crude energy weapons. They shoot down any ship that doesn't broadcast the codes of the compound's owners. You aren't familiar with the ways of this planet, Borelian. Trust me when I say you'd be better off to take your mate elsewhere to keep her safe. Muties and Mutie lovers aren't welcome among the tribes."

"The next time I hear that word I'm going to start shooting," said Zartah.

"Come, my Zartah," said Miriam, "You'd have to shoot all the humans in the world. Let's just go to a better place for the night. The hunters will be here soon anyway."

"What??? You've got hunters on your trail, and you came here?"

"No need to thank us," chuckled Gorda, his blaster leaping to his hand. Suddenly the camp was a very busy place as the fire was doused and everything dragged inside the cave. Great stones were pushed across the opening and spear points bristled outwards.

Zartah grinned as he watched then turned to Miriam. "Lead on, my love."

Blushing, she turned and ran, the two men close behind. The trail soon began to climb steeply, then it turned to a narrow ledge on the cliff side. As it became almost too narrow she suddenly disappeared into a cave. They followed close behind then she rolled a huge stone across the trail outside. The two men nodded admiringly at her strength.

"We can have fire for warmth," she said. "The light cannot be seen from above or below. The ledge is the only path into this place. Welcome to my home."

"Cozy," Zartah said admiringly, as he gazed around. There were animal skins, some quite large, smaller pieces of leather, piles and piles of firewood, and a few bags of dried herbs all stacked neatly. There was also a pile of shattered stone and nearby a small stack of spear shafts. "Looks like you haven't been here in a while."

"It's for the rainy season only. If I come too often in warm weather the hounds might pick up the scent. In the times of rain the scent gets washed away and I'm warm and dry; life is good." She was smiling and Zartah was gazing at her like a love-struck teenager. Gorda just grinned and settled down by the fire pit. A moment later he had a cheerful blaze going.

———— ◉ ————

RATHBONE AND KEIRA had barely begun their search of the planet when they spotted a large plantation. Keira brought the small ship in close to the main house and set it down gently. As they stepped out a large man appeared from inside the house. "Welcome, welcome. We don't get a lot of visitors from the rest of the galaxy. You are most welcome. Come inside; come inside."

He ushered them into the large house. It was richly appointed and very comfortable. "Come, we will share food and drink and you can give me all the news of the hub worlds. My name is Delgar of Ramia."

"I'm Rathbone of Nova," smiled Rath, "and this is my hand-mate, Keira."

"Well met and welcome, Rathbone, Keira." He shook the hand of each, but gave Keira a puzzled look.

"Keira can't speak, Delgar. She was injured in the wars."

"Oh, I'm so sorry to hear that, Keira. Please, both of you; come into the study here and sit. Salla!" At his call a tall woman with stooped shoulders entered and knelt before him. She was dressed in a simple shift and sandals with a silvery metal collar around her neck. "Fetch food and drink. The Arcadian special blend for wine, I think." The woman sped away.

"Was that a slave collar?" asked Rathbone.

"Oh yes, all the slaves have to wear one. I have them made on Elliston Prime. They cost a bundle to get them here, but they're well worth it. You see if the slave attempts to remove the collar it inflicts terrible pain. If they run away we can track them by its signal, and they're there writhing in pain when we find them. Those collars are wonderful deterrents.

"Now, it's been years since a ship of the company has arrived. Tell me all the news."

"Well," said Rathbone, "there are only two companies left, the rest have been absorbed."

"Oh my oath, that is startling. Has R.I.M. come to its senses and replaced O'Loran as CEO yet?"

"They tried, but failed. O'Loran has seized complete control of R.I.M. and declared himself Loran the First, Emperor of the Galaxy. He controls all of R.I.M. territory except for sector nine. The Borelian Clans rose up and declared sector nine as the Borelian Free Alliance. For the moment the emperor is playing nice about that.

"The black witch has returned and cleared the atmosphere of Nova Prime. It's being resettled as we speak." At this point the food and drink appeared, carried by four slaves, all wearing the same metallic collar. They drank a toast to happy times then Rath continued. "That brings me to the point of our visit. We're searching for a fellow clansman, Kathan of Borealis Three. We think he'd look like this now."

Rath handed their host the vid tablet. The man's reaction showed he clearly recognized the picture. "Yes," he said at last, "he was a most troublesome slave. He had a very high pain tolerance though. Now, who was it I sold him to? That was a few years ago, after all. Just let me go check my records. Enjoy the food and drink; I'll be back shortly." He rose and swiftly escaped the room.

A few moments later the wine was gone and the food tray empty. It was only then Rathbone realized they'd been drugged. He cursed Delgar soundly as his world began to fade and he toppled to the floor beside Keira.

Rathbone awakened to a blinding headache. He quickly became aware that he was bound, naked, and chained to a wall with a slave collar around his neck. Keira was chained nearby and starting to regain consciousness.

"Ah, welcome back," said Delgar cheerfully. He was standing nearby with several uniformed men beside him. All were heavily armed. "I don't know who you two truly are, but I do have my suspicions. You were far too heavily armed to be mere detectives or kinsmen looking for a fellow clansman. I think you're bounty hunters.

"I think there's a big reward out for Kathan. I think if I can find and return him I can finally earn my way off this rock and go home.

"Torgon, wait until they're fully recovered then take them to the slave pens. Put him to work and use her for a breeder. She can't speak so I won't have to listen to her screaming." With that he marched out and closed the door behind him.

As soon as the door closed the man called Torgon smirked and held up a controller device. He pressed a button and Keira screamed with pain. "Well, how about that," he said. "She can scream after all." Rathbone surged against his chains as Keira hung limply in her bonds, breathing in deep sobs. Torgon smirked again as he hit the button and Rathbone was consumed in fiery pain.

"That's just a small sample of what you can expect if you try anything," said Torgon.

Rathbone hung in his chains, slowly regaining his breath and getting his feet under him again. He looked at Keira who was recovering. "This is getting old, girl." She just nodded and drew in a deep breath. Rath did the same then grabbed the slave collar in both hands. His world exploded in pain.

Taken by surprise, Torgon hesitated for a moment, and then it was too late. He turned the device up to full, but Rathbone had already ripped the collar from his neck and hurled it aside. A heave of his cyborg enhanced muscles and the chain anchors were ripped from the wall. Swinging the chains like a weapon, Rathbone charged. Two men fell instantly; the third had tried to run but ran into Keira. She snapped his neck then ripped away the collar and threw it aside.

They quickly stripped the dead men and dressed in their uniforms. "Are you all right, my love?" Keira gave him a weak smile and kicked Torgon's body before scooping up a weapon. She kissed Rathbone's cheek as she stepped by and cautiously opened the door. From the door of the building they could see the back of the main house and their ship just beyond. Keira motioned to the ship.

Rath shook his head no. "That bastard knows something, and I want to find out what it is. I also want some payback for those damned collars." With a wolfish grin she winked at him then raced for the main house. He was close behind her. They reached the nearest door just as a slave stepped through it.

The man blanched as Rathbone signaled for silence then raised the controller he'd taken from Torgon. The man began to sweat as Rath pressed the button. To the man's great surprise, his collar unlocked and fell away. It took a moment for him to realize that there was no pain, no pain and no collar.

"Take this, my friend," grinned Rathbone. "Free as many as you can."

"Can I lock one on Torgon?" the man asked, returning Rath's grin.

"Torgon is dead," replied Rath.

"Then it's a good day. I owe you, friend. Run swiftly, as far and as fast as you can. He's called in all the troops. There're at least three troop carriers less than a turn away." Rath gave him a friendly slap on the shoulder as he and Keira brushed past and into the house. The newly freed slave sped away towards the fields, the controller clutched tightly in his hand.

"We must be swift," signalled Keira as she leaped to a closed door. She swept it open and Rath leaped through. It was just a pantry and it was empty of people. From room to room they searched, but found only a few slaves. Finally they discovered a small study where their clothes and weapons were laid out for inspection.

They quickly dressed in their own clothes and took up their weapons and comms. The first of the troop carriers had just landed and their own ship was now beyond their reach. "Skeeter," muttered Rath as he watched out the window. Then the alarm sounded. Their host fled the house and joined the troops outside. He and Keira watched as the man gave directions and the troops began to move towards the house.

"Looks like we have to do this the hard way," signalled Keira.

"Don't we always?" he chuckled. "Let's see if we can surprise a few of them."

The troops fanned out, surrounded the house, and took up aggressive positions at the main doors. One officer, obviously the commander, spoke over a loudspeaker. "Escaped slaves, you're surrounded. Come out peacefully and your punishment will be less severe."

"Not much of an incentive, that," muttered Rathbone. Keira giggled and took careful aim out the second story window.

"This is your only chance," continued the commander. "Come out now and save yourselves. Refuse and the pain will be more than you can imagine. If you..." He got no further as Keira squeezed the trigger and a small neat hole appeared in his forehead. He fell slowly to the ground.

At a barked command from their former host the soldiers charged the door and smashed them in. They swarmed through the house, looking for the escaped slaves. Calls of "Clear" rang out as they moved from room to room. Finally, after clearing the main floor they gathered at the base of the stairs to the upper floor.

Cautiously, they began to make their way up the steps. Most of them were already on the stairs, some near the top, when Rath and Keira leaped out and opened fire with blasters. The men in front were hurled back on those behind them and all went tumbling back down in a pile of tangled and injured bodies. Rath put a few shots over their heads for emphasis. They withdrew out the main door.

A second troop carrier was just landing. As the uniformed men came pouring out onto the grass, Delgar spoke to the commander who took charge of the assault. The troops charged the house, several falling to the ground, wounded. Keira was accurate and deadly with that projectile weapon. She could be killing them, but as Rath often said, wound one man and another has to stop to help him. That takes two out of the battle.

The troops poured into the house and up the stairs only to be knocked back again by Rath's blaster. At a shouted command, several men put down covering fire so the rest could safely climb the stairs. When they reached the top, all was quiet. Cautiously, they began to check each room.

Rathbone had fired his blaster then retreated. He and Keira slipped into the laundry chute and dropped to the basement. It was a tight fit and a hard landing, but they made it. A startled female slave was staring at them. Rath winked and motioned for silence. "Hide someplace safe," he said softly. She nodded and hurried out of the room. They followed more cautiously.

They found her waiting just outside the room. "Those steps go to the main floor pantry," she said, pointing to a set of stairs. "Those go out to the slave pens."

"Go to the pens," said Rath. "There should be a man there who can remove your collar. If not, you can always say you fled the gunfire."

She stared at him for a moment with wide eyes. Finally his words sank in. "Thank you," she smiled as she fled to the exit. Rath nodded, then he and Keira began to cautiously climb the stairs to the main floor.

They found the main floor unguarded as everyone believed them to be on the top floor. Grinning, Keira signalled then they slipped outside and around the building. Peeking around the corner of the house Keira could see a few soldiers and Delgar between them and their ship. A few quick signals to Rath and the plan was set. They'd regain their ship, taking Delgar hostage in the process.

They burst around the house and charged towards their ship, but the third troop carrier suddenly appeared. They wouldn't be able to make it. Shouts of alarm sounded from the house as well. Without breaking her strike Keira changed direction and headed for the forest. Rath was right behind her followed by gunfire from the troops.

They gained the trees and vanished from sight. It was nearly dark, and they sought out a safe place to spend the night.

Rath tried the comms, but the signal was being jammed. He sighed and cuddled Keira close. "You sleep, my love, I'll take first watch."

"Shouldn't we attack in the darkness?"

"They'll be expecting that, besides, they'll have the place lit up like a summer's day. We'll hide out for a few days so they think we've fled. Once they relax their guard we'll go back in. First thing we have to do is break that jammer so we can contact Micha. Delgar recognized the face and he knows something. I want to know what that is."

Keira nodded then snuggled closer and laid her head on his chest. She was soon asleep. Rathbone would watch, all his senses alert, and if there was danger she would know it the instant his body tensed. He kissed her hair then laid his head back against the tree and closed his eyes. His hearing would be more useful than his eyes in the darkness.

Rath let her sleep through the night. The empty sky was oppressive and unsettling. No need for Keira to deal with that so soon after the collar. She awakened to the first grey light of dawn. A quick glance told her she had slept the night through. She slapped his shoulder, shook her finger at him then kissed him deeply.

Keira pushed him back against the tree and smiled lovingly. "Sleep now," she signaled, "I'll watch." He returned her loving smile then closed his eyes again. This time he slept.

Rathbone awakened instantly at her touch. He'd managed a few hours rest, but the soldiers were in the trees now, hunting them and all the escaped slaves. Delgar had been incensed when he found the fields and pens empty with a pile of damaged slave collars in the latrine. Rathbone could faintly hear the distant screams of pain.

Quietly, they melted deeper into the forest. Once they were ready for the day they began to circle around, heading back towards the big house and their ship. They couldn't get close as more troops had arrived in the night.

They slipped further back into the trees and tried the comms. They were still being jammed. A swift and silent discussion followed. By mutual agreement they turned their backs on the house and headed deeper into the forest. With luck they could get out of range of the jammer and call Micha. Delgar knew something. Rathbone was certain they were on the right track.

———◆———

FAR ACROSS THE GALAXY, the emperor sat on a troubled throne. His plan had been set in motion; soon he would be engulfed in a war that would consume the galaxy and destroy all civilization, or he would be the unopposed ruler of it all. All except Sector Nine which he would leave for another time. He needed the witch's help; he dare not attack her yet.

"All in good time," he muttered to himself. "All in good time."

A New Plan

Micha paced the bridge, his face impassive, but his mind working at speed. "Talk to us, Micha," said Edie as she stepped into his path and took him into her arms. He squeezed her gently then released her.

"Sorry folks, I'm a bit distracted."

"Edie's right, Micha," smiled Lessa. "Talk it out. Let's get a look at it."

"All right," he sighed. "Here it is. At a time when we should be on Nova we're out here beyond the galactic rim. We've been sent on a wild goose chase, our crew's been divided, Zartah is on the run and Keira's disappeared. I'm not happy about any of it."

"Nor am I," said Lessa. "What do you want to do?"

"I want to gather up the crew and make a new plan. This has gone sideways from the start. I should have gone down myself."

"My love, you sent some of the most capable people alive to gather information for you. Trust them to do their jobs as they would trust you." Edie smiled and kissed his cheek as she spoke.

"They trust me to keep them alive," he sighed, "and it's time I started doing my job." He gave her a gentle squeeze then reached for the comms. He called for Zartah. Zartah was requesting extraction when another call came in. It was Rathbone.

"Defender, this is Rathbone, come in Defender."

Micha could hear weapons firing in the background. "Micha here."

"Boss, we're pinned down defending a group of freed slaves. We have intel, but time's running short. Requesting immediate extraction."

"On our way. Zartah, can you hold through the night?"

They could. "Jorge, get this ship to that second planet."

"I've already got a fix on Rath's comm unit, Boss," replied Jorge. The ship swung around and shot towards the second planet.

"All right folks, man the fighters. Jorge, take her in; pick up Keira and whoever she's got with her. Once you're loaded go for orbit. Make sure Rath and Keira are on the guns. I'm getting tired of being ambushed, I want to send a message. Let's go folks, two to a ship."

Mere moments later the cargo bay doors opened and an Arcalian Royal Fighter led two small Company fighters out into space. Like stooping hawks the dropped into the atmosphere followed by the larger intruder class ship. They all sped straight for the battle zone.

Rathbone grinned as he heard the scream of engines followed by the chatter of weapons fire. He and Keira were huddled on a jumble of boulders with a dozen escaped slaves hiding from the firefight. This crazy man had promised to protect them, and he was doing just that.

His mate was even scarier as she fought, both hand to hand and with weapons. They had appeared and set them free for the second time in two days, then led them away. The big merc and his mate had fought off several bands of slave hunters, but were eventually cornered by superior numbers. That's when he'd called for help. To their great surprise, it came.

The smaller fighters attacked the troops, destroying the transports and driving the men back into the trees. They continued to buzz around while the bigger ship landed and a cargo bay dropped open. Keira led the former slaves into the ship with Rathbone guarding their retreat. He was the last to board.

Rath slapped the control and the big bay doors closed. "Clear," he barked as he slapped the comm unit on the wall. They felt the rush of extra gravity as the big ship leaped skyward again. The inertial dampeners cut in and the artificial gravity won out as the ship cleared the atmosphere.

"Come on folks," grinned Rathbone. "Let's go get you something to eat before the boss gets back." He and Keira led the way to the mess hall. Timidly, the freed slaves followed.

As soon as the Defender rose into the skies Micha called off the fighters and they followed the larger ship into space. The bay doors opened and they flew inside. The doors closed and the air rushed back in. Micha was already out of the ship and hurrying to the bridge. He slapped at the comm unit on his shoulder.

"Jorge, get us back to planet one as fast as you can."

"We're already on course, Boss. Rath and guests are in the mess hall."

"Thanks Jorge." Micha turned down a different passage way and headed for the mess, the rest of the crew right behind him. "Report," he barked as he came through the door.

"We met a man named Delgar," said Rathbone as he rose to his feet. "He offered food, wine, and information. The wine was drugged and we woke up in slave collars. Delgar thinks he can find our man, and he wants to use him to buy his way back into the company's good graces."

"I assume you didn't like the collars, so you took them off," chuckled Micha.

"Of all the nasty things I've encountered over the years, those slave collars are the most vile," growled Rathbone. "Anyway, once we were free of the collars we tried to reacquire Delgar, but he'd already called in the troops. We took down a few, but there were too many and they were jamming our comms.

"We headed into the trees, trying to get outside the range of the jammers. We met up with these good folk there and decided it would be fun to make sure Delgar didn't get them back. Once we made contact, you came. The rest you know."

Micha grinned and turned to the newly freed slaves. "Welcome aboard the Defender," he smiled. "I'm Micha."

"You're the one they called the boss," said one of the women.

"That's right. Folks, we have a mission in this area of space, but as soon as we're finished we'll be happy to take you back to Borealis Three or Nova with us. You can start a new life there.

"Now, you can be a big help to me here and speed up this process. Tell me what you can of Delgar and/or Kathan of Borealis Three."

"He calls himself Kat now," one man said. "He was bought by Delgar years ago. He'd already been maimed on Exile and his mind wasn't quite right. He kept running away, no matter how bad the punishment. He almost seemed to enjoy the pain. One day, a few years ago, he killed Delgar's older brother and escaped into the forest. With Ogham gone, Delgar inherited the plantation.

"We hear tales from time to time; tales of a madman who's attacked and destroyed a plantation, freeing all the slaves and killing the owners. They say it's Kat and that he kills and eats the owners."

"There's another tale," put in one woman. "I've heard that he gathered a crew, stole a ship, and returned to Exile to destroy the compounds there. Others say he took the captured ship and went back to Borealis."

"Well, that he did not do," said Lessa. "Are you finished, Micha?"

"I am Lessa. As soon as these folk are fed you can take them to the infirmary and heal their hurts. Please be swift; I want you with me if we have to go in after Zartah."

"Understood, Micha. Come good people, Edie and I'll tend to you in the infirmary."

THE FIRE WAS WARM AND they sat contentedly beside it as they ate the last of the protein bars. Zartah squirmed around on the hard packed cavern floor until he was comfortable. Tentatively, Miriam came to him. She settled in beside him and looked away shyly when he put his arm around her to draw her closer. He felt her stiffen in his arms. "Miriam?"

"I know what a mate must do for her chosen, Zartah. I won't deny you; I'm just afraid. I was captured and taken into a compound once. Every night I was held down while the owner took me. Eventually I stopped struggling and he no longer had me held down."

"Miriam..."

"Once he felt safe I killed him and fled the compound. Zartah, I know you have no wish to hurt me, but I'm fearful and you're such a big man..."

"I'm not so big," he grinned. "Miriam, my love, relax. There'll be time enough for that when you're more comfortable with me. I just want to hold you close, feel the nearness of you, breathe in your scent, and..."

"Make certain I don't run away in the night?"

"Exactly," he chuckled, as he gently kissed her forehead. "I want to keep you."

"I want you to keep me." She snuggled closer and he gently enfolded her in his arms. "What will happen tomorrow?"

"Micha will come with the ship, and we'll go off planet, tell him what we can, and then wait while he decides what to do next. You'll meet the whole crew, Lady Arlessa and Brenna, her companion, Rathbone and his mate Keira, Jorge, my brother Murtah and his mate Ena, Edie, Micha's companion, and Jip."

"I hope they don't drive you out for choosing a Mutie for a mate."

"Hey there, I don't want you using that word either. You're a woman, a vibrant exciting woman, you're my chosen companion, and they'll all love you."

"Are you so certain?"

"Yes I am. They will accept you or I'll return here with you."

"You would do that for me?"

"In a heartbeat."

"He would," chuckled Gorda, "believe me. However, that won't be necessary. Micha will see you as a valuable member of the crew, Brenna will teach you the ways of our clothing, and Keira will teach you the uses of our weapons. Micha will pick your brain for the information he needs then you'll be a part of the crew; you'll see."

"You have such powerful weapons, and your clothing is far better than any I've seen since I escaped the compound. What use could I be to such advanced people?"

Zartah laughed heartily and hugged her gently. "Miriam my darling girl, listen to me. We crashed on this primitive planet and were ready to walk up to the most dangerous people here. You appeared and saved us from being captured and enslaved. Your clothing and weapons are quite finely made, obviously by your own hand, and you're in perfect health. This means you know how to find food and shelter.

"Girl, we know how to survive in space or on modern planets, but all too often we end up on more primitive planets where we have no real survival skills. If anything goes wrong, we're in trouble. With your skill set you could keep a team alive and functioning where the rest of us would perish.

"Gorda, did you notice how sharp her spear is; could you make one?"

"No, I couldn't, nor could I throw it with the skill Miriam did. Believe us girl; you have skills that will be valuable to the crew."

Miriam sighed and relaxed against Zartah's chest. Her mind was more at ease now that both men had assured her that she would be welcomed and useful. She drifted off to sleep listening to his heart beat and inhaling his scent.

Dawn found Miriam at the entrance of the cave, a snarl on her face. At the sound of her low growl Gorda and Zartah rose and joined her. There were hellhounds at the base of the cliff. "They've found us," breathed Miriam. "Within moments they will be on the trail, the hunters will keep us inside with arrows until the hounds can reach us."

"I'm getting tired of this skeeter," growled Gorda. "What say we flatten the lot of them?"

"There are too many," replied Miriam. "We must go out the back way and hope they haven't found that as yet. Come, this place is safe no longer." She scooped up her spear and raced to the back of the cave.

The two men followed close behind. There was a rough trail carved out of the rock wall leading upwards. Miriam scrambled up as quickly as a squirrel. Zartah and Gorda had to work a lot harder to reach the top. A small hole, hidden from below appeared. Miriam was already outside, gesturing for them to hurry. As they reached the ground she raced away.

Miriam led them into a deep canyon between the cliffs. She would have preferred more open terrain, but there was no choice; the hellhounds were behind them again. The canyon began to disappear into the solid wall of towering cliffs. Without hesitation she began to scale the cliff. It was only after she heard the weapons fire that she realized the two men weren't behind her.

Seeing there was no way for them to climb the cliff in time, Zartah and Gorda took up defensive positions. The first few hounds that closed on them were met with blaster fire. The rest turned and leaped among the jumbles of rocks.

The riders arrived on the scene and began firing arrows from a safe distance. Zartah put away his blaster and took out another weapon. He aimed carefully then squeezed the trigger. There was a loud bang and a rider fell lifeless to the ground. The rest of the riders instantly took cover.

Miriam scrambled back to his side. "Zartah, you must come; they cannot climb the cliffs."

"Neither can we, sweet lady. We make a stand here." Just then his comm unit squawked.

"Micha to Zartah."

"Here, boss."

"Status."

"We're under attack, boxed in, and pinned down, Boss. We could use a hand here."

"On our way."

"The compound has energy weapons, Boss."

"Understood."

"Gorda, the boss is coming in. Let's hunker down and let the crew take care of this."

"Works for me," he replied. "This rock overhang will protect us from the arrows."

Zartah and Miriam quickly joined him. A few moments later they heard the scream of big engines overhead as an Arcalian Fighter streaked past and attacked the nearest compound, knocking out the energy weapons.

The fighter circled back and swept low over the attacking riders' position. It turned gracefully and hovered, the hatch dropping open. Four heavily armed warriors dropped out and opened fire. A huge man and a battle scarred woman charged at the enemy at alarming speed. The hellhounds attacked, but a blur of brown savagery leaped from the ship and shot past the warriors and attacked the crazed animals.

There was instant mayhem and blood flying everywhere. A moment later, two hellhounds were dead, torn apart, and the rest were on their bellies in a submissive posture. Miriam had never seen a hound like this one who stood commanding the field. She watched in awe as the hellhounds slunk away and the big beast trotted over to the heavily armed man who patted him on the head.

The riders who survived the first onslaught were cowering away, not trying to shoot arrows, but trying to escape from the madness that had suddenly appeared. As they withdrew, Zartah fairly tossed Miriam up into the ship then followed with Gorda close behind.

Miriam scrambled out of the way and found a hand reaching out. A woman with pale skin and golden hair was smiling warmly. She took the proffered hand and the woman pulled her gently to a seat beside her. Zartah and Gorda quickly manned the gun turrets. The man at the controls barked an order and the troops returned to the ship.

Once everyone was on board, the ship streaked into the sky then out into space. Wide eyed, Miriam watched as the planet fell away and a ship grew larger until their smaller ship was able to fly right inside.

A few moments later the man at the controls spoke. "All clear folks; everybody gather in the mess hall. Jorge, standard orbit then join us for a bite to eat."

"On it. Boss," said the metal thing attached to his shoulder.

"Now then," he smiled as he turned to Miriam. She could see he was young, barely more than a boy, yet it was clear he was in command. Even her Zartah deferred to him. "You must be Miriam, Zartah's chosen companion."

"Yes, I am," she replied shyly, still trying to hide from the huge beast that seemed determined to approach her.

"Miriam, we're all pleased to meet you and have you join us. Don't be afraid of Jip; he's just trying to make friends."

"What manner of beast is he?" she asked. "I saw him defeat and control a whole pack of the hellhounds. How can such a savage beast be friendly?"

"Jip is a friend, Miriam," smiled the golden haired woman. "Here, just hold still and let him smell you. Once he gets your scent he'll decide if he wants to be friends. If he doesn't he'll move away; if he does he'll lick your hand and wag his tail."

"Come on folks, let's go. Miriam can meet everybody once we've given her a proper meal," said Micha as he dropped down out of the fighter ship. He walked away and the others followed. Miriam was both surprised and enchanted as Jip nuzzled her hand and wagged his tail. She sensed no threat from him, and his coat was so soft and warm. By the time they reached the eating area Jip was trotting contentedly at her side.

As soon as the crew gathered Micha nodded, then Zartah rose and introduced Miriam as his chosen companion. He then introduced each member of the crew to her. Each in turn gave her a smile and a warm welcome. There were tears in her eyes as well as a blush on her cheeks.

As Zartah finished Miriam smiled and spoke shyly. "Good people, thank you all for welcoming me. Zartah told me you would do this, but I was afraid. Muties aren't welcome anywhere I have ever been before."

"What's a Mutie?" asked Micha.

"A mutant, a deviant, a mistake made in the experiments..."

"My love," sighed Zartah as he put his arm around her shoulders, "that isn't you. Please don't use the M word here."

"Zartah, you must accept the truth. My mother was a mistake of the lab and I'm her child, a Mutant."

"Actually, you're not," Rathbone said. "Your mother was a Devan, but since you're in such good health, I'd say your father wasn't. Did your mother have problems with her bones breaking when she used too much of her strength? Did she die young because of the wasting sickness and brittle bones?"

"Yes, but how could you know that, and what is a Devan?"

Rathbone leaned his elbows on the table and smiled gently at Miriam. "Miriam, a long time ago, over a thousand years or more, a large ship filled with settlers was damaged in an ion storm. The ship crashed on a planet that hadn't been terraformed; the gravity was too heavy.

However, the air was breathable and the settlers managed to survive for a few years. As the first generation began to die off, the children seemed to be better adapted to the world the called Deva. After a few more generations, the human population of Deva had exploded; the Devans had adapted to their new home and the heavy gravity.

"Deva is in Sector Two and I once hid out there for a few weeks. I was strong enough to survive the gravity, but my pursuers were afraid to go there. Let me describe a Devan to you.

"A true Devan is short of stature with thick sturdy bones. They're extremely strong, intelligent, and possessing musical voices, a result of the language they developed. Their features are broad, their eyesight exceptional, and they have a natural gift of compassion. They prefer a more pastoral lifestyle, are exceptional hunters, and they're fierce when threatened.

"Miriam, it's my guess your mother was a full blood Devan while your father wasn't. You have the looks, strength and natural skills of your mother, but there is enough of your father's genetics to help you survive the lighter gravity. Your mother couldn't for she was from Deva. When a Devan leaves Deva their bodies deteriorate rather quickly in the lighter gravity.

"I suspect the lab failure with your mother wasn't her birth, but rather an inability to make her immune to the lighter gravity. She was probably taken as a child then experimented on in various levels of gravity over the years."

"Are you saying there are others like me? I am actually a true human?"

"There are millions of folks like you on Deva," smiled Rathbone. "Yes girl, you're all human, just from two different peoples. That's all."

Tears filled Miriam's eyes as she processed this information. She was human, not a Mutie. Her children would be born human with full rights as human. Zartah smiled at her then spoke to Micha.

"Boss, Miriam and I have sworn a life bond with Gorda as witness. Miriam has skills the crew can use; she would be a real asset."

"What skills are those, Zartah?" Miriam looked up, concerned until she saw the twinkle in Micha's eye.

"Survival skills under primitive conditions, Boss, Miriam kept us alive and safe when we'd have been in trouble otherwise. She also has working knowledge of Exile that can help us."

"I don't know, Zartah. The crew's getting pretty big and all." The twinkle in his eye and Zartah's wink put Miriam's mind at ease. "What do you think, Gorda?"

"I think we should keep her, Boss. She's strong, smart, and she can keep Zartah out of trouble."

"That works for me," laughed Murtah. "I say keep her."

Keira rose and stepped closer to Miriam. After gazing into the girl's eyes for a long moment she nodded, grinned, and sang a high sweet note.

"Keira's vote is in, Rath?"

"Keep her, Micha. Devans are natural hunters and trackers. We get outside the cities and she'll earn her keep."

"Lessa?"

"Keep her, Micha. I like her energy." Brenna agreed, as did Ena and Jorge.

"What say you, my beloved?"

"Jip says keep her, Micha," laughed Edie. "I'll trust that."

"All right, Miriam," smiled Micha, "what say you? Will you join the crew?"

She just gazed at him for a moment then spoke softly. "I get to choose?"

"Of course you do, girl," replied Micha. "Our's is a risky life and our lives are in danger far too often. If you'd rather, we'll take you back to Nova with us where Zartah can make a home for you, or we can put you back on Exile if you'd rather go back to something familiar."

"If I join you what will I have to do?"

"Whatever the Boss says," said Zartah softly. "You can trust him, my love."

"Miriam," said Micha, "the first thing I'd want you to do is learn the uses of our weapons and teach us the way of yours. That spear intrigues me. Also, I'd want you to be our guide and advisor on Exile."

"With all this power you want to learn what I can teach about my spear?"

"Micha wants to learn everything," laughed Edie. "Come on, Miriam, join us, be one of the family."

Miriam was overwhelmed at this. This normal looking woman, these normal people wanted her to be one of them. To them she wasn't a Mutie, she was a person. "I'm honored to be chosen," she said. "I'd love to be one of you. I swear you'll be more precious to me than family."

"They are family, darling girl," smiled Zartah. "They're the best family you can find."

"Done then," said Micha. "Miriam, each member of the crew has a speciality. Everyone is always combat ready, but each has a special skill set. You'll be our wilderness tracker and survival expert.

"Edie will take you to get clothing like ours and check you out in the infirmary while we get back to the second planet."

"Overlord?"

"Is that what it's called?"

"Yes, people are captured and made slave. Some are kept in the compounds and others are sold to the ships from Overlord. I was taken, but the manager of the compound tried to keep me for himself. I killed him and escaped. They're still trying to recapture me."

"We won't let that happen, Miriam," smiled Micha. "Get a good meal people, then gear up. We're not playing nice-nice any longer. I want to find our man then get our collective buttocks back to Nova Prime."

On the Hunt

As they approached Overlord a ship rose and tried to move past them. Jorge tried to hail them, but there was no answer. "Take us closer, Jorge," said Micha. "All hands, man the guns."

"They're trying to evade, Micha," said Jorge. "Pursuing. They're still evading."

"They're not armed, Micha," said Edie as she continued looking at her instruments. "I'm not scanning any weapons. I don't think they have a great range either."

"This is annoying," sighed Micha. "Keira, put one across their bow. That should get their attention."

With a wide grin Keira sent a shell to explode right in front of the fleeing ship. Micha grabbed the comms. "Attention fleeing ship. Power down and prepare to be boarded. The next shell will be amidships. You have ten seconds to comply."

"They're powering down, Boss," grinned Jorge.

"Very good people," said Micha as he spoke into the comms. "I suggest you suit up and abandon ship within one minute. One minute from now I'll blow that ship to the nine hells and back."

"Wait, wait, we don't have enough space suits. You can't just shoot us down."

"Yes I can."

"Wait, what do you want? Just tell us what you want."

"Are you the one in command there?"

"Yes."

"Suit up and eject; we'll collect you. Play me straight and I'll put you back on your ship and you can go your merry way. Mess with me and I'll be unhappy."

"Understood." A few moments later a single space suited figure ejected from the ship and drifted slowly towards Defender. The air lock opened and he made his way inside then waited for the air to cycle through.

As the lock filled with air a gray haired man unclasped his helmet and removed it. "Suit off, hands empty," barked a voice over the comm unit in the wall. He obeyed.

A moment later the door opened and a huge man with a gun in his hand stepped aside. "The boss is waiting in the mess hall," rumbled that deep voice. "Down that corridor then left at the end. It is the second door on the right after that."

He nodded then walked carefully down the passageway. That big man moved too easily, and he was armed. There was no need to alarm him in any way. As they entered the mess hall there were a few people relaxing at tables. He was led to a young man, barely more than a boy. "You? You're the one in charge here? What the hells is that Mutie doing here?" He pointed at Miriam.

Before anyone else could react Micha was over the table and on him. The man gulped as a sharp blade appeared at his throat. Micha was nose to nose with him. "Miriam is a member of my crew. Disrespect her again and I'll throw you out the air lock then send for another. Understand?"

"Understood," gulped the hapless man. Micha's blade disappeared as the boy released his victim and turned away.

"Sit," commanded Micha as he kicked a chair over to the man. "See this woman sitting over here, she's witch trained and can tell if you're lying. You lie, you die."

"Understood," nodded the man respectfully.

"Why did you try to run from us?"

"We didn't want to die."

"Explain."

"You're the bounty hunters sent to collect the madman. We were afraid you'd try to eliminate the competition."

"Where were you going?"

"Exile."

"Why?"

"No other options, all we have are short range ships. You have the only ship in the area capable of escaping this system."

"Tell me what you know of Kathan."

"I don't know anything."

"Try again," said Ena as she leveled a blaster at him.

"Don't test Ena again," said Micha. "She doesn't like it. Tell me what you know about Kathan."

"All I know is he's crazy, he likes pain, and he's loose somewhere on Overlord or Exile. Delgar bought him years ago, but he'd been too messed up on Exile. He kept running away. The punishment got worse every time we caught him, but he just laughed at the pain. A few years ago he finally got free of the collar and we haven't been able to catch him since.

"He leads some sort of outlaw band that attacks the plantations and frees the slaves. We catch most of them and bring them back, but he keeps trying."

"Why do you say he is crazy?"

"I've turned that damn collar up until a normal man would pass out from the pain, but he just laughs as his body writhes. He actually bit my ankle once."

"Does this picture look like him?" asked Micha as he pushed the tablet across the table.

"Pretty much, but he has a scar across this side of his face; it goes from the corner of his eye down to his jaw bone."

"The scar," said Miriam as she stepped forward. "Is it red and shaped like a lightning strike?"

"Yes," replied the man. "You've seen him?"

"Once before when Father was still alive; father called him kinsman. I saw him again two winters ago. He was in a ship that was shot down. I tried to take him to safety, but he laughed and ran to the Insider's hunters."

"Who are the Insiders, Miriam," Micha asked.

"The Insiders are the people who live inside the compounds, safe from the predators. They hunt and capture the Outliers, those who live outside the compound, to make them slaves."

"So he ran right to them?"

"Yes, it seemed like he wanted to be captured, however, after he showed himself to them he led them away from me before letting them take him."

Micha nodded as he absorbed this final piece of information. He turned to the prisoner again. "Do you have an approximate location for Kathan?"

"No. He attacked Delgar's plantation last night, freed a few slaves then fled. We lost track of him in the forest. He's like a will of the wisp in the trees. No one can catch him there."

Micha snorted then grinned. "Delgar is on that ship isn't he?"

"Yes."

"All right, my friend. I'm sending you back. You tell Delgar that we're not bounty hunters." He leaned forward and pulled aside his tunic collar to show his tattoos. "We're Kathan's kinfolk and we've come to take him home. We'll be very upset if any harm comes to him. You tell them that, and then you take that ship back to Delgar's plantation. We'll be right behind you with all guns locked and loaded."

"Understood," the man gulped. Rathbone hauled him to his feet and led him back to the air lock. Once he was suited up again the lock opened and he kicked off toward his own ship. It manoeuvered gently to pick him up. Soon after that it turned back toward Overlord, Defender following close behind.

As the ship descended toward the vast lawns of the plantation Defender opened up and two Arcalian fighter ships dropped out. The two fighters followed the troop carrier to the ground while Defender remained in close orbit. Heavily armed mercs poured out of the two Arcalian ships as they touched down. Delgar was visibly sweating as he recognized Rathbone and Keira.

"I'm sorry, I didn't know he was your..." Delgar got no further as Keira put a blaster to his head and laid her finger along her lips in a gesture calling for silence. Delgar complied, the fear clear in his eyes. At close range that blaster would turn his skull to jelly. He watched as the mercs spread out and entered his house. They soon began to return with all his slaves.

The young man who seemed to be the leader marched up to Delgar, carrying a female slave in his arms. It was the woman he had beaten that morning. He thought she was the one who'd let Kat into the grounds.

"Tell me how to get this collar off her," said Micha as he gently lowered the girl to the ground.

"You'll need a controller, Boss," said Rathbone. "He'll have one on him for certain."

"Get it for me. Edie, see what you can do for this woman."

"Yes, my love," said Edie as she knelt beside the woman and opened her med kit.

"Got the controller, Rath?"

"I do," replied Rathbone as he dropped Delgar's unconscious body to the ground.

"Get the collars off these people."

"Aye, Boss." In a trice the slaves were free of the collars.

"Can any of you fly this ship?" Micha asked of the freed slaves.

"I can," said one woman as she stepped forward. "Where do you want me to fly it to? I won't go back to Exile."

"You'd rather stay here, a slave?"

"Yes. At least I can survive here."

"Why not fly it back to a better place?"

"These are all short range ships, Sir. They can't navigate open space and they haven't the fuel capacity to..."

"Understood," sighed Micha. "Gather what you'll need for a long flight. Take the ship into orbit. Our ship is there; she'll protect you. When we leave for home we'll lead you out of this system and back to Nova territory."

"Nova? The plague planet?"

"No longer; Nova Prime is whole once again and seeking hard working settlers," put in Lessa. "You'll be welcomed there and you'll all be free citizens. Slavery is against the laws of Nova."

"Truly?"

"Truly," smiled Lessa. "Go now, gather what you need." The woman sped away with several of the others following.

"We're wasting time here," growled Micha. "Miriam, take Zartah, Gorda, Rathbone, and Keira; find the trail and we'll catch up as soon as we can."

Miriam was startled and a grinning Zartah took her arm to guide her. "Come on sweetheart, time to show your stuff." Miriam blushed as she saw the others smiling at her. She understood this was both a test and Micha's way of showing his confidence and trust. She nodded then trotted toward the forest, her eyes sweeping the ground before her. The trail was easy to find.

Miriam was enjoying herself as she followed the tracks left by the raiders. Her new clothing was warm, comfortable, and her new boots were wonderful. She was only carrying her spear as she wasn't yet familiar with the modern weapons of her new people.

Miriam smiled with delight as she looked up from studying the tracks. Her new family were watchful. No predators or enemies would ever be able to sneak up on these people, especially the silent one, Keira. Miriam was in awe of Keira and her mate. She smiled warmly and continued along the trail.

The man she was tracking was completely at home in the forest. He and his people went through water, over hard stone, climbed trees, and walked backwards to leave a false trail. All this was possible for Miriam to decipher, but it would easily confuse anyone without good tracking skills. When you had to develop these skills to survive you learned them well; Miriam had.

The day was growing dark when she finally stopped. "I can't follow them in the darkness, Zartah," she sighed as she rose from studying the ground.

"What do you want to do, Miriam my love?" he smiled.

"What???"

"This is your mission, Miriam. You're in command here until Micha catches up with us. Tell us what you want us to do."

Miriam smiled. This wasn't so hard for her to do; it was much like when she rescued people from the downed ships. "We should find a place to be safe for the night. We need to eat then rest. I will watch."

"There, by that rock outcropping," said Rathbone. "It's well hidden and we can defend it easily if need be. Will that do?"

"Yes, I like it," replied Miriam.

Keira sang a few notes then stepped off into the trees. "Keira says you've worked hard, Miriam," smiled Rathbone. "Keira will take the first watch. I'll take second."

"I'll take the dawn watch," said Gorda. "You need to be fully rested, Miriam. You'll have a hard day tomorrow."

Miriam looked bewildered and Zartah pulled her close to hold her gently. "You don't need to protect us, sweetheart. You need to be alert to lead us. We can watch and protect."

"You people are all amazing," sighed Miriam. "I will try to be worthy of your company."

"Miriam, you are worthy," chuckled Gorda. "Most of us would have lost that trail long ago." He reached for the comm on his shoulder. "Gorda to Micha."

"Micha here."

"We're camped for the night, Boss."

"How's Miriam doing?"

"Boss, this girl is amazing. She's still on the trail. We'd have been lost long ago, but she can track them easy."

"Tell Zartah he's a lucky man, but she'll always know where to find him." There was a round of chuckles at that then they settled down for the night.

Miriam startled awake, she'd heard a sound. She was on her feet and her spear was in her hand at the ready. Keira was squatting by a small fire. She smiled and nodded approvingly at Miriam. It had been the crackle of the fire that awakened her.

Keira placed two small carcasses on a spit to cook. Miriam just shook her head. How had this woman arisen, hunted, killed, and started a fire without waking her. Her admiration for Keira continued to grow. She returned the woman's smile then slipped into the trees to relieve herself. When she returned the others were all awake. She slipped away to mark the trail then returned to the fire.

Zartah appeared and sat beside her, lightly kissing her cheek. "Did you rest well, my love?"

"Yes, I sleep well in your arms, my mate," she said, "but I'm concerned."

"About what?"

"How is it I sleep so soundly? It isn't safe to do so. Keira arose, hunted, killed, made fire, and didn't awaken me."

"Don't give it another thought, Miriam," grinned Rathbone. "Keira does that to me all the time." They all chuckled at that.

Miriam was both surprised and bemused at this. She was even more surprised when Keira brought her the first portion of meat. This human woman, actually a superhuman woman, had just shown her respect and friendship. Miriam's heart swelled and there were tears in her eyes as she accepted the gift. Truly she had fallen in with remarkable people.

———◉———

WHILE MIRIAM ENJOYED the warmth of belonging to a greater family, one man sat at the controls of a small ship. He'd had the demon's own time sneaking past that damned Intruder class Raider. Kathan had no idea who these people were, but he knew he had no friends on Overlord or Exile. It was better to avoid contact with them and deliver his cargo. The ship held his small crew and the three slaves they had freed.

Neither did Kathan have any idea why Nodran wanted these three, but as always, he'd been more than happy to raid Delgar's place again. It would be nice to spend a few days in safety. It would give him time to think about the bounty hunters who were looking for him.

Why? Why were they here and who would put a price on his head? Okay, lots of people, but who had the money and pull to get a high class merc unit on his trail? Better yet, how could he steal their ship and get back to Borealis Two and kill that damned Viceroy?

If there was one thing Kathan wanted above all else it was to kill the Viceroy and set his sister Marla free. He also had to find his beloved Deela and free her. The very thought of the possibilities that merc ship represented sent a thrill through his tortured mind. "One thing at a time, Kat my son, one thing at a time," he admonished himself. "Step one is to escape."

———◉———

THE EMPEROR SAT BROODING on his throne, as he had christened the plush chair behind his desk. He was a patient man, but this time it wasn't easy. His agents had been working tirelessly for many turns and the time was drawing near. Soon he would be the undisputed emperor of the entire galaxy, or he would be embroiled in a war that would destroy all known civilization. The stakes couldn't be higher.

Worse yet, the second controller had not as yet been found. Out there somewhere was a device that could control him completely, and he had no idea where it was or how to find it. He had dozens of agents looking for it, but they had no idea of what it truly was or the power it represented.

He sighed and shook his head sadly. The longer he went without finding it the more dangerous it became for him. Someone would surely discover it and its uses. The Emperor's only hope was his greatest enemy, his daughter-in-law, the black witch of Nova Prime. The day was drawing closer when he'd have to seek her out. Emperor Loran the First wasn't looking forward to that day.

He arose and began to pace slowly about his opulent office, muttering under his breath.

The Making of a Union

Miriam set out along the trail once again. She didn't go far when she stopped and took a hard look around. Something wasn't right here. She held up her hand and the others stopped. The trail looked easy for them to follow, too easy compared to what she had encountered so far. She sat down and studied the path before her.

No one disturbed her and eventually she rose to her feet. Miriam cast about until she found a long stick which she snatched up. Using the stick to poke at the path ahead she moved cautiously. A few steps later her stick tripped a wire and something jumped into the air and snapped shut. It was a leg hold trap that was big enough to break a man's leg.

"There are at least four more between us and that turn in the path," she said softly. "I must find and spring them carefully."

"Let me, my love," smiled Zartah as he stepped up beside her. "Watch me; this is one of the possibilities of this weapon." He raised his blaster and aimed it along the trail in front of them. As he pulled the trigger the shock wave tripped the springs that set the traps. The traps snapped shut on empty air. He winked at her and lightly kissed her forehead.

Miriam smiled and patted his arm. "Well done, my mate. Let's proceed." She stepped along the path until they reached the turn. The trail wound around a huge boulder then into an open space. Zartah stepped past her then she heard a crackle of sound.

As the ground fell away from Zartah, Miriam leaped to his side and hauled him back onto solid ground. In so doing she lost her balance and fell into the pit. Sharply pointed wooden stakes pierced her body and she screamed. Consciousness left her as Zartah leaped into the pit with her.

Zartah jumped down into the pit, easily avoiding the sharpened stakes below. He carefully broke off the stakes that pierced her body then passed her up to Keira. Rathbone was scanning for enemies and Gorda was on the comms as Zartah climbed out of the hole.

"Gorda to Micha, emergency, emergency."

"Micha. Speak."

"Miriam's been hurt bad; we need healers; hopefully not the dispatcher."

"Keep the channel open, we're coming."

It was mere moments later an Arcalian ship streaked toward their position. The big bird swept in and barely touched down before Edie dropped out of the hatch followed closely by Lessa.

"This is beyond my abilities, Lady," said Edie, as she examined the unconscious Miriam. "Can you help?"

"I can. First we need to remove those stakes."

"Divans are tougher than you think," rumbled Rathbone. "This girl's strong; she can take it. I'll hold her; Keira, you pull out the wood. Once we've got them clear the Lady can heal her."

"Just one at a time, Rathbone," said Lessa. "Pull one out then let me heal the wound before you pull another."

"Aye, Lady, which do you want first?"

Lessa indicated which stake they should pull out first. Rathbone held Miriam steady and Keira pulled out the weapon with a firm strong draw. Lessa's eyes were already out of focus as her hands closed the gaping wound in the girl's chest. Next came the one from her side then the shoulder and last the thigh.

"She's sleeping peacefully now," sighed Lessa, as she sat back and placed her palms flat on the ground. "She will awaken soon, but she should take it easy for a day or two. Miriam was lucky; none of the stakes pierced a vital organ."

"Lady, how can I ever thank you for this?" asked Zartah, as he sank to the ground beside her.

"No thanks are necessary, Zartah. Tell me, what is it about her that caught your attention?"

"It was her strength, both of mind and body; and yet there's something of the wounded child about her that makes me want to protect her. Lady, it makes my heart sing to see her smile."

"Oh my, you've got it bad, my friend," laughed Lessa. "She'll be fine. There was a bone beginning to deteriorate, but I've fixed that issue, then enhanced her as I have the rest of you. Miriam will have a long and healthy life."

"Lady..."

"Hush now, Zartah, she's stirring. You attend her while I see what Micha's up to." With that, Lessa arose and walked away to where Micha and Gorda were studying the ground with Rathbone and Keira.

Miriam opened her eyes and gazed up at Zartah's smiling face. "What happened? Why am I still alive?"

"The Lady healed you, my beloved. Not only that, but she enhanced you as she has the rest of us. You're now stronger and faster than you've ever been. Your injuries will heal faster as well."

"Why has she done this, Zartah?"

"This crew is her personal guard as well as the guardians of Nova Prime, her home planet. There aren't many of us, but we're quite effective. You're now one of us, my beloved."

Miriam gazed into his eyes for a long moment. She reached for his hand and squeezed it earnestly. "I will strive to be worthy of this, Zartah my mate; both of your love and of her gift."

"You are worthy, make no mistake," he smiled. "Ah, here comes the boss."

"Miriam, are you ready to travel?" asked Micha as he approached and sank to the ground beside her.

"I believe so, Micha," she replied. "I'm sorry I failed you."

"Failed me? No girl, you were completely successful. You tracked Kathan to his hidden launch pad, found the traps, and kept my First Man alive. That looks like a big success to me."

"But I didn't find him."

"There was a small ship here; it launched before you arrived. You couldn't see it because it was hidden from you and probably left over those mountains, away from your view. It tried to sneak away, but Jorge spotted it and traced its path back to Exile. He thinks he can find where it entered the atmosphere. No, Miriam, you've put us right on his track.

"Zartah, take Miriam and Gorda and return to Defender. Send Gorda back with the ship."

"Aye, Boss," grinned Zartah as he helped Miriam to her feet.

<hr />

MIRIAM AWAKENED IN Zartah's arms. They were lying in a comfortable bed aboard the ship. It took a moment for the memories to clear, then she shook her head and smiled. She had saved her mate's life, but had taken terrible wounds. He had called the witch who had healed her then made her stronger, so she'd said.

Zartah had brought her back to the ship then they had retired to this small room and the bed. Miriam had succumbed to sleep immediately, her body still adjusting to the healing and the enhancement. She stretched and tested her muscles. There was no pain, only smooth and powerful movement.

"How are you feeling, my love?" asked the deep voice beside her.

"My body feels strong, renewed, but I'm concerned, my mate."

"What concerns you, my love?"

Miriam lay down beside him, place her hand on his chest and gazed into his eyes. "Zartah, you claimed me as your mate, you speak to me as a man does his mate, and you've brought me away from a life of danger. You brought me to a new life and your friends have welcomed me."

"So, the problem is?"

"I'm afraid. I find I'm holding myself apart from you and that's wrong. I know how a woman is to be with her mate and you deserve to have that of me. I try to bring myself closer, but the fear holds me back; I'm so very sorry. I'm making you a poor mate."

"You're making me a fine mate, Miriam. You're the only mate I want. Don't push yourself too hard; it'll all come in time. I understand that you've been abused, and it'll take time to get past that..."

"Thank you, my gentle man, but that's not the real problem."

"No? Well then, what is it?"

"You're such a big man, I'm afraid you will hurt me."

"Miriam, I will never hurt you. I promise ..."

"Zartah, I trust that you would never deliberately hurt me. You don't understand my meaning."

"Miriam, I..."

"Here, Zartah," she said, her eyes downcast as she lightly patted his groin. "You're such a big man; surely you must be the same here. I'm only small and I'm afraid you'll split me asunder..."

"Miriam, Miriam, Miriam," he chuckled as he gently pulled her closer, "You have nothing to fear at all. I'll confess my dread secret to you. The little man who hides in my britches is really quite small. Oh, he can rise to the occasion when duty calls, but ..."

"You're lying to me," she said as she pushed away to arm's length and look right into his eyes.

"No, no I'm not," he protested, the laughter clear in his eyes. "It used to be big, but as a boy I was attacked by a bear. I managed to kill it, but not before it bit off most of my..."

He grunted as she grabbed his manhood through the clothing and squeezed him. She stroked him a couple of time and his body responded. Her eyes opened wide, and she released him, pushing away. She retreated to the door. "I have to find the witch." With that she was out the door and gone.

Zartah looked down then slapped at his rising erection. "This is a fine mess you've caused. Why couldn't you just sleep for a few more minutes?" he sighed and lay back on the bed to stare at the ceiling.

Miriam found the ship was in flight, on its way back to Exile. It took a few minutes, but she managed to locate Lessa with Edie in the infirmary. Lessa noticed her standing shyly by the door, waiting to be noticed.

"Hello Miriam, how are you feeling?"

"I am well, Lady. Lady, may I please speak with you in private?"

"Of course, Miriam, come this way; there's a small office in here we can use." She led the small woman into a tidy office then closed the door. "What's on your mind?"

"It's Zartah, Lady."

"Zartah? Has he done something unworthy? Do you believe you chose in haste...?"

"No, Lady, no, not that. Zartah has been a blessing and a gift. He has taken me to a new and wonderful life."

"Then what...?"

"Lady, he is so big, and I'm so small."

"I have known many couples where the man is ... Oh, I see." Miriam had made a gesture at her crotch and, despite the look of deep concern on her face, Lessa nearly laughed aloud. However, she could not keep the merriment from her eyes.

"You can laugh at me if you wish," said Miriam sadly as she turned to go. "You're so tall and beautiful and human. I'm just a M..."

Lessa reached out to touch Miriam on the shoulder. "Please, forgive me, Miriam. I see your concern, and I will confess to be amused at the way you expressed it, but I can see this is serious for you. Please stay and tell me all of it. Why does this concern you so?"

Miriam sighed and returned to sit beside Lessa. "I know what a woman must do for her mate. I'm not unwilling, but I was taken slave once and men held me down and used me. They were much smaller than Zartah and they hurt me. I'm afraid he will split me open like a ripened Orta fruit."

Lessa was serious now, her eyes filled with compassion. "Miriam, your mother died when you were still young, didn't she?"

"Yes, Lady. She died the year before I began to bleed as a woman."

"There was much she didn't have the chance to teach you, Miriam. Please allow me to explain."

"Lady?"

"When a woman is unwilling, even a small man will cause pain. When a woman is willing, no, more than willing, filled with desire, her body will expand to accommodate a much larger man without pain."

Seeing that Miriam was still skeptical, Lessa decided to include a small deception. "Miriam, you know of my power. When I healed you, I enhanced your abilities in all things. Seeing that Zartah is much larger than you I also enhanced your ability to expand in that area. You'll need to be patient, but with time and patience you will be able to be a full mate for Zartah.

"Zartah is a good man, Miriam. Speak to him of your concerns and ask for his understanding and patience. I'm certain all will be well for you both."

"You fully enhanced me, Lady?"

"Yes, I did. I thought it best."

"Lady, I have no words to thank you for this. Do you truly believe he will understand?"

"I'm convinced of it, Miriam. Go now; go back to him and sort this out." She hugged the small woman then shooed her out the door. Miriam fairly ran all the way back to the room where she'd left Zartah. He was still on the bed.

"Miriam?"

"I've spoken with Lady Arlessa."

"Oh?"

"She explained some things I should've learned from my mother, but didn't get the chance to do so."

"Really?"

"Yes, she also explained the nature of the enhancements she gave me. Realizing the size difference between us was so great, she enhanced other of my abilities as well."

"Indeed?"

"Yes. Zartah, I want to be a good mate for you, and now I believe I will be able to do that. Lady Arlessa said I should explain my concerns to you and ask you to be patient with me until my body adjusts to you. Will you do this for me? She said that if I was willing, my body should be able to accept you without pain given time to adjust."

"Of course I'll be patient with you, silly woman."

This time, when he pulled her closer she came willingly. As she pressed herself into his arms she felt the now familiar tingling in her body. She trembled as he held her near, but she did not try to move away, instead she snuggled closer. Zartah cuddled her closer and kissed her hair. "We can take all the time you need, my love. I care not as long as I get to keep you."

He kissed her hair again and she tilted her face up to look at him. Without another thought he kissed her mouth. Miriam stiffened, then moaned as she melted under the fire of that kiss. Electric shocks flowed through her body as it responded to his touch. Thus encouraged he deepened the kiss.

She was gasping for air as their lips parted. Fighting to clear her fogged mind, she asked, "Why did you do that?"

"Oh my girl, I've wanted to do that since I first laid eyes on you."

"Why?"

"It is a thing lovers do, my sweet, and I've wanted you for my lover since I first saw you."

"Why?"

"Hush, Miriam," he chuckled, as he pulled her closer and kissed her again.

Miriam trembled both from the kiss and the feel of his rising manhood against her belly. It excited and thrilled her as well as scaring her half to death. She gasped and trembled even more as his hands began to explore her, gently removing her clothing. She struggled with both the instinct to flee and the desire for more of his touch.

Her confusion and distress were heightened as his lips sought her body and his hands began exploring her most intimate parts. This wasn't like before when she was held down; this time she was held down by the power of the emotion coursing through her. By the time his lips found her thighs all sense and reason had left her. Miriam suddenly released herself fully to the madness and desire of the moment.

Much later she lay atop him, breathing deeply and nearly asleep. Yes, it had hurt, but it had been a pain of pleasure, and eventually the pain had vanished in waves of ecstasy. "Well, how about that," sighed Zartah as he lightly kissed her hair, "it fits after all."

"Hush, silly man," she laughed. "I'll be lucky if I can walk straight for days."

———— ◉ ————

KATHAN SIGHED AND RELAXED back under the tree. The drug was taking effect and soon he would be free for a time; free of pain, free of the demons that plagued his mind, and back with his beloved sister, Marla. He knew that by now she had been brain dead for many years, a victim of the Viceroy and the inhibitor. That didn't matter once the drug took hold. Once the drug reached his brain he could go back.

The small garden with its lone tree was heavily guarded. No one would disturb him here; Nodran would see to that. Not for the first time Kathan wondered what Nodran's agenda could be. It didn't really matter, Nodran kept him in fuel and weapons. The gods only knew where he got the supplies.

He'd arrived with the three slaves Nodran had requested. The three had been whisked away and he never saw them again. Nodran must have been pleased; he'd included a little extra in the goodie bag. Kathan sighed deeply as pain and reality slipped away from him.

He was still lost in the drugged dreams when the merc ship arrived overhead days later. Kathan was completely unaware as the huge Mutie scooped him up and carried him out through the secret passage and into the forest, his crew following close behind.

On the Trail

Zartah and Miriam appeared on the bridge just as Exile came into view. Micha looked up, first at Zartah then at Miriam. He grinned and she blushed. His grin broadened as he returned to the task at hand. A few moments later he spoke.

"Jorge, are you sure this is the trajectory?"

"Yes, this is it, Boss. He slipped off the sensors right about here."

"All right, let's see what's of interest in the area. Miriam, come here please. What can you tell me about this area?"

"I'm sorry, Micha. I've never seen any of Exile from above before. I don't recognize anything."

"Understood. Jorge, find a clear spot and set her down."

"Aye, Boss."

Jorge set the big ship down lightly in a small clearing. He stayed on board when the rest of the crew spilled out onto the ground. As soon as they were clear he locked the hatches again.

"All right, Miriam," smiled Micha, "anything look familiar now?"

She gazed all around for a few moments then trotted to the edge of the clearing. They followed and found her at the beginnings of a hidden trail. "I've been here before, but it was long ago. There are six compounds that I'm aware of, all are dangerous, but number six is the worst. We are near number six."

"How near?"

"Three days through the forest will bring us to the hills overlooking the compound. They have many weapons and men in uniforms to use them. Number six controls all the other compounds. I was caught and sold to the leader there, a man called Nodran."

"What happened?" asked Edie.

"I escaped while we were en route," she replied. "I knew if I was taken within those walls I wouldn't return. That was the second time I was captured."

"Miriam, do you know what's so special about number Six?" asked Micha.

"Nodran makes the dream drugs there."

"Dream drugs?"

"At first he said it would take away the pain, and many Muties volunteered to try it. None returned alive. I went to see what had happened to them. I found only twisted and distorted bodies.

"There was a large Mutie carrying one of them. He dumped the body with the rest then limped away. I followed and asked him about the bodies, about what happen to those people. He said that Nodran bought people, took them below the compound and made them help him. Sooner or later most die and he sends the bodies out for the predators, but the predators won't eat them. They have too much of the dream drug in them."

"Tell me more about the dream drug."

"All I know is it takes away pain and gives pleasant dreams. It comes from a plant that grows here. Many Muties use it to dull their senses and to keep the predators away."

"Is that why you show them respect and compassion, Miriam?" asked Zartah.

"Yes. They've been distorted; their lives filled with pain and madness. I won't add to that."

Micha smiled at her approvingly. "Can you lead us to the compound from here, Miriam?"

"Oh yes. It's three days away, two if we hurry, but we must go carefully."

"Lead on," smiled Micha.

Miriam took the lead at a fast trot. It seemed like complete chaos to the crew, but she was sure in her twists and turns. When she was certain there would be no problem keeping up with her, she picked up the pace.

Through most of the day she ran on, the crew close behind. She led them down twisting forest trails, over rock faces, across streams, around bogs, and she didn't tire. Miriam exulted in the new powers the witch had given her, and she was still glowing from her first true experience of loving sex with her chosen mate.

They encountered the occasional gigantic predator, all fang and claw, but no beast can stand up to combined blaster fire. They were safe enough. As darkness began to fall she led them to a cave with a small opening, but a large interior. "We'll be safe in here and you can't see the sky," she said.

"Why would we not want to see the sky?" asked Brenna as she dropped her small pack and sat on it.

"I've noticed the sky makes you folk uneasy," replied Miriam.

"There're no stars, Brenna," sighed Gorda. "It gives me the creepies."

"There's probably a few, Gorda," said Rathbone, "distant galaxies and such, but I know what you mean. I felt the same at night on Overlord. The cave is a good idea."

"Miriam, how did we do?" asked Micha as he and Edie spread open their bed rolls.

"We should be able to see Compound Six late tomorrow," she smiled as she sat beside Zartah. "I remember much of the way and the crew travels faster than I did alone trying to avoid danger and seeking the path."

"You said it has been a long time since you passed this way, yet you remember the trails?"

"It's her nature, Micha," said Rathbone. "The Devans have amazing memories; they never forget anything."

"That's good to know," chuckled Micha, as he settled himself by the opening to take the first watch. "Get some rest people." He focused his attention out into the forest. The others lit a fire for warmth and to prepare food, but Micha didn't once turn his head. All was quiet behind him and had been for some time when he heard a soft footfall.

Keira patted his shoulder then moved aside to let him pass. As Micha stepped back into the cave to seek out his blanket and Edie, Keira took up his seat and focused her attention out into the forest. It was well into the night when Brenna relieved her, and it was Gorda on watch as daylight returned.

They ate a light meal and then Miriam led them onward. The day was well advanced when she stopped and pointed to a rise in the land. "We can see the compound from there," she said as Micha caught up to her.

"Show me. Everybody take a breather."

She led him up the hill to where he could see. Spread out below in a shallow valley was an enclosed compound surrounded and protected by a tall wire fence. Inside were a cluster of large buildings surrounded by smaller living quarters. Well-cultivated fields were also in evidence. This place had old company outpost written all over it.

He signalled for the others to come up. Once they had time to look it over he spoke softly. "What do you think, Gorda?"

"The fence will be charged, Boss, but we can jump it easy enough. I'm seeing a few armed troops, not very well trained by the look of it, and three small ships. I'll bet our boy's ship is one of them."

"Miriam, what else can you tell me about this place?" asked Micha.

"That large building is where they take the captives. I was told they take them underground once inside. All the armed men will go inside as darkness falls. All the rest of the people will go inside the smaller buildings, then the hellhounds will be let loose."

"Do they have lights?"

"Lights?"

"Do they turn on big lights to light up the fence?"

"No, that would draw too many predators. The hounds will keep the people in and warn of any danger from outside. See, there are the hounds in that pen. They've already caught our scent."

"I see. Okay folks, you got the layout in your mind?" Everyone nodded then he withdrew to the sheltered spot below the crest of the hill. The others followed.

"Suggestions, options?"

"We haven't met a lot of friendly helpful folk since we arrived in this system, Boss," grinned Zartah. "I'm thinking we should be a bit more insistent in our approach."

"I second that, Micha," said Lessa. "Like you, I'm getting nervous about being away from Nova for so long."

"Agreed, Lessa, and I want to know what the nine hells is going on. The time for diplomacy is over people. Gorda, how do we take down that compound?"

"We go in at first light. We go over the fence, use blasters on the hounds and anybody else who gets in the way."

"I don't want to wait that long. I'm getting seriously uneasy about home. Lessa, can you make enough light for us to see?"

"Of course, Micha. Shall I put the hounds to sleep as well?"

"Thanks, Lessa, I wouldn't ask, but..."

"Understood. I too feel that we're running out of time."

"All right then," sighed Micha. "Get some rest folks, we go in later tonight."

They settled down to rest; Miriam curled up in Zartah's arms. She was excited, but terrified of what would happen. It wasn't safe to travel in the darkness and it wasn't even close to wise attacking Compound Six. Ah well, even if she died in the raid it was all worth it for the love and respect she had come to know with these folks; especially the love from her mate. Miriam fairly glowed with the memory of it. She fell asleep as darkness descended over the forest.

Miriam had no idea of the time when Zartah kissed her awake. There was a soft glow of light from several sources as the crew geared up for the invasion. Once ready, Miriam led them cautiously through the forest to the compound's fence. The hellhounds charged, baying as they neared the wire.

As the hounds charged Lessa stepped forward and held out a hand. "Stop," she commanded in a terrible voice. The hounds instantly flopped onto their bellies, whimpering. A soft glowing light emanated from her hands, and by that light the crew leaped over the fence. Once everyone was over Micha turned on his light and Lessa let hers fade. She took two running steps then leaped over the fence to join them.

Lessa spread her arms and the compound was bathed in light. It was faint, but gave enough for them to see. The crew headed for the main building. When the sun came up they were all in place and everything was ready. Micha spoke into his comm unit. "Jorge."

"Here, Boss."

"Bring her in; make a fuss as you land."

"Aye, boss." A few moments later there was a loud peak of thunder as the ship rose up, broke the speed of sound, then made a swift run and landing in Compound Six.

As the ship landed the compound's armed men came racing out to surround it. Lessa thrust out her hand and they all fell to the ground, unconscious. Meanwhile Micha and the other were rounding up everyone they could find inside and herding them out to the open area near the ship. They finally found the office of the leader, Nodran. His bodyguards were no match for the crew.

The armed guards were reviving as the last of the inhabitants were herded into the large group beside Defender. "Which one of you is Nodran?" demanded Micha. No one spoke so he shot the nearest man. As the man crumpled to the ground, he asked again. "Which one of you is Nodran?" again no one spoke. Micha shot another.

"That's him," babbled the next man Micha looked at. He was pointing to a small balding man amid a group the troopers.

"Come here," Micha said to the man who'd been pointed out. Instead he cringed and hid behind a larger man. "Murtah, fetch him." The big mercenary moved at lightning speed. The hapless Nodran was soon grovelling in the dirt at Micha's feet.

"I'm looking for my kinsman, Kathan of Nara Clan. Where is he?"

"I don't know what you're talking about," snivelled Nodran. Several others had gasped at Micha's mention of that name. He turned to the closest.

"Where can I find Kathan?"

"You don't want to find that one," replied the woman.

"Why not?"

"He's drug crazy. It happens when they get too addicted; their minds don't work right anymore. They have to stay on the drug to function and they need extra to get high."

"Understood. I still want to find him; where is he?"

"His house is there, but the Mutie is gone."

"Explain."

"When he's in the house a giant Mutie guards the door. When he's gone the Mutie hides. Since the giant is gone, then Kat must be gone as well."

"Rathbone, Keira, check that house." They were gone in a flash. A short while later they returned.

"The place is empty," signalled Keira. "There is a passageway leading out under the fence and into the forest. He has escaped." No one could interpret her signals except the folk of the crew. Micha liked it that way.

"Zartah, take Miriam, Rath and Keira. Get on his trail now. Stay in contact."

"Aye, Boss. Keira, take us to where Miriam cam pick up the trail." She nodded and trotted back towards Kat's abandoned house.

"Now for you," said Micha as he turned to Nodran. "Tell me what you've done to Kathan and what I can do to help him. Tell me why he works for you, what work he does, and what the nine hells is going on."

"I don't understand," he said, still trembling.

"Lessa, please demonstrate what will happen if he lies to me or tried to evade my questions again."

Lessa stepped into the open and raised her arms high. Her hair was blown back by a wind only she could feel. The well-worn uniform shimmered into flowing black robes and the sky darkened. Suddenly she was wreathed in flame, yet untouched. "Behold, the sword of Nova."

The flames coalesced into a burning sword in her hand. She leveled it at a nearby building and the flames shot out. The building exploded. Lessa laughed cruelly then pulled the dark flames back inside herself. Her robes shimmered back to her uniform and the sun returned to the sky.

"This woman is Ena, she'll know if you lie," said Micha. "Lie to me and Lessa will get to play. When she's finished you'll be ready to talk."

The man was white with fear. He glanced towards his men, but there was no help to be had there. "All right, I'll talk. Can we go to my office and have a civilized drink together?"

"Give you a chance to drug me, I don't think so. I have no time for this. Talk or die, your time's up."

Nodran slumped further, but Murtah hauled him back to his feet. "I got the drug from the Muties, they use it to kill pain. I'm a chemist, or I was until O'Loran sent me to this hell hole. I determined to find a way to escape, but I needed help; lots of it. Korath was running the place back then, but I got him addicted then took over. I began trying to produce a viable fuel from local minerals, enough to power one of these short range ships to sector three. That's what I'm working on.

"Kat brings me the people I need. When I learn the location of a person who can help, Kat makes a raid and retrieves them. This last trip he brought an engineer and two navigators."

"So why the drugs? Won't these people help you on their own?"

"Most would kill me in my sleep and try to take over. They think it is better to have some small power here than to go back and risk a worse fate at the hands of the company. As long as I control the drug, I can control them."

"What about Kathan?"

"He was useless, tortured beyond hope when I got him. His pain tolerance was impressive, so I gave him the drug to kill the pain. He raids the plantations and frees the people I need here, and I pay him with drugs. The fool is completely addicted to the overdoses now. He'll be out in the forest somewhere, guarded by that Mutie."

"Why did he run from us?"

"You're flying a company intruder class ship. He hates and fears the company. We got word that bounty hunters were after him. He thinks you're those bounty hunters come to kill him."

Micha sighed deeply then turned away. "Let them go back to their lives, we're done here; everybody back on the ship."

Once they were all aboard the ship she rose gracefully into the morning sky. Micha was deep in thought as they reached a low orbit once again. Finally he roused himself. "Gorda!"

"Here, Boss."

"Take that long range Arcalian fighter and head back to Nova as fast as you can. Something is going on somewhere and I want to know what it is. Jorge will send the coordinates for the jumps. Do you want company for the trip?"

"It can be a little unnerving out there, Boss. Aw, what the heck, I'll be fine. I'll take a couple of those freed slaves with me for company."

"Take Murtah and Ena with you too. No crew member goes alone."

"Okay, Boss, I'm on it." With that he was gone from the bridge.

DEEP IN THE INNER HUB worlds the emperor sat brooding on his throne. His mind wandered ceaselessly over his plans. All was about to change as soon as he got word that the stage was set. He looked up expectantly as a man hurried in and knelt. "Ah, Hoaka, my friend, you bring good news I hope."

"Yes Sire, I do. The assassins are all in place, just waiting for the signal." He held out a control device. "One push of that button, Sire, will send the signal. The key leaders, both military and civilian, of A.S.Inc will die and your forces will invade at the same time. In the confusion they will be easily defeated long before the Borelians can be alerted and come to their aid. Press that button, Sire, and you'll be emperor of the entire galaxy before morning."

Emperor Loran smiled as he held up the device. "We're committed now, Hoaka. I shall be Emperor of all as you say, or we'll be embroiled in a war that'll destroy civilization as we know it. Nothing ventured, nothing gained, eh?" With a chuckle of pure delight, he pressed the button.

The signal went out in the secret code, leaping through the relays, reaching every hidden assassin in A.S.Inc territory. Each checked his timepiece and at the precise moment, struck. Hundreds of people in positions of command fell to the attack. Before anyone could begin to understand what had happened the Emperor's forces were attacking key military installations.

The takeover was completely successful. A.S.Inc. surrendered without a fight. Emperor Loran was now undisputed emperor of the entire galaxy, all except for Borelian territory. The Borelian free Alliance was now the last of the free states. They would be easy prey.

Viceroy Lortax and High Priestess Marla were enjoying a quiet lunch in her office when the news arrived.

Elusive

Kathan fought the intrusion. Someone was shaking him, trying to get him to drink something. No, there was pain out there; he wanted to stay in the dreams. Marla was there, his friends were there, life was sweet in the dreams. Damn that voice anyway. Kathan began to get angry and tried to lash out at his tormentor.

"That's it, Pyne, keep going. He's coming around."

"Stand back," said the huge Mutie. The three men stepped back out of harm's way. They well knew how violent Kat could be when he was dragged out of the dreams. This time they'd been afraid he'd overdosed. He had still been unconscious when the merc ship arrived.

It was Pyne's superior hearing that had saved them. He'd awakened them and pointed out the light. They caught glimpses of the mercs in that soft light and fled through the tunnel. Now the mercs were tracking them. Whoever was leading those mercenaries was one hell of a tracker. Worse yet, the hunters seemed to have no fear of the predators.

Kathan lashed out at his tormentor, but his blows had little effect on the giant Pyne. "Wake, Kat. Danger comes. Wake and think." With a groan of protest Kathan sat up and tried to shake off the dreams. Sweet Nara, how much had he taken anyway? Reluctantly he took a sip of the vile liquid Pyne was pushing at him. Gods that tasted awful, but it helped to clear his head.

"This had better be good, Alad," he muttered, as he took another swallow and grimaced.

"Kat, we've got real trouble this time," said the man he'd addressed.

"We've always got trouble. What is it this time?"

"The bounty hunters," replied the man. "They took the compound in the night. Pyne heard them coming and we were able to get out through the tunnel, but they're tracking us."

"Huh, let them try. Nobody but a Mutie born on Exile could track us in this forest."

"Well they must have one then, because they're on our trail and gaining. Pyne's been carrying you, but he's tiring. Running isn't going to be enough to shake these guys. We need you functional."

"I need to eat something, and then we'll start playing dirty. We'll set traps on the trails to slow them down. See if you can kill something to bleed out and draw in the predators. We'll confound these fools then we'll take them out. Maybe we can catch one or two alive and sell them back to Nodran." The others chuckled at that as Pyne passed him some dried fruit.

———⋄———

"WHAT'S WRONG, MIRIAM?"

"This has all been too easy, Zartah, my beloved. They don't hide their tracks well. There are three men and the Mutie. I know him, his name is Pyne."

"You know him?"

"Yes, we met long ago when I came here before. See, he limps, you can tell by these tracks."

"Hmm, I'll take your word for that, sweetie."

"Yes, well, they stopped here for some reason. I believe Kathan was still in the dream world and Pyne had to carry him. They stopped here and then went on, four men this time and Pyne. Kathan is awake now.

"Here their tracks are far too easy to follow. We must be wary of traps. They know they're being followed and are trying to lead us astray."

Miriam proceeded cautiously, probing at the ground with the butt of her spear. She soon triggered a trap. A dead tree with jagged branches suddenly fell across the path. It would have killed or maimed anyone trying to follow those tracks. Zartah was impressed. Miriam continued to poke around and soon found the faint traces of where the quarry had gone. She grinned as she took up the hunt.

Throughout the rest of the day she tracked Kathan, steadily gaining on him. It took him longer to set the traps than it took her to find and spring them. He was getting frustrated and angry. He couldn't take a ship because that damned intruder class warship was hanging in orbit. He couldn't seem to catch their tracker unawares either, there was nothing left to try but to run. He did.

By nightfall it was apparent to him that running wouldn't work either. These mercs seemed to be tireless. Worse yet, the predators were wary of them; the mercs had learned that blaster fire was a fine deterrent. "All right, let's see if they can travel after dark without moonlight or stars," he muttered as he caught a glimpse of Miriam on his trail.

"Dammit, I know that woman; she's a Mutie. How the hell did they recruit her? We'll never lose Miriam, I'll have to think of something else."

"WE'RE CLOSE, MY MATE, but we won't catch them before darkness falls," said Miriam.

"It's nearly dark already, my love," replied Zartah. "Find us a place to camp for the night. We'll take up the chase at first light."

"They may move at night," rumbled Rathbone.

"Yes," agreed Miriam, "they might. Pyne could lead them safely, but they couldn't go far and they'd be more tired in the morning. Tired people are easier to track."

"Point taken," chuckled Rathbone "I'll take first watch."

Once again Miriam awakened in Zartah's arms. She had been aware when he rose to take a turn at watch, but she hadn't felt him return.

"Why did no one wake me to a turn at watch?" she asked as she stood and brushed her mane of hair back from her face.

"You're the tracker, Miriam," said Rathbone. "Only you can track our quarry and find the traps on the trail. You need to be well rested. The rest of us can stand watch. The next time we're in a city somewhere you get to stand watch."

She looked him in the eye for a long moment then nodded. "Understood. Where's Keira?"

"She's..." a sudden piercing whistle interrupted him. A huge man limped into the clearing, Keira right behind him with a weapon at his broad back.

Miriam recognized Pyne. She stepped before him then bowed her head in a gesture of respect. "I remember Miriam," the giant said gently. He too bowed his head in greeting and respect.

"I remember Pyne," replied Miriam.

"You have returned to the dark forest. Why?"

"I ask forgiveness of Pyne," said Miriam. "My mate seeks a kinsman who has been lost for many turns."

"What name does the kinsman carry?"

"He is Kathan of Nara. My mate is Zartah of Nara. Kathan is called Kat, or so we believe. If you see Kat, will you tell him Marla, High Priestess, has sent Zartah to find Kathan? We are to bring him safely home to her."

"If he crosses my path I will speak of this."

Zartah started to speak, but Miriam's out flung hand stopped him. She knew as well as the rest that Pyne was stalling so Kat could get farther away, but it would be unwise to offend Pyne. It would also go against Father's teachings of the code. "We wish Pyne joy of the journey."

"Joy of the journey to Miriam. May she find what she seeks."

"It was good to speak with you again, Pyne." He nodded then proceeded down the trail.

"Miriam, should we follow him to see if he goes straight to Kathan?" asked Zartah.

"No, Pyne will lead us far from the one he protects. He'll deliver our message when next they meet, but that could be seasons from now or it could be tomorrow. He was here to slow us down and to lead us away if possible. Kathan will have been moving away from us while we spoke with Pyne."

"Miriam..."

"Peace, Zartah, my beloved. We will now go catch Kathan."

"What did I miss?" asked Zartah.

"Kathan will move quickly now, but his trail will be easy to follow and there won't be traps to slow us down."

"How can you know that?"

"The traps were Mutie traps, designed to kill predators or food. Pyne is the only one of them strong enough to set those traps. He no longer runs with them. Come." She set off down the trail.

Her eyes constantly scanning the ground and the surrounding forest, Miriam pushed the pace. The sun was not yet high when the forest gave way to a rocky terrain. This might have stopped another tracker, but not Miriam. Her quarry had passed through some muddy areas and small bits of fresh mud on sun baked stone were like a street sign to her.

The ground began to rise steeply, and Miriam exulted. They would have him soon. Kathan and his companions were no match for those with her. Zartah, Rathbone, and Keira would scale those rocks with ease. There was only one track up the rocks that a human could have climbed so she attacked the slope with a will.

As they topped the rise they were met with gunfire. 'That's far enough, Bounty Hunter," called a voice from the rocks ahead.

"We're not bounty hunters," bellowed Zartah. "We're Nara Clan. Lady Marla sent us to bring her brother Kathan home."

"You lie, Bounty Hunter. I saw Marla accept the inhibitor myself before I was sent here to this hell."

"Yes, she took the inhibitor, but the old Viceroy has been killed. Lortax of Nara is Viceroy now and Marla is once again High Priestess. A lot has happened since you came here."

"It was a nice try, Bounty Hunter," a maniacal voice laughed as a hail of gun fire pinned them down temporarily. A moment after the barrage stopped a small ship rose into the air and sped away, keeping close to the ground.

"Dammit," muttered Zartah as he grabbed at his comm unit. "Zartah to Micha. We caught up but he escaped in a small speeder heading southwest."

"Got him on scans, Zartah. Sending a ship for you."

The Hunter and the Hunted

"Where are we going, Kat?"

"Compound Two, they're the only ones with weapons to bring down that ship."

"Do you think they can?"

"I don't know, Alad, but they're our best chance. I just hope they're not too bitter about our last visit." Alad chuckled but said nothing more. He just hung on as Kat sent the speeder through some tight twists and turns. Kat kept the machine close to the ground, hoping the terrain would confuse the bigger ship's sensors. It was a vain hope.

They came in hard and fast, keeping to the weapon's blind spot. There was a wild panic in the compound yard as the speeder swept in and landed. No one tried to disembark from the small flyer; it had been instantly surrounded by hellhounds and armed hunters. There was no reasoning with either of these mindless beasts. Kat would wait until they were called off.

When the speeder made no threat, a tall man walked out from behind a building and whistled. The hounds and hunters backed off a bit. "You in there, Kat?" he bellowed.

"How did you know it was me?" Kat's voice chuckled over the speaker system.

"I heard from Nodran that the mercs were on your trail. They sound like a tough and persistent crew."

"Indeed they are. What are my chances of sanctuary?"

"After your last visit to our peaceful home? I'd say there will be a high cost."

"Name the terms," sighed Kathan.

"I get the merc ship if it survives and any surviving mercs, plus a full shipment at your expense."

"A full shipment? Good gods, it will take me years to pay for that."

"Not my problem, Kat." The tall man was grinning with delight now.

"Understood," Kathan replied through clenched teeth. "All right, you get the mercs, their main ship, and a full shipment; I get any small fighter ships on that intruder."

"You get one small ship, if there are any, nothing more."

"You're killing me here." Kathan sighed in defeat. He knew he was out of options.

"Time's up, Kat, take it or blast off. The mercs will soon be within range."

"I have no choice, do I? Alright, deal, but you'd better get them while they're in the air. You don't want to face this crew on the ground."

"I know, Nodran told me about them. They've got a full-fledged witch with them. You make the most interesting enemies, Kat."

"Tell me about it," grumbled Kathan as he stepped out of the speeder. "Alad, fuel her up. We want this ship ready if the mercs break through."

"Have a little faith, Kat," laughed the tall man. "We've increased the power and the range of the weapon. We're ready for the mercs." Kathan didn't reply, but he had serious doubts. These mercs were like something out of the old legends of heroes and gods. He wasn't sure anything could stop them.

ZARTAH WAS MUTTERING impatiently when the Arcalian fighter swept in and landed gracefully. The hatch dropped open and they all leaped inside. The ship was instantly in the air again, Brenna at the helm. Miriam buckled into a chair while Zartah took the co-pilot's seat. Rathbone and Keira manned the guns. The ship was already of the trail of the speeder. "Brenna to Micha, I've got them and we're on the trail."

"Good work, Brenna. Jorge will give you the co-ordinates for where they landed."

"They'll go to Compound Two," Miriam said. "Compound Two has a weapon for shooting down ships."

Brenna relayed that information to Micha. He quickly responded. "We'll draw their fire, Brenna, you take out their weapons."

"Understood."

Keira gave a whistle and hand signal. "Guns ready," called Rathbone.

"You've got this, Brenna," said Zartah. "I'll go man the tail guns." He kissed Miriam's hair on his way by.

"He's gone to ground. I've got the co-ordinates," called Brenna. "We're going in."

———⟫●⟪———

THE COMPOUND YARD WAS a mad scramble. The big weapon was uncovered and aimed at the sky, seeking its prey. It was only a few moments later they heard the warning as a ship came screaming through the atmosphere. The weapon fired, but missed. The mercs knew about the weapon and were taking evasive action.

The big ship dodged two more salvos then disaster struck the compound. The intruder dodged away and an Arcalian fighter swooped in just above the ground. It was moving far too fast to swing the weapon around. Gunfire swept the yard, sending everyone scrambling for shelter. As the fighter passed over the compound a missile launched from the port wing. A moment later the compound's weapon exploded in a thousand shards.

The fighter ship and the huge intruder both settled to the ground. Heavily armed mercs poured out onto the yard and engaged the hunters and hounds. It was no contest. The people watching were horrified at the speed and efficiency of the mercs. They asked no quarter, and they gave none. The battle was over quickly.

The compound was searched, but Kathan was gone. Jip took a quick walk through Kathan's speeder then checked the compound yard. He soon located where Kat had escaped through the wire and into the forest.

"This man is starting to annoy me," muttered Micha. "Miriam, take your hunters track him, take Jip with you."

Grinning, Miriam set out on the trail, Jip leading with his nose to the ground. Zartah, Keira, and Rathbone were close behind.

"This guy is slippery as an eel," Micha grumbled as he clenched his fist in frustration.

"It's what has kept him alive in this place," said Lessa. "Miriam will have him soon."

"I sure hope so, Lessa, I'm really getting a bad feeling about how long this is taking."

———⟢———

KATHAN FLED INTO THE forest, not trying to hide his trail, just trying to put some distance on the mercs. "Who in the nine hells are these guys?" he muttered as he ran. He knew of only one last possible sanctuary; he only hoped he could reach it. That and Pyne would be there waiting for him.

His men ran behind him, uncomplaining. This wasn't the first time they'd been on the run. For the past number of years they'd stayed with Kathan, ever since he'd set them free of the slave collars on Overlord. He had always managed to find a way to outsmart his pursuers and they were certain he would this time.

Kathan wasn't so confident. He'd never encountered hunters as determined, or as efficient, as these mercs. They reminded him of stories his father had told them when he was a child. His father had regaled him with the heroic tales of the early days of Nara Clan. A time in the far past when a group of mighty warriors had broken free from their masters and formed the free clans.

Maybe these people were telling the truth. Could the Viceroy be dead? Could Marla be high priestess again? No, that was impossible. He'd watched in chains as the inhibitor was placed on her head and the light of reason had left her eyes. Whatever these mercs wanted, he was determined they shouldn't have it.

Darkness fell and they climbed a tall tree to be safe from the predators. They dared not travel at night without Pyne. Sleeping in trees was a trick they had learned from the Muties. The Muties knew lots of great things about survival in the forest and Kathan had taken pains to learn as many as possible.

Kathan's biggest problem now wasn't the mercs on his trail; it was the shakes from coming off the drug so fast. If he shook too hard he might fall from the tree. Cursing softly, he removed his belt and used it to lash his arm to a branch. If he fell he'd probably dislocate a shoulder, but at least he'd survive.

Morning found him on the ground searching for herbs to quell the shakes and nursing a sore shoulder. It was barely light, but Kathan was desperate. He managed to find one and began chewing thoughtfully. He knew he couldn't outrun the mercs for long and there was no way to shake them off his trail, not with Miriam as their tracker.

So why the hell was Miriam working for them anyway? She was as independent as a person could get, fully convinced she was a Mutie, and she was a friend. At least she was the daughter of a friend and he had protected her more than once. What could make her turn on him? What could have happened to make her hunt him with such determination?

The herb did the trick and the tremors eased off. There was no more time for musings, the men were awake and it was time to run. They didn't try to hide their tracks; that was a waste of valuable time now. They just fled towards their last hope of escape. A place Kat called Mutie Central.

———◉———

"THEY SLEPT IN THIS tree last night," said Miriam as she studied the ground. "He's pulled some of this herb to chew. He must be going through withdrawal from the drug; the herb will ease the tremors."

"Tremors?" asked Zartah.

"If one comes off the drug too quickly the body goes into shock. There are violent tremors. He would have had difficulty staying in the tree."

"Why would they sleep in the tree, Miriam?" asked Rathbone.

"They must not have weapons to repel the predators," she replied. "Also, they all rested in hopes of being fresh enough to outdistance us."

"That won't happen," signalled Keira. Miriam looked puzzled so Rathbone translated for her.

"Keira, I must learn your speech," she smiled.

Just then there was a shriek in the trees and Jip returned carrying the carcass of a small animal which he began to devour. He didn't look like he wanted to share so they contented themselves with ration bars.

Zartah was grinning as Jip finished his meal, rose and found the scent then trotted off down the trail. Miriam laughed and followed with the others close behind her. It was midday when she suddenly stopped and gazed all around. In a moment she called softly and Jip returned to her.

"What is it?" asked Zartah, on full alert.

"I know where he's going," she replied. "We can go faster now, for I know other ways to get to the place. It's a place few humans have ever seen and far fewer have returned from."

"Miriam?"

"It's the secret place of the Muties. There is one place where the Muties are safe and where no human can go unless he is escorted there.

Pyne must have hidden Kathan there before. I'll bet that's where Pyne went after he left us. We can travel faster now until we get close then we will have to follow a careful path."

Zartah would have inquired further, but she was already running down a different trail. Jip bounded happily along at her side and the others followed closely. They ran until darkness forced them to stop. "Tomorrow we'll proceed more slowly," said Miriam. "We're nearly there. With luck we'll arrive first. If we can present our case first we'll get a chance to face Kathan and explain to him. If he arrives first we may not be allowed to see him."

"I don't believe I'm willing to take no for an answer, Sweetheart," said Zartah. "I know Micha won't be."

"Please promise you won't hurt the Muties, my companion. They've done no wrong in this."

"Miriam, we're not trying to force Kathan to return with us. We're just trying to speak with him and offer him the chance to go home. If he chooses not to go then he can send messages for Lady Marla. This is all we're trying to do. We need to verify this Kat person is indeed Kathan of Nara; then explain our mission to him. I'm just afraid he'll keep this up until Micha gets angry."

"What will happen if Micha gets angry?"

"He'll set Lady Arlessa loose on this planet."

"I have seen what she can do, and I don't want that to happen."

"No, my love, you haven't yet seen a tiny fraction of what Lady Arlessa can do, especially when she's angry. She's already annoyed at this affair, but she'll hold herself in check as long as Micha remains calm."

Miriam rose with a sigh. "We will not rest this night," she said firmly. "We'll go cautiously, but we must arrive at Orlem before Kathan. Come; follow very closely and as quietly as possible."

AT THE HEART OF THE empire the slow steady click of the Emperor's heels on the floor were the only sounds in his opulent office to indicate his agitation. As he paced, his mind raced over the upcoming parliament he had organized. The newly appointed leaders of the various sectors would be there to claim their reward for the part they'd played in his victory.

Emperor Loran the First knew better than anyone what he had to do. He had to grant them power, but not too much. The authority had to be spread out enough so none of them got delusions of seizing the throne. It would be a delicate balance, but nothing beyond his capabilities, under normal circumstances.

The big problem for Loran was that these weren't normal circumstances. Somehow the power to the building had failed in a winter storm. It had been lost for only a few moments, but it had been enough. The security record in his office had a gap of several minutes. Had someone engineered the power failure? Had he been compromised? Had that damned controller device surfaced in the hands of another man?

Cursing inwardly, he paced and mentally reviewed each appointment and promotion he planned to give. None seemed to be excessive or out of place. Perhaps he was just being paranoid. "Ah well," he sighed, "even paranoids have enemies, and I have far more than the rest."

His reverie was broken as his trusted friend and chief of security entered and knelt. "Sire."

"Rise and be seated, Hoaka. Is all in readiness?"

"It is, Sire. They're gathering in the great hall even now. My men are double checking all security and seizing all weapons. Sire, these people have come expecting to be granted wealth and power; you have nothing to fear from them. It is far too soon after the coup to expect an assassin, but we're being doubly vigilant."

"Never forget Rathbone of Urn and his damnable vendetta," sighed the Emperor as he lowered himself into a chair.

"He can't get to you here, Sire," replied Hoaka then he chuckled. "Yes, I suppose you've heard that before. I've told my men to go under the assumption that Rathbone will make an attempt. If he does we'll be ready, and if he doesn't then no harm done."

"What of the progress with the rebellions?"

"They spring up as quickly as they're put down, but they're losing steam," replied Hoaka. "Once you hand out the titles to the new gentry, it'll be up to the new lords to quell their sectors."

"Indeed, Hoaka, but we'll have to keep an eye on them none the less. Is there any news from Sector Nine?"

"The Black Witch has taken her hounds and fled the galaxy, so the reports say, Sire. I believe she's gone to Exile for some reason of her own."

"You know of Exile?"

"I do, Sire. I was part of the security team that carried old Baran of Borealis Prime to that distant place. I was assigned to company headquarters as my reward for service. I cannot imagine why she would be out there unless she's trying to prepare a bolt hole in case of disaster."

"You mean invasion."

"I mean Sector Nine being brought into the Empire," grinned Hoaka.

"Perhaps you're right. She could be quite comfortable on Overlord, but cut off forever from the rest of the galaxy. I quite like that idea, Hoaka. Thank you. I shall give this some thought. Now, about the security recording of this office and my rooms, how are you doing with that?"

"Everything is on extended independent power source now, Sire. Redundant backups are also in place. There won't be another lapse. The guards at the doors swear no one came in or went out during the black out."

"Then all is well, Hoaka. Come, let's not keep the new Lords of the Empire waiting." He rose and strode toward the door, his trusted Security chief close behind.

It was many hours later the emperor was back in his office, his mind still troubled. All had gone according to plan; the galaxy was fully under his control. Well, all except for the Borelian Free States, but they were no threat to him.

Keeping an eye on them would be more entertaining than conquering them would be. The witch would keep Brenna and her mother safe, and that fact gave him a strange sense of relief. In spite of it all Loran loved his rebellious daughter and wanted to keep her safe from harm.

His biggest problem right now was finding a way to convince the witch to help him. After their last encounter she wasn't likely to be easy to convince. There had to be a way; there had to be something she wanted that he could use as leverage. What was she really after out on Exile, he wondered?

Meeting at Orlem

It had been a night Zartah was in no hurry to repeat. It was one thing to stand watch and fend off predators at night, but it was another matter to move through their territory under a starless sky. His blaster was nearly drained and so was he. Thank the gods it was getting light. The total darkness of nights on Exile was unnerving.

How Miriam managed to find her way in the gloom was a mystery he doubted he would ever solve. However, she had found her way. The travel had been slow, but they had arrived at their destination in one piece. There, on a low cliff face, was the entrance to Orlem. Another hour's walk would put them there.

Zartah sighed and dropped his small pack to the ground. Rathbone scooped it up without a word. They were tired, but that wasn't so unusual during a mission. Many times they'd gone for long periods without sleep then fought a hard battle at the end of it. Such was the nature of life in the crew. Zartah nodded and Miriam led them onward.

The low cliff loomed larger as they approached. Closer inspection showed it to be the rim of a crater, an ancient crater. There were caves leading into it and Zartah nodded as his keen eyes took in everything about the place. Those caves would lead to open ground inside most likely. This sanctuary would be vulnerable to attack from above.

Miriam's arm swept out to stop him and Zartah froze in his tracks. She moved a fern that was in his path and he saw the nasty leg hold trap. She nodded approval as he stepped in behind her. She continued slowly, the others stepping in her footsteps to avoid any further traps.

Miriam stopped several yards from the largest cave and dropped to one knee. She gestured for the others to do the same. They did, grateful for the rest. Kneeling they waited.

"Miriam?"

"They're watching, dear companion. We're being judged. If they decide to speak with us we'll have the chance to convince them we mean no harm to them, Orlem, or Kathan."

"What happens if they decide otherwise?"

"They'll drive us away or kill us."

"I'm getting tired of all this diplomacy," grumbled Zartah. "I'm tired, hungry, and I'm running out of patience. They'd better start talking soon."

"Please be patient, my love. Please let me speak for us."

Before the conversation could go further a figure appeared in the mouth of the cave. As it advanced slowly, a dozen figures rushed out and brandished crude weapons. Miriam heard Jip growl softly and she put out a hand to scratch behind his ear.

The figure turned out to be an old woman with a distorted face and abnormally large hands. She leaned on a wooden staff for support. "I remember Miriam. Why does she bring armed humans to Orlem?"

"I remember Wista, she who speaks for Orlem. This one is Zartah, my mate. These folk are armed to defend from predators. They bring no harm to Orlem. We wish only to be heard."

"The words of Pyne have already been heard," replied the old woman as the giant Mutie appeared at her side. "We are cautioned to be wary of your words. You would bring harm to one who has been a great friend to the folk of Orlem."

"We wish only to speak peacefully to Kat who is Kathan of Nara and kinsman to my mate."

"Kinsman? You can prove this?"

"Zartah, show her your markings."

Zartah opened his shirt and exposed the tattoos on his neck. "These are the marks of my clan," he said rising to his feet and turning to give her a better look. "I wish to speak with Kathan, to tell him of events that have happened since he was taken away. I wish to explain why we came and to take him back home, but only if he chooses to go. If he chooses to remain here, I'll carry messages to his family for him. This and only this is my purpose here."

"If this is truth," said Pyne, "then why did you attack Compound Six?"

Zartah shook his head in frustration. "Listen carefully. When first I came here I was shot down, attacked, tracked, and Kathan fled in fear. Everywhere I go people attack first without letting me speak. I will not leave until I've spoken with Kathan. Please help me for everyone's sake."

"Explain what you mean by everyone's sake," demanded the old woman.

"My boss is in a warship high above this place as we speak," replied Zartah. "He is also of Nara Clan and a determined man. If I report you've refused me he'll rain down destruction from above. Orlem will fall just as Compound Six and Compound Two have done. He will take Kathan by force and many people will die. I don't want that to happen. Please help me."

There was a pause as the woman and Pyne conferred. At length she turned back to them. "We don't believe your threats. Go from this place or suffer."

Suddenly Rathbone surged to his feet and charged; Keira right at his side. Before the woman's guards could react the mercs were on them, hurling them aside and batting down the crude weapons.

Pyne swept Keira against the cliff face with a force that would have killed a normal woman, but she shook herself and came at him again. His next blow struck only empty air as she ducked and lashed out at his knee from behind. The huge Mutie began to topple over, but Keira was on him, powerful legs squeezing the air from his lungs and steely arms choking the life from him. Pyne went limp and sagged to the ground with her on his back. Rathbone was standing guard over her.

"Don't kill him, lover," rumbled Rathbone. "We need him alive."

She replied with a few sweet notes that hung in the air. With a grin she released Pyne and leaped to her feet. Again she sang and everyone gazed at her in wonder. "She says we have defeated you easily," translated Rathbone, "but we've harmed no one. You can now see the truth of Zartah's words. Help us to complete our mission peacefully."

"You truly will not force Kat to go if he doesn't wish to?" The old woman asked fearfully.

"As one Mutie to another," Rathbone said gently, "I promise we have no desire to harm Kathan. His sister is the supreme commander of us all. She wants to learn of his fate and to see him again if possible. This is why we have come."

"You are Mutie?"

"How else could I do the things I do?" he replied gently. "They experimented on me too, but I escaped them."

"These humans allow you among them as an equal?"

"Yes. They are now my family, my people. They'll hold to their word, Wista. See, my mate hasn't harmed Pyne. She didn't kill."

"She is Mutie?"

"Keira cannot speak. That power was taken from her. I'm Rathbone."

"Rathbone has proved his worth to us. The words of Miriam's mate will be heard. Come." Wista turned and led them into the cave.

The cavern wasn't deep; light could be seen coming from the other side. They quickly emerged to a gentle slope that went down to a glittering lake. There were huts clustered along the shoreline and others scattered up the sides of the crater. Everywhere misshapen figures could be seen moving about. There were a few humans as well.

"I see some humans," said Zartah. "So I'm not the first to see this place."

"Some humans have come to us seeking sanctuary," replied Wista. "No, you aren't the first. Those who come to us remain until they decide to leave. When they leave they're given the forgetting root to chew so they won't remember the way to Orlem."

"The forgetting root, is that the one Kat uses?" asked Zartah.

"Yes it is. He first used it to forget the pain, but he became addicted to the drug made by Nodran. Now he chews the root so his body forgets the powerful effects of the drug. It is a sorrow to watch him deteriorate this way.

"When Pyne first brought him to us it was for healing. Soon after Pyne took him away he returned with freed slave Muties. Since that time he will occasionally come to us with more freed Mutie slaves. Those people are all here. They will defend him utterly."

"As I have said before, he needs no defense from us. We only wish him to hear us."

"I will make that happen, but you must not harm him, and he must be allowed to decide what to do with the information you bring to him. Agreed?"

"Agreed, Wista, and thank you."

"Kat has yet to arrive, but Pyne says he is coming. You're all tired. We'll provide food and fire. You may rest until he appears then we'll negotiate the time of the gathering. All will hear the words of Zartah as well as the words of Kat."

They were led to a resting place near the water. A fire was built up and food was soon roasting by the fire. Once they'd eaten and exchanged a few pleasantries with their hosts they were told to relax and rest. They easily found comfortable positions and began to fall asleep, all except Keira. She was fully alert.

"Keira," Zartah called softly, "wake me for next watch." She smiled and nodded then turned back to keeping an eye on the locals while her crew mates caught some much-needed rest. Even though they were safe they'd keep watch. Exile had presented them with far too many unpleasant surprises. Zartah wouldn't let his guard down.

Once Keira wakened him, Zartah took up a lookout post. The daily life of Orlem went on all around them, but they were given a wide berth so they could rest. Stepping a bit away from his companions, Zartah reached for the comm unit at his shoulder.

"Zartah to Micha."

"Micha here. Report."

"We've been allowed entrance to Orlem and we have a promise we'll be heard."

"That's good news, if he actually shows up."

"I believe he will, Boss."

"But you think he'll bolt as soon as he learns you're there, right?"

"Right. These folks will warn him for certain."

"All right, Zartah, I'll take steps to prevent that. Get some rest. Micha out."

It was late in the day when Kathan arrived.

———————◈———————

THE SHIP SWEPT IN FAST and low, bearing down on the temple of Nova. A woman dressed in black robes stood waiting for it to land. Commander Darks had already relayed to her news of the inbound ship.

The big bird alit gracefully then Gorda, Murtah, and Ena spilled out of the hatch. Murtah and Ena went to check on their children while Gorda approached the woman in black. He dropped to one knee before her, but she raised him up and stepped into his arms. "Gorda."

"Lady."

"I'm Norlene when we're alone, dear man. Tell me what's happened?"

"Lady Marla's brother is alive and as slippery as a company spy. He thinks we're bounty hunters and is doing his best to evade us. Micha is getting restless and he's getting nervous; he sent me back to find out what is happening. Both he and Lady Arlessa are becoming anxious."

"Their instincts are as sharp as ever," chuckled Norlene as she took his arm and walked him into the temple. Once in her rooms she brought him food and water.

"Well, they're right to be anxious, Gorda. Much has happened since you left. First, the Emperor has staged a takeover and now has control of the whole galaxy, all except for us. I doubt it'll be long before he turns his attention to Sector Nine. Marla and Lortax are already in conference with all the leaders of the free states. If the Emperor comes at us there's not much hope we could survive."

Gorda gave a long low whistle. "Dang, girl, you sure don't sugar coat it much."

"Sugar coat? How could I sweeten that bit of news?"

"Point taken," he chuckled. He reached for the comm unit on his shoulder. "Murtah, better fuel her up. We're going back and we're not wasting time."

"Understood, Gorda. We heard the news."

"Gods, this is not making for a quiet old age for me," sighed Gorda. "Norlene, have you any good news at all?"

"I missed you," she replied with a twinkle in her eye.

"I've missed you too," he chuckled. "With any luck this news will bring the crew home for a while."

"Do you really think Micha will abandon the mission?"

"No, I don't. It seems odd that I'd willingly follow such a young man, but he's an old warrior."

"That's the truth of it; Micha is an old soul all right. Gorda, what's plaguing your mind?"

He sighed and looked away for a moment before speaking. "I have a problem that I can't seem to find a solution for."

"Oh? Can I help?"

"Perhaps. Zartah's taken a mate. I watched as he patiently overcame the woman's natural fear and mistrust to claim her."

"This has relevance to your problem?"

"It does. Zartah seemed to instinctively know what to do. Sadly, I don't."

"Are you saying you wish to bond with a companion but can't find the courage or the words to ask her?" There was merriment dancing in her eyes and Gorda was blushing deeply, something quite unusual for a battle-hardened mercenary.

"Yes."

"Oh my, that can be a problem."

"The problem is, the woman is well above my station in life."

"Gorda, I'll stop teasing. I'm still in mourning, but the time for that has passed and I freely admit I'll accept you if you ask me. Please just grant me this. Go back to Micha and finish the mission. When you return to me, my time of mourning will be passed, and I'll be ready. Ask me then."

"You'd truly accept me, Norlene?"

"Yes I will, silly man, but my people had a certain ritual for a witch to end her period of mourning. I just need a few days to set myself free."

Just then his comm crackled to life. "Gorda, ship is fueled and ready."

"On my way, Murtah. Warm her up."

Gorda rose to his feet, gently pulling Norlene close. She put her hands on his chest and smiled. "A few more days, Gorda, that's all I ask, and then we'll declare the bond before Arlessa. If the Emperor comes, I'll stand at the side of my mate."

"If the Emperor comes, Lady, you'll defend the temple and I'll defend you," he smiled. She lightly kissed his cheek then watched him stride out of the temple. She smiled with delight at the new spring in his step.

Gorda leaped easily into the ship. "Let's go," he said as he clipped a harness on.

Murtah worked the pilot's controls and the ship rose through the atmosphere. Ena was in the co-pilot's seat. She grinned at Gorda as she spoke. "Gorda, you seem to be in good spirits for a man who has just heard the worst news of our lifetimes."

"The news wasn't all bad, Ena."

"Really? So Lady Norlene got tired of waiting and spoke first, did she?"

Gorda blushed deeply as he spoke. "Dammit, Ena, that's not fair, using witch training on me. Murtah, control your woman."

"I'd love to, Gorda. Have you any idea how that might be accomplished?"

"Hush you," laughed Ena as she slapped Murtah's broad shoulder.

Caught

"I think we did it, Kat," said one of the three men following Kathan. "There's been no sign of them all day. I think we lost 'em."

"I hope you're right, but I doubt it. There's no way in hell for us to lose Miriam. No, she's figured out where we're going. I just hope we got here first," sighed Kathan as he stepped out of the forest at the entrance to Orlem. Wista was there already. Kathan's instincts screamed of danger and he was on full alert.

"I remember Wista," he said as he bowed in her direction.

"Wista remembers Kat. Come, we have been expecting you."

"You have? Why?"

"Pyne has been here for days. He and the others await your arrival."

"Others?"

"Others came claiming to be your kinfolk. They've agreed to the laws of Orlem. They will speak, you will speak, and when all words have been heard then decisions will be made. They've promised no harm will come to you."

"Wista, these people are very dangerous. They've taken Compound Six by force. You can't trust them to keep their word. I believe I'll just be on my way."

"That's a bad idea, Runner," said a voice from the edge of the forest.

Kat stiffened in place at that voice. Slowly he turned to face the newcomers. His heart froze in his chest. He couldn't hope to escape these people. The young man who spoke was armed to the teeth. To his left was a witch in full flowing black robes, fire dancing about her body, yet burning nothing it touched. To the man's right was a small woman, full black, dressed in battered fatigues, armed, and wearing the black armband of a dispatcher. Her face was masked, but her eyes were hard. His only hope lay in Orlem.

"I claim sanctuary in Orlem," Kat said as he spun back to Wista.

"Granted," replied Wista. "Come, Micha, food and rest await inside."

"Wait, you know these people? They bought you?"

"What could they offer to buy a Mutie, Kat. Your remark is not respectful."

"I beg forgiveness of Wista," sighed Kathan, resigning himself to his fate. "Please allow my men to go free, Bounty Hunter. There's no gain in harming them."

Micha stepped up beside Kathan as they came out the other side of the cave and into Orlem. He opened his shirt to show his tattoos. "I'm not a bounty hunter, Kathan," he said. I'm just a messenger. However, I am a mercenary. I insist you listen to my message so I can get paid."

"You're truly Nara Clan?"

"I am and so are a number of my crew. So, will you listen, or do I have to tie you to a post to make you listen?"

"Promise me you won't harm these people and I'll listen."

"Done. Tell me, Kathan, why do you pretend to be a madman? I suspect you're as sane as the rest of us."

"I suspect you're wrong about that one, Mercenary. Only a madman would lead a life such as mine. So, does the condemned man get a meal before facing the music?"

"We'll play by Wista's rules here," grinned Micha, "but I warn you. Try anything slippery and I'll hunt you down, tie you up, and sit on your chest while I deliver my message."

Pyne appeared as Micha spoke. "I ask forgiveness of Kat, but I was defeated in combat. The silent woman spared my life. Kat, these people have shown respect for Orlem and the people."

"It's not your fault, Pyne. You've never faced people like this. Neither have I for that matter."

"They are Mutie also, Kat. This is why you can't defeat them. Their abilities are different than normal humans."

"I believe you, Pyne."

Kathan was led to the place where Zartah and the rest of the crew were waiting by a fire. Smells of food were everywhere, and he was starved for real food. He was also starting to get the shakes again. Without a word, Pyne handed him some dried root. He chewed it thoughtfully and the tremors ceased. Only then could he keep real food down.

Kathan frowned at Miriam as he chewed. "Why did you betray me?" he asked at last. "What could they offer you to make you betray everything you are?"

"I've betrayed nothing and no one," she replied gently. "I haven't harmed you or any of your people, and I haven't brought harm to you. You're behaving stupidly; you should listen to these folk."

"What did they give you, Miriam?"

"A life, Kat, and the knowledge of what I truly am; that's what they gave me."

"Oh, and what do they say you truly are?"

"She's a Devan," rumbled Rathbone, "but you already knew that."

"She's only half Devan," replied Kathan, "and the only success those fools on Overlord ever had. We brought her out, her father and I. We took Miriam and her mother and brought them to Exile where they could live free. We had to keep Miriam out of the hands of the Insiders, and we had to protect Orlem, that's why we never brought her here."

"You knew?" said Miriam. "You knew and Father knew but neither of you spoke to me of this?"

"We couldn't, Miriam. If we told you, you'd have demanded to be equal to the humans, and then one of them would've sold you to the Insiders. You'd have ended up back in a company laboratory. This was the only way to protect you."

"I should have been told."

"Miriam, these mercs will sell you to the company for profit. Run now while you can still escape them."

Confused, Miriam looked at Zartah and then at the others. She didn't want to believe Kat, but the seeds of distrust had been planted. Suddenly Lessa reached over and gently gripped Miriam's arm. "Remember, Miriam, remember what life has been like with the crew. You're one of us now; we won't betray your trust."

As the witch touched her Miriam felt a wave of warm loving energy flow through her. She remembered Lessa's gentle kindness and guidance when she was upset. She remembered the sweet joy she'd found in Zartah's arms and the acceptance in Micha's eyes. She reached for Zartah's hand as she spoke.

"These are my people now, Kat. They won't betray me, and they won't harm you unless you force them to. Just listen to what they have to say; they ask nothing more of you. If you wish to be rid of us then listen."

"Nice touch, Witch," grumbled Kathan, "but I've seen that one before."

"Miriam spoke the truth, Kathan," replied Lessa, her voice going cold. "Beware you don't push me too hard. I grow weary of your suspicion and stupidity." She grew silent as the dispatcher reached out to lightly grip her shoulder.

"Enough," declared Wista as she approached. "It's time. Come."

They rose and followed her towards a small rise in the heart of the community. Kathan knew he had no chance to escape; the mercs kept him surrounded and watched him carefully. Worse yet, Pyne seemed to trust them since the silent woman had spared his life. He was going to have to play this one out and see what would happen next.

Wista made her way to the raised dais and raised her arms. "People of Orlem, we are gathered today to hear two groups of people speak. The humans have agreed to abide by the laws of Orlem. Does this satisfy you?"

"It satisfies us," came a chorus of voices.

"Then let us begin. Micha, you will speak first. You may direct your comments to one person or to the many."

Micha stepped forward to stand on a lower dais as he was directed. "I'll speak first to all and then to Kathan of Nara," he began.

"Many years ago there was a tradition that forced a High Priestess to marry the reigning Viceroy. At the time of marriage an inhibitor was placed on the Priestess to numb her mind and control her. In the days of Kathan's youth, this was the way of things. Kathan's sister Marla, who was high priestess at the time, suffered this fate.

"In the years that followed Lady Arlessa came to be High Priestess. She broke this tradition, refused the marriage, and refused the inhibitor. In the struggle that followed the Viceroy was killed and replaced by Lortax, Chieftain of Nara Clan. Lady Marla was released and returned to the seat of the High Priestess. I personally witnessed these events as did many of my crew.

"A short time ago Lady Marla came to me and asked me to find her brother, Kathan of Nara. She wishes to know if he yet lives. She had recently learned of the existence of Exile and she sent me here to find him. I believe the man known to you as Kat is the man I seek.

"Kat, I believe you to be Kathan of Nara, my own clan. Lady Marla, High Priestess of all the Borelian Free States wishes to know of your fate. She wishes with all her heart to see you again and verify for herself that you are alive and well."

"I'm alive anyway," sighed Kathan, as he stepped onto the other small dais facing Micha with Wista on her high Dais between then as mediator.

"So you confirm that you are indeed Kathan of Nara Clan."

"Yes, I'm Kathan. Mercenary, I wish to all the gods there was some way I could believe your tale. What you say is a dream of mine, a dream from the drugs. I've been addicted for so long now, sometimes I have such dreams even when I'm not using. See, my hand isn't shaking, that means I'm on the drug and dreaming."

"In that case, why not enjoy the dream to its fullest. Come back to Borealis Prime with me, see Lady Marla for yourself. Hold her in your arms and see that she's whole once again."

"Nice try, Merc, but I'm not that gullible."

"You will not relent?"

"No, I won't fall for your tricks."

"Very well then, do you have any message for Lady Marla?"

"If you see my sister," said Kat, a faraway look in his eye, "just tell her I love her. Tell her to be regal."

"She said to tell you to be noble."

"Tell her I do try as best I can."

"Very well then," sighed Micha, "my task is complete here. As soon as the rest of my crew returns I'll leave this system and relay your message. I'd be happy to leave now, but this system is hard to find and I don't want to miss my people in passing. It may take a day or two. I'll keep my ship in orbit above Orlem until I'm ready to leave. If you change your mind and decide to come with me, just hail the ship. She's called the Defender."

Wista looked at Kathan. "Are you satisfied, Kat?"

"I'm satisfied if he promises not to hunt me any further."

She turned to Micha. "Kat is satisfied if you swear an oath to no longer hunt him."

"I swear this hunt is finished. At first light I'll take my people back to my ship. I will no longer hunt the man called Kat."

"Are you satisfied, Kat?" asked Wista.

"I'm satisfied."

"Micha, are you satisfied?" she asked.

"I'm satisfied. I've fulfilled my mission, I've done my duty, and I will get paid. I'm content."

"Are there others who wish to speak to this issue?" There were none. "Then we're satisfied the ways of Orlem have been respected." Wista smiled and stepped down. She led them back to their resting place then left them, well pleased that violence in Orlem had been avoided.

As they settled down for the night, Micha took the first watch. Kathan and his men were settled near them as was the custom of Orlem. "You don't need a watch here, Merc," said Kathan. "Not unless you're afraid I might slip away in the night."

"Friend, I don't give a Relevian rat's ass what you do now, as long as you offer me no threat. I've done the job; now all I want is to get paid and go home."

"Is that all life is about for you, getting paid?"

"Far from it," said Lessa as she joined the conversation. "Micha is the Chief Guardian of the Temple of Nova Prime. As such he's far more interested in his people than in money. Unfortunately, a new colony needs many things and they all cost."

"So this is how you support your people?" asked Kathan.

"It is," sighed Micha, as he slid down to a seat on the grass. "I have a big crew and most of them have families. They need to be paid, so I have to find ways to make that happen. Lady Marla is going to pay a heavy price for you making me stay extra time and having to chase you all over creation."

The older man chuckled at that. "Merc, I mean Micha, you're the most determined man I've ever met. Nobody has ever stayed on my track like that. The funny part is, you have no idea what a great favor you've done for me."

"I did you a favor? What favor might that be?"

"You took the smug out of the Insiders of Compound Six, and you destroyed that damned weapon in Compound Two. That threat was a serious problem."

"Oh? I thought they were friends of yours."

"Far from it," chuckled Kathan. "They've been a pain in my butt for years. I nearly got killed several times trying to engineer Miriam's escape from there."

"You engineered her escape?"

"No, she managed that on her own. She's every bit as amazing as they'd hoped. You'll get a big price for her. Congratulations."

"Miriam's not for sale," replied Micha. "She's part of my crew, no more, no less."

"You're serious."

"I am. So what do you do here that makes some people hate you and other risk their lives for you?"

"I free the slaves, or as many as I can. I started doing it just to annoy the Insiders, but it soon became more than that. Some slaves I just don't give a damn about, but most I'll set free if I can. The slave Muties I find I bring here."

"Why?"

"Because they're people, just like any other. Yes they're damaged, but so are we all in one way or another. They deserve respect, but instead they're treated like dirt."

"You don't like that?"

"I saw my sister enslaved," growled Kathan. "I saw her treated like dirt, then I was shipped off here and left to rot or be fodder for the predators. Ah what the hells, you wouldn't understand anything like that."

"I was born slave," Micha replied softly. "I've seen a lot more than you know. It looks to me like you could use a few decent weapons."

"I could at that. I don't suppose you could spare a few?"

"I'll think about it. Tell me more about what you've been doing here."

"Why?"

"Because Marla will plague him for information," laughed Lessa.

"Now that does sound like Marla all right," grinned Kathan. "All right, I guess there's no harm in you knowing. That idiot in Compound Six is trying to build a ship that'll make it back to the Galaxy. He plans to take a few people, and a ship load of the dream drug to sell. What he doesn't know, and I haven't told him, is the first place he will reach is Borelian territory. The clans won't look too kindly on a drug dealer moving into their space."

"That's the truth," chuckled Micha.

"I work for him to get the damn drug, but also because he has enough influence to protect me while I work."

"Work at what?"

"Finding a way to kick every damned human, including myself, off this planet. Humans created the Muties then discarded them; they deserve a home world."

"That's what you're trying to do? Why?"

"Because since I was first taken prisoner I've been abused and tortured by humans. It was a Mutie that first set me free and showed compassion and respect for me. They're more deserving, and I need a purpose in life. What's the point of a life without a purpose?"

"Now that I do understand," sighed Micha. "All right, here's my comm unit. Use it to contact me if you decide to come with me. You could ask the High Priestess and the new Viceroy for help here. On the other hand, if you decide to stay I'll contact you before I leave to let you know where to find the weapons."

"You're serious? You'll give me weapons?"

"I know I shouldn't. I should kick your butt for making me chase you all over the place when I should be home defending Nova. However, I guess we can spare a few bits. If you've got one of those little ships handy Rathbone could arm it for you."

"Sorry friend, you guys captured the last ship I had. I don't suppose you could spare me a fighter, could you?"

"I'll see," grinned Micha. "Pass back the comm unit." Kathan handed him the unit and Micha called the ship. "Micha to Defender. You awake Jorge?"

"Edie here, lover, Jorge is on sleep cycle. What do you need?"

"How many company fighter ships do we have on Defender?"

"Just a minute. All right, we had our two fighters plus eight company fighters. Zartah got shot down so we have seven left. Why? Is everything okay?"

"All's well, my love. Lady Marla just bought her brother an early Solstice gift. Tell Jorge to load one up to the hilt with weapons and ammo, then bring it down first light. You pick us up in one of our own ships."

"Understood, Edie out."

"You're serious?" asked Kathan as Micha tossed back the comm unit.

"You heard me; your ship will be here at first light. It'll be a short range fighter ship, fully fueled and fully armed. I'm sure Jorge will toss in a few small arms just for luck. If you decide to come with us you can fly your ship right into the hangar bay; if not then good luck to you."

"I couldn't go back even if I did want to," sighed Kathan.

"Why not?" asked Lessa.

"It's the drug, Lady. I've been addicted for years and now it takes stronger and stronger doses to get me past the pain and into the dreams. Worse yet, it takes more and more herb to keep me even when I'm not dreaming. I'm tied to this world, like it or not."

"Sounds like you're tied to that drug dealer too."

"Sadly, that I am. I curse the day the bastard got me hooked, and I swear there will be a day of reckoning for that. However, for now I need him to help finance my activities."

"Is there anything you could do for him, Lessa?" asked Micha.

"I believe there is, Micha," she replied. "Kathan, it would take a few sessions, but I believe I can take away the addiction for you. I would need your permission to do so."

"Woman, unless you're as powerful as the black witch herself, I doubt there is much you could do for me."

"I am," replied Lessa. "I'm Lady Arlessa, she who freed Lady Marla and destroyed the old Viceroy. I was temple trained and then I was trained by Lady Norlene, the black witch of legend, herself. She came through time to aid me in the restoration of Nova."

"Lady, that was a tale worth hearing. You're wasting your time as a merc. You should be in the entertainment sector."

Lessa caught Micha's hand to keep him from leveling Kathan. "There's only one sure way to know the truth of the tale," she grinned. "Accept the healing."

"You tell me the greatest witch in ten generations is out here running about on Exile as part of a merc crew, and you expect me to believe it? Go for it, Great Lady. Cure me of the drug addiction."

"With extreme pleasure," smiled Lessa. "Lie back here and relax."

He did. Lessa ran her hand above his body from head to toe and back again. Micha heard him sigh as his breathing deepened. Lessa then slipped in behind Kathan and cradled his head in her hands as she sang a healing song.

As her song went on, his sleep deepened, and he dreamed. He dreamed of Marla, he dreamed of home, he dreamed of running through the forest of Exile, and he dreamed of being free of the need and the pain. He didn't waken until morning. When his eyes finally opened he was alone with his men.

"Kat, are you okay?"

"Yes, I believe I am. I haven't felt this good in years. Where are the mercs?"

"They said they'd wait for us outside the caves. The leader said your Solstice gift is ready. The witch said the healing would last for a few days, but she'll need to do it again a few times for it to be permanent."

Kathan stood up and stretched out his hand. It was steady. "When was the last time I had some herb?"

"Yesterday, and there wasn't much to give you," said Pyne. "The witch has removed the need for a short time."

"But there's no pain either," marvelled Kathan. "Come on." He leaped away and raced up the hill toward the caves, his men struggling to keep up.

Kathan burst from the cave to see two ships just at the edge of the forest. One was a fighter of the Arcalian guard, probably the leader's ship. The second was a sweet little fighter ship, bristling with weapons. Kathan stopped right beside it.

"Well, you look happy," grinned Micha. "The fuel's been topped up and weapons are fully charged. There are two extra boxes of ammo for the small missile launchers and there are a few hand weapons, blasters and the like, inside."

"By all the gods, you are serious."

"I never wanted to harm you, Kathan. I just wanted to deliver my message and to invite you to come home."

"How are you feeling today?" asked Lessa as she appeared from around the ship.

Kathan dropped to one knee instantly. "Lady, I beg forgiveness for my attitude yesterday."

"Rise, Kathan, no harm was done, and no offence was taken. I could feel the pain emanating from you. Is that how you got addicted, to mask the pain?"

"It was, Lady. Lady, how can I ever thank you for this gift?"

"It won't last long, Kathan, a few days only. If I give you another healing before we leave it will last for a few months. Ideally I'd like to give you four treatments, one week apart. That would eliminate the addiction as well as the pain that caused it."

"Lady, I'll cherish these next few days free of pain and need. If your ship is still in these skies one week from today I'll call and beg another healing."

"And I will grant it," smiled Lessa. "Micha is getting anxious to leave. Until we meet again, Kathan of Nara, brother of my friend Marla, may you fare well." With that she leaped easily into the larger ship and it lifted gracefully from the ground.

"Kat, what's happened, and what does it all mean for Orlem?" asked Wista as she approached cautiously.

Kathan smiled broadly as he turned to her. "We've been given a ship, Wista. More, with this ship we can defend Orlem from an aerial attack as well. Once the mercs leave the system we will own the most powerful ship on the two planets. Oh Wista, we'll be able to do so much more now."

"Pyne said she's healed you from the drug and the pain."

"Yes, for a few days anyway. If they're still here in a week she'll give me another treatment. That should last much longer."

"Perhaps you should consider going with them to complete the cure."

"Wista, I won't leave Orlem undefended, nor will I leave the people vulnerable to the Insiders. We've been given this gift, Wista; I intend to enjoy it." Just then the comm unit in his pocket squawked.

Kathan pulled it out and responded. "Kat here."

"Stop standing around and go play with the new toy," laughed Lessa's voice.

He looked up but couldn't see the Arcalian fighter get swallowed up by the intruder class vessel, they were in orbit, yet he knew where to look. With a grin of delight Kathan keyed open his new ship and climbed into the pilot's chair. There were additional weapons and ammunition piled in the other chairs. He and his men were now far better equipped than they had ever been.

"Let's go," he shouted and closed the hatch. His men hurriedly clipped themselves into seat harnesses as he sent the ship leaping into the air.

"There he goes," said Lessa as the small ship leaped into the air and shot into space. It broke atmosphere and hurtled toward Overlord. "Where do you think he's going?"

"He had a mate once," said Miriam. "She was taken slave and sold to Overlord. It's said he has searched for her for years. Perhaps he's going to find and set her free."

"May his search be fruitful," said Lessa. "Micha, since we're not doing anything important except waiting for Gorda to return, do you think we could..."

"Follow Kathan and provide a little back-up?" grinned Micha.

"Exactly."

"Excuse me," said a timid voice from behind. They turned to see one of the freed slaves peering in. "I'm sorry; I just wanted to see the bridge. Did I hear you say Kat's going to free his mate?"

"Yes," replied Lessa, "why does that frighten you?"

"We should leave now before he finds her."

"Come here to me," said Micha. She came closer. "Explain."

"Kat was mated to Deela," said the woman. "Deela's a Mutie with a rare psychic talent. She was captured and bought by Delgar. He kept her until he became afraid of her then he sold her. They say she's kept hidden in total darkness. They say she was blinded, but that didn't stop her visions."

"How did she frighten Delgar?" asked Lessa.

"Deela sees things, things she shouldn't be able to know. She saw the death of Delgar's brother and she forsaw Delgar's death in the jaws of a beast. He caused her great pain to make her change what she said, but she couldn't. Finally he sold her."

"That's the trouble with seeing the future," sighed Lessa. "You don't often see what you want to see. Also, you only see snippets of reality, not the whole context."

"You know how she does this, Lady?"

"Not how she does it, but there are ways, and in my youth I did dabble with it for a while. Now, my curious one, have you seen enough? The bridge is truly off limits for passengers. Come, let's go to the mess for a snack, you and I." With that Lessa led the woman away.

"What do you make of all that, Boss?" asked Zartah as the two women left.

"Trouble," muttered Micha. "I don't need psychic abilities to know that. Gorda can't get here fast enough to suit me."

———————⊙———————

HOAKA ENTERED THE ROYAL office to find the Emperor relaxed back in his chair, his hands clasped behind his head and a big smile on his face. "What news, Hoaka?"

"All is well, Majesty. The governors have been successful in putting down the various rebellions and uprisings. Commerce is now flowing quite freely throughout the Empire, except for Sector Nine. Everything there goes through the Free Traders; unfortunately they pay no taxes to the Empire."

"Yes, well, we'll address this soon enough, my friend. However, you came to me; I didn't summon you. Therefore you have one small bit of information for me that you feel is important. Be seated and spill it. I have yet to shoot a messenger."

"Yes, Majesty," grinned Hoaka as he settled into a chair facing the Emperor. "News has reached me of a plot to assassinate you at the grand conference later this year."

"I want you to oversee the security precautions yourself, Hoaka."

"Yes, Sire. I'll be happy to take on that task."

"I have another task for you as well, my friend."

"Sire?"

"I'm taking a vacation, Hoaka. I want you to reign as regent in my absence."

"Majesty, no, please, that's a task for more skillful men than I."

"I need you to do this for me, my friend. The governors are already accustomed to working through you. They report to you, you come here, and then take the orders and decisions back to them. All you have to do is bring everything to this office as per normal, then take the appropriate messages back to them. If there's something big just say I'm thinking it over and will get back to them."

Hoaka did not respond for several moments. Finally he agreed, but he did not look happy about it. "What troubles you, Hoaka?"

"Several points, Majesty, if I may."

"Please do."

"Sire, I don't like the idea of you going off on your own without proper security. Also, in truth, I fear I might enjoy the power far too much. I don't want to meet the same fate as my predecessor."

"It's because you're aware of your own limitations and emotions that I've chosen you for this task, my friend. Just don't raise the taxes too high, don't start any wars, and don't antagonize anyone in Sector Nine."

"Sire?"

"I'm going into Borelian territory. I don't want them stirred up too soon, and I truly don't want them aware of me until I'm ready for them."

"Sire?" Hoaka had nearly risen from his chair.

"I'm going to visit my daughter, Hoaka. I don't think showing up with the entire fleet would gain me a hearing. I'll travel incognito. I hope to establish a truce with her and the witch. However, I'll need a few bargaining chips. Give me a few days then slowly start building up a military presence of the border. After two weeks, put up a heavy border tax on all goods coming out of that sector."

"I'll do as you ask, Sire, as always, but are you certain this is the only way?"

"I'm convinced of it, my friend; otherwise I wouldn't even consider it. I'll leave tonight. Please have a small speeder rigged out and provisioned for a long trip. Nothing fancy, Hoaka, I want a ship that'll pass unnoticed into Sector Nine. Once I'm in their territory you can start tightening the noose."

The new Regent left the Emperor's offices with a stony face. Those who worked for him knew something was in the wind, but he wasn't talking, and they knew better than to ask. Later that night there was a power loss for a few moments. When the power was restored, Hoaka hurried to the Emperor's offices then returned reporting that all was well with Emperor Loran.

When the power failed Loran slipped out of the office and joined Hoaka. They hurried up one floor to the roof where a small ship was waiting. The emperor climbed in and checked it out. "I said a small speeder, Hoaka. This has a few more comforts than I envisioned."

"I know, Majesty, but you did say it would be a long trip. The three man speeder is faster and has a bit more room to stretch out. This is a much older model that's been upgraded. We took it off a smuggler last week. I did plan to keep it for myself, but this seemed like the right ship for your journey. May you have a safe and successful trip, Sire."

"Thank you, Hoaka. Make sure I have an empire to come back to." He closed the hatch as he finished speaking. A moment later the small ship rose into the sky and disappeared. It was broadcasting Hoaka's personal codes. No one challenged it.

Prophecy

"Keeping an eye on me, Micha?" crackled the comms.

"I don't want you breaking that new toy," replied Micha, as he stepped closer to the vid screen so Kathan could see him more clearly. "Since we've got nothing to do except wait for Gorda, we thought we might fly back-up for you."

"Back-up? Are you serious?"

"Lady Marla wouldn't like it if I let you get into trouble and didn't help out."

"Marla always did watch out for me. Do me a favor; don't interfere unless I call for help."

"Agreed. Kathan, don't be shy about that call."

"Understood. Kat of Exile out."

"Something about that Kathan isn't quite right," muttered Zartah.

"Agreed, Zartah," sighed Micha. "Sadly, we have a few more days to wait for Gorda, and I highly doubt Kathan has stopped causing me trouble."

"It should prove to be an exciting few days," grinned Zartah. Micha just chuckled as he switched the vid screen to long range and scanned for Gorda's ship. It was way too soon for that and he soon turned his attention back to Kathan's small ship. It was just reaching Overlord's outer atmosphere.

"We're armed and ready, Kat. Are we doing recon or do we have a mission?"

"We're going after Deela."

"Kat, no. We don't even know where to look and..."

"And you don't want to find her anyway, do you? I need to know right now; can I depend on you three or not?"

"You can depend on us, Kat. If you really want to find her this is our best chance. We have a fighter ship that is fully equipped, and we have that intruder class full of super mercs as back-up. We're with you."

"Then let's see if we can track her down."

It was late in the day when the small ship swept down onto Delgar's plantation. It made a strafing run and knocked out the two troop carriers that were still parked there. The soldiers came boiling out onto the lawn, weapons blazing, but they had nothing that could harm a fighter ship. Kat made another strafing run then brought the ship in to hover near the main entry to the mansion. He grabbed the loudspeaker.

"Attention the house, send Delgar out here to parley."

"Delgar's not here," came a shouted reply.

"Send him out or I'll blow the house down around your ears."

"He's not here, dammit," bawled the officer who stepped out onto view. "He's been staying Melhome's plantation ever since your last raid."

"Contact him and tell him Kat is coming to visit," replied Kathan as the ship suddenly rose into the air and pivoted around. In another moment it vanished from sight.

"Melhome's place," mused one of his men. "That'll be tough to crack."

"You could be right," sighed Kat. "However, I'm willing to bet that's where they've got her. We've hit every other damned plantation on this cursed continent. There's only a few outliers on the bigger islands and the rest of the planet is water. I'm betting they've got her on Melhome's territory, that or they'll know where to find her."

"That place will have plenty of soldiers and firepower," said another of the men. "Even with this new ship and weapons we don't stand a chance of taking down Melhome."

"We could try a surprise raid," mused Kathan, "but I gave away that when I told them we were coming. I think we need a lot more fire power."

"Kat, you can't trust those mercs, can you?"

"Well, he kept his word about this ship, and he did let us go when he could have taken me. I think it may be worth a chance." With that Kathan sent the small ship out into space.

"Kat to Micha," he said as he picked up the comm unit.

"Micha here, are you having fun with your new toy?"

"Yeah, listen, Micha, were you serious about helping me?"

There was a deep sigh over the comms. "I was and I am. Somehow I knew you weren't finished causing me trouble. Want to come aboard Defender and tell me about it?"

"On my way. Kat out."

"Kat, are you seriously going onto that ship?"

"I am. He could have taken me a dozen times if that was his plan. You men stay on this ship. If things go sideways; make a run for it."

"Alright, Kat; I sure hope you know what you're doing."

"So do I," muttered Kathan as he brought the small ship into the launch bay of the intruder class ship.

The big merc who had been waiting for him at Orlem was waiting for him again. Zartah led Kathan to the mess hall where Micha and most of the crew were waiting. He was given a plate of food and shown to Micha's table.

Kathan ate slowly, watching Micha's face and trying to gauge the man's responses. He wasn't having much success for Micha could be as closed as a stone. Kathan broke first. "I need your help. Sadly I can't pay, but you can have all the loot you can find and I'll record messages to Marla asking her to pay you."

Micha did not blink; he just sat, stone faced, in thought for a long moment. "What's the job?"

"I have a mate," sighed Kathan, as he leaned back in his chair and pushed away his plate. After a moment he leaned forward again, resting his elbows on the table. "They took her from me years ago. I want her back, and I believe she's being held prisoner in one of the plantations below."

"I gave you a ship, isn't that enough to dig her out?"

"No, sadly, it isn't. They'll have lots of fire power and soldiers."

"Are you certain that is the right plantation? There seems to be quite a few of them on this continent."

"I've raided most of them. I always hear about her being there, but she's never where I expect to find her. This plantation is the one place I've never been able to break into. It has to be the right one."

"That or they keep moving her around," rumbled Rathbone. "They'd only bother with that if she was extremely valuable."

"She is," sighed Kathan. "Deela can see the future, or bits of it. She's a Mutie. She sees what the rest of us can't, and she scares the hell out of most people."

"But not you," said Micha.

"No, not me. All I wanted to do was protect her, but they caught us both and took her away. I'm told they torture her to tell them where I'll strike next. That may be one of the reasons they seem to be waiting for me half the time."

"What is it about her that frightens people, and why does it not bother you?" asked Lessa.

"What she sees is often the darkest moments a person will face. She's seen my darkest moments, that and more. She foresaw the madness and the addiction; she saw the pain and the torture as well as the sorrow. She also saw our being ripped apart. She begged me to leave her, but I couldn't."

"I can understand that," said Micha. "All right, Kathan, we'll help you. Her name's Deela?"

"Yes."

"Send the co-ordinates of the plantation to the bridge then get ready to fly. I'll bring Defender in close to draw their attention; you keep an eye on them from a distance to make sure there are no tricks. Zartah, you, Miriam, Rath, and Keira take the Arcalian ship and fly on his wing. If things go sideways Miriam can track anybody and the crew will deal with any of the nasties."

As Miriam rose to go, Jip stood and padded along beside her. "Two trackers are better than one," laughed Miriam. "What sort of predators are there on Overlord?"

"Only humans," grinned Kathan as he rose and joined them. "The only wild animals on Overlord are some farm stock that got loose."

"That's good to know," chuckled Zartah as he led the way back to the hangar bay. "I'm tired of strange critters trying to make a meal off my poor old bones."

While they went to the hangar bay and strapped in, Micha headed for the bridge. As he strode on he began to arrange his suddenly smaller crew. "Lessa, you're on sensors, Brenna on comms, Edie, you've got weapons."

"Aye, Boss," came a chorus of voices.

"Jorge, have you got the new co-ordinates?"

"I do."

"Take her in and make it showy."

"Aye, Boss," grinned Jorge.

"Fighters away, Micha," said Lessa as Kathan and Zartah's ships left the hangar bay and slipped in behind the larger ship. At Micha's nod Jorge sent the battle cruiser into the atmosphere of Overlord.

Defender swept down on the plantation, her hull glowing from the speed of her entry. She spun around as she settled quickly to the ground. Micha spoke over the loudspeakers. "Hello the house. Send out the owner and nothing bad will happen. Hide from me and I'll blow your house down."

"Who are you? What do you want? How dare you threaten me in my own home?" It was a voice over a loudspeaker. Micha signalled with his hand and a grinning Edie targeted the high peak of the roof and launched an energy beam. The corner of the roof disappeared.

"I said step outside," said Micha. "Don't make me repeat myself again. Gunner, lower your sights. If no one comes out by the count of ten, blow the top floor off that house."

Lessa grinned as she watched her sensor screen. "They've evacuated the top floor, Micha. There are several leaving out the back and several more gathering inside. I think they're going to put up a fight."

Even as she spoke three missiles were launched through a window. They slammed into the side of the ship, but the armor-plating held. In fact it was barely scratched. "Fire," barked Micha, still holding the comm so those inside the house would hear. Edie fired and the top floor of the house exploded away.

"You're starting to annoy me," said Micha. "Gunner, lower your sights. This time blow them all to the nine hells of Porapix. We'll search the rubble for what we want."

"Stop, stop," shouted a woman as she ran out onto the lawn and stopped in front of Defender. "What do you want?"

"Are you the owner here, or his mate?"

"I'm the owner," she replied as she stood taller. "What do you want?"

"You keep a slave named Deela. I want her, unharmed."

"There is no such person here."

"Micha, there are a number of people entering the forest," said Lessa. "Zartah is right behind them, but it looks like he'll be ambushed."

"Brenna to Zartah," said Brenna as she switched the comms. "trap!"

"Understood!" came the reply. Brenna switched the comms back so Micha could talk to the woman.

"Woman, did you have Deela here and did you send her away with an armed escort? Don't lie to me; it will just make me angry. You won't like me when I'm angry."

"I hate you already," shouted the woman. "Yes I did. What do you want with the slave?"

"That's my business," replied Micha. "Bring out your people, quickly. Bring your slaves to the ship. Hurry!"

Reluctantly she obeyed. When they were all gathered on the lawn, Micha spoke again. "All slaves board this ship." The ramp lowered and the slaves fearfully climbed aboard. "I've taken your slaves because you annoyed me. Now move your people aside." Micha motioned with his hand and the big rail guns moved to aim at the rest of the shattered house. The people, including the dozen soldiers, began to run as Edie opened fire, levelling the rest of the house.

"Micha to Zartah."

"Here, Boss."

"Report."

"A bunch of them got out through a tunnel. We've locked down the ship and are following on the ground. Kathan is with us, but he's left a man on his ship."

"Stick with it," replied Micha. "I'll pick up the fighter and go back up. Keep me posted."

"Understood. Zartah out."

Micha grinned as he reached the ramp area. The former slaves he had taken on before were removing the collars from the new people and showing them to their quarters. He nodded his approval as he passed them and descended the ramp to face the people on the ground. He was just one man alone, but they shied away from him.

They watched him carefully as he jogged swiftly around the rubble of the house and disappeared from sight. A few moments later the fighter ship rose and shot out to space. The intruder class battleship followed. "We should have just handed over the woman," muttered one man.

"Oh shut up," snarled the owner, gazing at the rubble that had been a magnificent home only moments before. Sadly, the man was right, she should have given the bounty hunter whatever he wanted. "How many men did you send with them?"

"Thirty men, fully armed, Ma'am."

"Delgar and that misfit Nodran will pay for this, and they'll replace every slave I've lost. Call in the reinforcements."

"Yes, Ma'am." The soldier reached inside his pack for a comm unit and made the call. Shortly, two troop carriers arrived, but there was no one to fight and the mercenaries didn't return. The woman boarded one of the ships and flew away seeking refuge elsewhere.

Micha brought the fighter into the launch bay and then hurried to the bridge. "Report."

"Smooth as glass here, Boss," replied Jorge.

"I've got Zartah and company on sensors, Micha," said Brenna. "Lessa and Edie are down in the healing bay attending to our new passengers. We're getting close to a full house, if you know what I mean."

"Understood," sighed Micha as he eased himself into the captain's chair. "Have you got Miriam's quarry on sensors?"

"I do, and it isn't good. They're all bunched up, but I estimate there are nearly forty people in that party. I've already alerted Zartah."

"Let me guess, he said they would be easier to find."

"Yes, and that it would be more exciting this way." Micha just chuckled and shook his head.

<hr />

"THEY'RE IN THE TREES," shouted Miriam as she leaped from the fighter ship. Jip landed beside her, his tail wagging furiously. "This way." She'd spotted the people fleeing into the trees just as the ship came round the corner of the house. Zartah, Rathbone, and Keira followed close behind. They were immediately joined by Kathan and two of his men. One man had remained with the new ship.

Miriam easily found the escape tunnel and the trail leading into the surrounding forest. Darkness was falling fast, and they would soon lose the trail. As she tracked them Miriam became apprehensive. There were a lot of people ahead and she had no idea if they were armed, could they set traps, prepare an ambush, or any of a dozen other dangers. She asked Zartah to call a halt. He agreed. Kathan didn't.

"You can't stop now; they'll get away. We've almost got them. Come on."

"Go on if you want to," sighed Zartah, "but we're camping for the night. They're on foot with an armed escort. I don't want to stumble into them in the dark. Someone could get hurt, perhaps even Deela. The idea is to get her back in one piece, right?"

"Right." Kathan wasn't happy, but he could see the sense of it all. "It's just that I've never been so close; I don't want them to slip through my fingers again. What if they have a ship?"

"The boss will be watching from Defender. If they have a ship, he'll deal with it. Keira, you get first watch."

Keira grinned and spun her fingers. His shoulders sagged as he surrendered. "Alright, best two out of three." Miriam watched carefully and recognized the game. It was one she had learned from her father. Rock, paper, scissors. Zartah lost and Keira kissed his cheek then snuggled down beside Rathbone.

"Dammit woman, that's the third time in a row you've beaten me. I'm starting to think you're cheating." Keira's silvery laughter hung on the air as he slipped into the gathering darkness to keep watch.

The night was well on when he roused everybody. "Shhh, easy now, we've got company," he whispered softly. Slowly, silently, everyone reached for their weapons. Zartah pulled Miriam away from the center of camp. Jip followed closely. It was only a few moments of waiting with their eyes shut tight before the flash grenade exploded nearby followed by a series of flares. The flares were followed by shouting men.

"Face down on the ground, now!" Several weapons fired at once, but no one was hit. "Get down, face down, now!"

As the shouting men charged into the small camp, their plans went all to hell. Instead of frightened people blinded by the flash, they faced hardened warriors who were already moving. Zartah charged into them from behind. As he did, Miriam's spear flew past his ear to skewer a man with a blaster. Before the man could hit the ground, Zartah's fists were taking a terrible toll.

On the other side of the small clearing Keira and Rathbone were creating mayhem. Each moved with blinding speed and showed no mercy. Keira was holding a big knife in each hand and Rathbone was using a short club he'd snatched up. Soon the attackers were trying to flee from these two demons, but they only ran into Zartah.

A few of them escaped into the darkness and silence fell. Just as they thought it was over there was a shout of victory. "Hold, hold or I'll kill the Mutie." It was Nodran. He had an arm around Miriam's throat and a blaster aimed at her head.

"Nodran, you bloody fool, what do you think you're doing?"

"Kat, grab their weapons, quickly. We've got them. I'll say you led them right into a trap. No one'll ever know the difference."

"Nodran, you idiot, let her go before she kills you. What the hells are you doing here anyway?"

"Protecting my investment. The blind witch belongs to me. Grab their weapons now..."

Nodran had let the blaster drift away from Miriam and that was his undoing. Her hand flashed downward, stopping abruptly at his genitals. With a groan he released her, the blaster firing harmlessly at the ground.

Suddenly there was a gray blur and Jip had the hapless man in his mighty jaws, shaking him violently. Nodran screamed and tried to fight but the big dog shifted his grip to the man's neck and bit down hard. Nodran fell lifelessly from the dog's relaxed jaws. Jip danced sideways to place himself between Miriam and the other fallen soldiers. His lips peeled back in a snarl that left no doubt about his intent to defend her.

Rathbone was suddenly at her side; Keira was already studying the ground. "Miriam, can you find those who got away?" asked Rathbone.

"Yes," she replied in a hard voice as she retrieved her spear. Miriam had no love for slavers and their hired guards. "Zartah?"

"Go, Miriam. Let Rath and Keira deal with them, but find them. We don't want them joining up with their buddies."

Miriam slapped her thigh and pointed to the ground. Jip got the idea and was off into the dark forest; Miriam, Rathbone, and Keira close behind. A few moments later they heard the dog's roar and the screams of his victims. Zartah turned to one of the wounded men on the ground.

"Kathan, kill any man who makes a wrong move."

"Aye, Zartah."

"Now then, my fine bold, ambushing friend, I want information. Speak truly and live; you lie, you die in pain."

"Understood," replied the man as he struggled to a sitting position with his back against a boulder.

"How many men were with you?"

"We were twelve plus the dealer from Exile."

Zartah nodded as he took a quick look around. "Seven are here; Jip took out the dealer and at least one other. That leaves four for Keira. All right, my friend, how many left in the party we're following and what are their capabilities?"

"There are eighteen more armed soldiers, three overseers, the plantation owner, Delgar, and the slave."

"Tell me the slave's name."

"I heard Delgar call her Deela. Apparently she's some great secret the plantations owners share among them. They say she's blind and that she's trained to the collar not to speak. If she speaks without being directly addressed by an overseer they deal out the pain. They also say she can tell the future, but I doubt that."

"Why?"

"It was my duty to guard her from time to time. She whispered that I'd die an old man in my bed if I could evade the hound." At that point they heard another scream in the forest then Zartah's comm came to life. "Rathbone to Zartah."

"Report."

"We've brought down five all told. Jip seems to have lost interest. Did we get them all?"

"Yes, come back in."

Zartah knelt down by the wounded man. "All right, let's have a look at you." He poked around on the man for a moment, eliciting a few grunts of pain but finding nothing life threatening.

"You've got a few bumps and bruises, but you'll survive," he grinned. "I don't have a med kit with me, but I've got a few pain killers. Jab this in your leg and you should be able to walk."

"Thanks, I think," replied the man as he gave himself the injection. "What are you going to do with me?"

"Not a damn thing," grunted Zartah as he regained his feet, "as long as you behave yourself. Now tell me if there is another ambush waiting for me."

"Yeah, there is. I owe you that much," sighed the man as the pain killer started working its magic. "I can't tell you where or when, but there will be one."

"Fair enough. Where were you taking Deela?"

"Back to Delgar's plantation. We went out the escape tunnel and took the path to the emergency transport. We were ordered to wait and capture anyone who tried to follow. We're the most highly trained professionals on this planet but you cut us to ribbons without a single loss. Who are you people?"

"They're professional mercs, you moron," grumbled Kathan. "Did you people actually believe you could take on real fighters? You've never faced anything except unarmed runaway slaves. That woman could have torn you apart without any help."

"He's right there," chuckled Zartah, "Keira is nobody to mess with if you want to live."

"So what are you going to do with me?"

"They say there're no predators on this world," replied Zartah. "I'll just make sure you have no comms or weapons on you then I'll send you home to report in and get some more meds. First though, tell me how far we are from that transport."

"Not that far," replied the man. "It was only half a day's march in the daylight."

"Good to know," said Zartah as Jip bounded into the clearing, followed closely by Miriam, Keira, and Rathbone.

"Anybody feel like sleeping?" asked Zartah.

"Let's get this done," grumbled Rathbone. "They seem to be following a well beaten path."

"There'll be another ambush."

"Oh good, that means they'll wait for us." Keira laughed and punched Rathbone's arm. Zartah nodded and Miriam set out with Jip, the crew following close behind. Since the enemy wouldn't be civilized and sleep at night, the crew would play it their way.

Deela

It turned out to be easier than they thought. Rathbone tied a short rope loosely around Jip's neck and passed it to Miriam. Jip took off down the trail dragging Miriam behind. Zartah was holding the butt of her spear, Keira was hanging on to his belt, Rathbone was holding her hand and so on.

They didn't travel all that far when Jip stopped and emitted a low growl. They'd found the next trap. "They're close, lying in ambush," whispered Rathbone. "I'll spring the trap."

"Sorry Rath," grinned Zartah, "as First Man, that's my job. Just make sure they don't mess up my hair."

"They won't even get close."

Zartah was still grinning as he started down the trail once more. He was making far too much noise and it didn't take long to attract the attention of the men lying in ambush. Just as he stepped into a small clearing several armed men leaped out of hiding, some holding lights focused on him and others were aiming weapons. "Get down on the ground, now!"

"You first," roared Rathbone as he waded into them from behind. Keira was right at his side, her blaster firing repeatedly. The man who had shoved his weapon at Zartah's face died with Miriam's spear in his neck, his weapon was in Zartah's hands and firing before the dead man reached the ground.

Miriam ripped the weapon from another man's hands then brained him with her fist. She hurled him into two others then leaped on them. She went down under them, but Zartah tore them off her. Even though the crew was outnumbered by three to one, they were soon victorious.

The security soldiers had never actually seen any combat except with terrified runaway slaves.

In moments the men were down, disarmed or dead, and defeated. "Where the hell is Kathan?" asked Zartah.

"He and his men went on," signalled Keira. Just then they heard the sound of weapons fire ahead.

Zartah turned to the defeated men who were still alive. "Follow us and you'll die."

"Understood," replied one of the men, not making eye contact with the big man. He didn't raise his head until he was certain they were gone.

It was a short run to where Kathan and his men were pinned down by the remaining three guards plus Delgar and a tall man holding a weapon to the head of a small woman. "Hold your fire, Kat," shouted Delgar. "Hold your fire or she dies." Kathan and his men complied.

The night was fading fast and there was just enough light for the crew to see as they arrived. They came in at a full run. Rathbone fired his projectile weapon and the tall man fell, relaxing his grip on the small woman. Delgar went down to Keira's fist, his neck broken. Rathbone and Zartah had disarmed the last three guards. Rathbone grinned as Keira kicked Delgar's body. She hadn't enjoyed the slave collar and Delgar had paid for that.

The small woman was cringing on the ground when Kathan reached her. "Deela, Deela it's me, Kat," he soothed. "Shhh, girl, Kat's got you. I promised I'd come for you. I'm sorry it took so long."

"Kat, how did you get here?"

"I had help from some friends."

"You mean the witch's hounds."

"We've been called that before, girl," rumbled Rathbone, "but I didn't expect to hear it out here. How do you know of us?"

"I've seen her in the dark worlds," replied Deela, her voice trembling. "I've seen the death and destruction she wields, and I have seen the devastation her faithful hounds can cause. Your alpha, the young wolf who leads you, is he here?"

"No," said Zartah, "Micha isn't here. You'll meet him soon, Deela, and the witch as well. I'm sure Lady Arlessa will want to meet you."

"No, please, just kill me swiftly so I don't suffer more. Please Kat."

"Deela, I'm sure the lady won't harm you. She's curing me of the addiction. Girl, these folk have chased me all over two worlds just to deliver a message from my sister. They've been generous and have helped me find you. Deela, without them I couldn't have set you free. We'll visit them then we'll return to Orlem together."

"No, Kat, take me to Orlem, please. I fear these hounds and the witch more than the slave masters."

"Deela..." Kat ceased speaking as Keira crouched down beside Deela. It took her only a moment to get the slave collar off.

As Keira started to rise Deela reached out to grasp at her arm. "You're the silent one, the woman of beauty who deals death; the one who cannot speak. Thank you, lady, both for freeing me and for allowing me to live."

Keira sat down beside the small woman and took the frail girl in her arms. Rathbone passed her a ration bar and gently she fed the starving woman. Kathan looked bewildered and confused. This wasn't quite the reunion he'd envisioned. "Deela, this isn't one of your dreams, girl. These people won't harm you, I'm certain of it."

"I've dreamed of them," she replied as she nibbled on the ration bar. "I have seen what they can do. I have seen some of what they will do. I know they're your kinfolk, but they frighten me."

"Kathan is armed, Deela," Zartah said gently. "He won't leave your side; he'll protect you."

"He can't," she replied, shrinking deeper into Keira's arms.

"Keira can, and she will," smiled Rathbone. "Already you feel safe in her arms."

"Yes, man of bone and metal, I do feel safe with the Woman of Silence. Alright, if I must face the witch and her hounds, then so be it."

Just as she spoke the Arcalian fighter swooped in and landed gracefully. Deela was gently lifted aboard and the others followed. She lay quietly in Keira's arms on the short flight to Defender, her hands clutching Kathan's tightly.

As they disembarked the fighter Lessa was waiting for them. "So, it's you, Watcher. I sensed your presence as soon as Keira touched your hand. Bring her to the infirmary, Keira." With that she marched away.

"Deela, how does the lady know you?" asked Kathan as Keira easily carried the small woman.

"From the dark lands, my love," sighed Deela. "The only respite I had from the slavers was to escape to the dark worlds for a time. It's deadly and dangerous there, but I could survive it and there I was free.

"The witch came there, with another, wielding fire and destruction on all who attacked them, and there were many. She saw me as I watched from hiding, yet she didn't pause in her dealing of death. I go now to my end, but I go reunited with my lover and in the arms of a friend."

Keira made soothing sounds as she carried Deela through the door. "Even you can't protect me from her, Silent One."

"There is no need," said Lessa, her voice somewhat kinder, "I won't harm you. I asked for you to be brought here for healing. You see much that was, is, and will be, but you can't see the context, only flashes of what actually is. Yes, you saw me in that dark place, but you don't know why I was there or for what reason I did what I did.

"Put her here on this bed, Keira."

Keira laid Deela gently on the bed then turned and stepped between Lessa and the woman. Startled, Lessa met Keira's eyes and saw the pleading there. With a visible effort, Lessa regained full control over her emotions. The hard lines around her mouth softened. "It's alright, Keira, I won't harm your new friend. She's been badly mistreated; I just want to heal her wounds then you can take her to the mess hall and feed her."

Keira relaxed her posture and smiled her thanks. She patted Deela's leg to reassure her then stepped aside. "I'm Arlessa of Nova;" said Lessa as she lightly touched Deela's forehead. "Forgive me if I've frightened you. I wish only to heal the wounds inflicted on your body by your captors. I swear I won't harm you. Will you permit this?"

Deela swallowed hard then found her voice, shaky as it was. "Yes. Do with me as you will for I cannot stop you."

Lessa began to glow with a golden aura. "You've seen me at my darkest, Watcher; now see my light." She moved her hands over the frail woman's body, singing softly as she did. The glowing light encompassed Deela as well, and she began to smile as she drifted into a deep restful sleep.

"She'll rest now," said Lessa. "You may remain with her if you wish, Keira." Keira smiled and patted Kathan's shoulder then left the room. Lessa followed and together they went looking for a meal. Kathan sat holding Deela's hand while she slept. She was smiling in her sleep, and he wept with joy to see it.

———◉———

THE SPEEDER CAME IN slow and landed with a thump. A tall man in a hooded robe climbed down and asked to be refueled. Reluctantly, he was drawn into small talk by the attendant.

"Come far, have you?"

"You could say that."

"Where you from, if you don't mind my asking?"

"I really don't remember, it's been so long. I move around a lot."

"Sometimes I wish I could do that. I've spent my entire life in this town; never even been off world. So where you headed?"

"Nowhere in particular. I'm a Seeker of the Tengar."

"Never heard of that one; what's it all about?"

"By our god's command we travel about at random, seeking."

"Seeking what?"

"That's the thing, we don't know until we find it."

"So you're a pilgrim then?"

"Afraid so. I thought I'd take a look at some of the rim worlds, see if there's anything interesting out there."

"Hunh. Well, she's all fueled up, Pilgrim. Good journey; hope you find what you're looking for."

"Thank you." The tall man paid his bill then climbed back into his ship and lifted off.

The attendant watched the ship until it vanished into the grey sky, then he went inside and reached for the comms. It took a few moments for his message to get through, then he got a response.

"Akron here, go ahead."

"Biton Three fueling station here. Beware. Old speeder. Tall pilgrim. Suspicious."

"Explain."

"Ship is spec'ed up, runs too smooth. Man's a bad liar and he paid in new empire script, not old company script."

"Understood."

As the Emperor flew on, cursing the fact he had to keep his pace down and pretend to be on a random course, word of his passing sped on ahead until it reached the ears of old enemies.

Kella relaxed back in the plush chair aboard the governor's ship. She had grown a deep affection for this old assassin. Besides, she was now doing a brisk trade in Arlen territory, something unheard of until he had taken over the alliance. They were chatting easily when a man rushed in with a message for her. She glanced at it then passed it to him.

"I think we might want to look into this," said Rathbone the Elder. "Every instinct I have is screaming of danger." He reached for the comm on his shoulder. "Captain."

"Sir?" came the response.

"Take us into comm reach of the refueling station on Biton Three as quick as you can."

"Biton Three, full burn, aye, Sir."

Kella and the elder Rathbone's conversation now shifted to speculation. That continued for a couple of hours until they got word they had arrived. "Biton Three on comms, Governor. Patching through."

"Biton Three here."

"Arka, Kella here. Tell me."

"That ship was running way too smooth for a pilgrim's ship," replied Arka. "The man was too stiff, if you know what I mean. He really didn't want to talk, and he stiffened every time I asked a question. This man doesn't like people poking him for information; seemed more like he is used to being the one asking the questions. He paid in new empire script, and he had a lot of it. Sending a likeness of his face through now."

A moment later their vid screen lit up with a clear image of the tall man's face. Old Rathbone sucked in his breath as he saw Kella's face when she looked on that image. "Great job, Arka," said Kella. "You'll get a bonus for this one. Kella out."

The governor cut the comm link then sat back, lost in thought. "Just who is that pilgrim; you've seen that face before."

"I forgot you never did get to see his face. That, my dear Governor, is Emperor Loran himself."

"Loran? Damn his eyes. What in the nine hells is he up to now? Your information channels are faster than mine and far more discreet. Get the word to Nova and Borealis Prime as quick as you can, Kella."

"On my way," she grinned, as she leaped to her feet and headed for the hangar bay. Moments later her speeder dropped out into space and was away. While the Emperor held his speed down and set a wandering course, Kella headed straight for Nova at full burn.

Forewarned

Defender was back in orbit around Exile by the time Deela awakened. She woke up in a panic. "Deela, easy, my love, easy, Kat's got you," soothed Kathan. "Kat's got you; you're safe now."

"Oh, Kathan, we're not safe; no one is safe. The man of steel comes and the hordes with him. Death, destruction, and slavery follow wherever he goes."

"Deela..."

"Please take me to the hound, he must be warned."

"The hound? You mean Micha?"

"Yes, the witch's hound. He must be warned. Please Kathan, there's no time to lose."

"All right, my love, all right. Breathe, girl, breathe." Kathan reached for the comm Micha had given him. "Kathan to Micha."

"Micha here."

"Micha, Deela is awake and says she needs to speak with you. Do you have the time?"

"We're in the mess; can you find it?"

"I think so."

"Keira is on her way, she'll lead you. Micha out."

Keira soon appeared and led them to the mess hall where room had been made at Micha's table. The rest of the crew gathered round as Deela was brought into the room. Keira put her in a chair facing Micha. The poor woman was clearly fearful, yet she seemed determined to speak.

"I sense the Lady near. Lady, I thank you for the healing; I haven't felt so good for long years."

"Now we need to feed you, Deela," smiled Lessa, as she placed a bowl of fruits and meat in front of Deela.

"Thank you, Lady of Magic, but first I must speak with the man known as the witch's hound."

"That would be me," said Micha gently. "I'm Micha. My hands are on the table near your own if you wish to touch me so your insight will confirm who I am."

"There's no need, young warrior. I've heard that voice in my dreams often enough. I dreamed of you again. I want to warn you."

"I prefer not to know the future, Deela. I have enough trouble coping with the present."

"The trouble that comes will test you beyond reason. A man of metal and cruelty comes, death and destruction in his wake. He has defeated you in battle before, but you must face him again. Much will depend on your luck and decisions.

"I've seen two futures; one where the galaxy is peaceful, civilization flourishes, and another where all is drowned in war. The decision will be yours. Inside you are two men; one is the farmer, a man of peace who nourishes his family. The other is the warrior who protects his family. The fate of us all rides on which of those men will make the final decision."

Lessa leaned forward and took Deela's hand. "Deela, please understand, you see two possible futures, but there are an endless number of possibilities. You see only fragments of what might come to pass. The future isn't set in stone."

"I truly wish I saw none of it at all, Lady. This ability is a curse. I was kept in chains, starved and beaten, because of it. Micha, a man comes soon with news of great importance. You must learn what the Woman of Exile can teach before he arrives."

Micha sat back and regarded Deela for several moments. Finally he spoke; what he said surprised all of them. "Zartah, can I borrow your companion for a while?"

Zartah looked surprised for a moment. "Sure, Boss, just don't break her."

"I'll be very careful with her, Zartah. Miriam, will you teach me how you made that spear point?" asked Micha. "I've had the sense I need that skill ever since I first saw you with it."

"Of course, Boss," replied Miriam, a smile playing at her lips. "We'll have to go down to the planet."

"Then let's go. Zartah, the ship is yours. Try to keep Edie out of trouble."

Edie laughed then called out. "Miriam, you bring him back in one piece."

Miriam was smiling as she followed Micha to the hangar bay.

The small fighter ship dropped towards the planet with Micha at the controls. He smiled to himself as he caught a glimpse of his companion's look of concern. "What's on your mind, Miriam?"

"I'm concerned. I can't teach you in one day what it took a lifetime to learn."

"I learn fast."

"Not that fast."

Micha's laughter was rich and genuine. "Miriam, there are two reasons we're here today. Reason number one, with all those extra people on board, the ship is a little crowded for me. I suspected you might enjoy a few hours in the open air too. Reason number two is I do want to learn what you can teach, but I expect today we will only gather some stones to work with. The instruction can happen later."

Miriam sighed with relief. "Yes, that would be the best way."

"You're still nervous around us, Miriam. I understand that. Aboard ship you're helpless as you have no knowledge of how the technology works. Keira can teach you modern weapons. Zartah will teach you the basics of technology, and you'll teach us all survival skills. As soon as we have time, we'll all head for the vast forests of Nova Prime and you can teach us all how to survive without modern technology. Today we gather a few stones and breathe open air."

"Thank you, Micha. You're not as I expected."

"Oh? What did you expect?"

"From listening to Zartah and Gorda, I built up an impression of a cold, efficient, and ruthless man. Forgive me."

"Edie says I'm two people," he sighed. "The man here today is the man who loves his farm and his people. The other man is the one who protects them. He's exactly what you expected; he has to be. If that man allows emotion to influence him then my people and my farm will fall."

"I think I understand now. The witch with all her power obeys you as do the rest. She knows the cold dispassionate man will make the best decisions. She sets the goals, but you have to achieve them. Is that right?"

"That's pretty much how it seems to work. I'm not sure how I got myself into this mess, but it's mine to deal with now."

"I'm sorry to add to your burden, Micha."

"Stop that right now, Miriam, companion to my best friend. You've added nothing to my burden; you've lightened it. Already Zartah is becoming less reckless. You bring skills that are badly needed for the life we lead. If you hadn't found them when they crashed, Zartah and Gorda might have had a much harder time of it. No, Miriam, you're not a burden; you are a welcome addition."

Micha landed the ship in an open space that had a lot of exposed ground. As they reached the ground Miriam took a deep breath and smiled. "Micha, you were fine on the ship, and you really are needed there, but you took the time to bring me here, to give me a respite from the close quarters and the people. You could have sent Zartah, but you came yourself to make sure I understand I have value to the crew; to make me feel welcome. Thank you."

Micha chuckled as he tossed a stone at a distant tree. "Are you always so insightful, Miriam?"

"Father always said it was one of my gifts."

"In that case I'll seek your advice often," he grinned. He bent and scooped up a large stone. "Is this workable?"

"No, that stone won't split, it's too hard." She picked up another and showed it to him. "This will split, and you can knock small flakes off the edges to make a blade or a spear point."

Micha nodded as he inspected both stones carefully. Finally he put the good one in the sack he had brought. "Okay, let's try again." A while later he showed her another. She beamed at him and nodded. Micha put his prize in the sack.

Hours passed and the sack was getting heavy when his comm crackled to life. "Defender to Micha."

"Micha here."

"Gorda's back, Boss. He'll be here in less than an hour. He says he has big news, and it isn't good."

"It never is," sighed Micha as he signed off. "Well, Miriam, it looks like out holiday is over."

Together they walked back to the fighter then returned to the ship. Their re-entry into the hangar bay was quite shaky and the landing bumpy.

"Looks like that fighter needs a tune up," said Rathbone as they descended to the deck.

"No, Miriam just needs a bit more practice," grinned Micha.

"Miriam, you flew the ship?"

"Yes. It was my first time. It was exciting."

"Well then, in that case," grinned Rathbone, "it was a good landing. Exciting eh? You and Zartah are a fine match."

Micha and the entire crew were on the bridge waiting for Gorda. All eyes turned to the door as he and his two companions entered. Gorda didn't waste any time or words. "Boss, this doesn't look good. Emperor Loran has taken over the whole damn galaxy except for the Borelian Free States."

The entire bridge was silent for a moment; then Micha spoke. "Jorge, if Kathan and his people have gone, then take us home to Nova, full burn."

"Aye, Boss, they left hours ago. Home to Nova Prime, full burn it is." The big ship swung about, oriented herself, and then blasted away from Exile.

"Ena, what did Gorda leave out?" asked Micha.

Gorda reddened and Ena grinned. "Well, Micha, it appears there may be a ceremony of union once we get home. It seems the black witch of legend will claim another victim."

There was a round of congratulations and Gorda endured it all with a red face. Lessa noticed Micha gazing into space, a smile playing at the corners of his mouth. "What is it Micha?"

"I needed to hear that last bit," he replied softly. "If there's hope for Gorda, then things can't be as dark as they seem."

"Geez, thanks, Boss," grumbled Gorda, bringing another round of laughter.

In less than two days they blew past FarStar, the beacon still cautioning one and all to go back, then then they faced the long lonely run back to Nova Prime. They were still three days out when Kella's speeder came hurtling towards them. "Kella to Micha, come in Micha. Please acknowledge. Kella to Micha."

"Jorge, drop to one half speed. I don't like the sounds of this," said Micha, reaching for the comms. "Micha here, go ahead, Kella."

"Micha, I have news that you need but won't like."

"Doesn't everybody? Come aboard, Kella. I'll meet you on the bridge."

"Understood. Kella out."

"All Nova Crew to the bridge, now. Rathbone, let Kella in then bring her with you."

"Aye, Boss."

A short while later they were gathered on the bridge. Rath brought Kella in then all eyes turned to her. Micha grinned and answered her unspoken question. "We've got a ship load of refugees. This is the only place on board where we can get any privacy. So, what brings you out beyond the edge of the rim?"

"I assume you all know about the empire swallowing up everything except The Free States."

"We do," sighed Micha. "I assume we're next."

"They're already starting to build up forces at the border. So far Lortax has been able to match them, but we all know that's hopeless."

"Yes it is, but that's not what brought you out here, is it?"

"No, Micha, it isn't. Something really strange is going on. A few weeks ago one of my people noticed a lone speeder slip into Sector Nine. We've been watching for it. That speeder is carrying high tech weapons, new engines, and the lone pilot is an old acquaintance of yours."

"Oh, do tell."

"It's the Emperor himself, traveling in disguise as a pilgrim, but he's headed for Nova Prime, there's no doubt in my mind at all."

"My father?" exclaimed Brenna. "Kella, are you certain it is him?"

"Yes, Brenna, it is Emperor Loran. I have no idea at all what his game is, but he's coming and he'll soon be at Nova. You'd better hurry if you want to get there first."

"Understood. Jorge..."

"Aye Boss, Nova Prime, full burn." The big ship swiftly regained her former speed.

"I wonder what he wants," mused Micha.

"I think I might have an idea," said Lessa. "Rathbone, do you suppose he has figured out where that little trinket has gone."

"I wouldn't bet against it," grinned Rathbone, "but why would he come alone? If it were me I'd send in the soldiers to retrieve it."

"As would I," mused Lessa. She noticed the puzzled looks on the rest of the crew and explained.

"After our hasty departure from Elliston, Rathbone presented me with a gift, a souvenir he had picked up there. It seems that the Emperor has replaced his body with a robotic version of himself. He's far faster and stronger even than our crew and he's impervious to pain.

"However, the man who built him put in a fail-safe device the emperor wasn't aware of at first; a remote controller that freezes him instantly. Also, in the frozen state, his mind is completely open to suggestion. As long as the controller exists he's vulnerable. The question is why would he come alone?

"Micha, divert to Borealis Prime. He's alone; Norlene can handle him for a while. We need to put our refugees in a safer place, we need to report to Marla, and we need to confer with Lortax before I face the Emperor."

"Understood and agreed," sighed Micha. "Jorge..."

"Borealis Prime, full burn, aye, Boss."

They continued to speculate on the possibilities, but everyone knew it was just a way to kill time. When they arrived on Borealis Prime the refugees were taken off the ship and to a hospice. They would be treated kindly and integrated into Borealian society. Meanwhile the crew was ushered into the private offices of the High Priestess. Viceroy Lortax was waiting there as well.

High Priestess Marla rushed to Micha, her face hopeful. "Micha, did you find him?"

"Yes, Lady," smiled Micha as she raised him to his feet again. "Your brother is alive and well. That man is as slippery as an eel. He thought we were bounty hunters and fled. We had the demon's own time trying to catch him. Eventually we caught up and made him listen. Lessa healed him and I gave him a fighter ship. Now I have gifts for you too."

"Oh?"

"Yes, the first is this full report, including vid and messages from Kathan."

"And the second is my bill?"

"Yes, Lady."

"I suppose I'm buying that ship you gave him."

"Well, you said whatever it took, so..."

Suddenly Marla leaped into his arms. "Oh Micha, you found him. I don't care what the cost; you've performed a miracle for me. You'll have your payment and more."

"Thank you, Lady Marla. Perhaps once things settle down around here you might want to go out past the rim for a visit. I'm still not sure he's convinced you're alive and back as High Priestess."

"I surely will do that, Micha, although I don't believe things will settle down around here anytime soon. That brings us to the crisis at hand. Lessa, the Temple officially calls upon Nova Temple for the assistance of the two most powerful witches in this realm."

"Of course, Lady," said Lessa as she bowed before Marla. "How can we best serve the temple?"

Marla laughed as she raised Lessa to her feet. "You and your crew of savages can come to table with Lortax and me. Let's see if we can devise a way to survive."

"With pleasure, Lady," replied Lessa as she sat gracefully, motioning for the crew to pull up chairs. "So, where do things stand now?"

"They're amassing on the borders," said Lortax. "They're building up slowly and we've been matching them, but that's a fool's game and we all know it. The Free States can't hope to match them militarily. We need something else. Also there's the Emperor himself. What in the nine hells is he up to anyway?"

"I'm wondering why you haven't dropped a couple of warships down on his speeder and blown it to the next galaxy?" sighed Rathbone.

"I'll admit, it is tempting," grinned Lortax. "However, there are other considerations."

"Such as?" enquired Micha.

"Peace, Micha," sighed Marla. "For the first time in living memory the galaxy is at peace. Say what you will about Emperor Loran; he's managed to bring peace to the galaxy. If we can find a way to co-exist with, or even within the empire..."

"An absence of war isn't peace, Lady Marla," Lessa said, as she gazed out the window. "Would you have the Temple bow to the Emperor, the very man who ordered the annihilation of Nova Prime's population...?"

"Easy, my love," said Brenna, as she laid her hand gently on Lessa's arm, "easy."

"Lessa, I understand; I do," Marla said kindly, "but think for a moment. If he's killed, his forces may attack us anyway. Even if they don't, the rest of the Galaxy will be plunged into warfare as thousands of leaders rise up to try to fill the void. The galaxy will be split into hundreds of warring factions. All will dissolve into chaos. Billions of people will lose their lives.

"If there is a way to prevent that, surely we must try. He's headed for Nova Prime. There may be a chance there, Lessa. Will you not see what he wants first?"

"I will," replied Lessa, as she gave in, "for Brenna's sake as well as your own, Marla. I do understand what you say, and I can see the big picture here. I'll do what I can." As she finished speaking she caught the hard look in Micha's eyes.

"If we fail, then what?" asked Brenna.

"If you and Lessa can't convince him to negotiate," said Marla, "then we have to try it the hard way. Every ship of the line facing the Empire's forces has a priestess on it. Most are newly promoted and haven't much strength with the magic. Their presence is mostly symbolic. However, if this goes badly, I want both you and Norlene on the Viceroy's flagship."

"If this goes badly," said Norlene as she strode into the room, "I have a different suggestion. Sorry I'm late, Lady Marla."

"Not at all, Norlene," replied Marla. "What do you suggest?"

"I suggest you, as High Priestess, should be on that flagship. Your personal assistant with you, of course."

"My assistant, Meggan?"

"Your assistant, Norlene. Lessa and her crew of savages would be more effective on their own. Nova Crew has a certain reputation; the sight of Defender flying beside the Viceroy's ship with the cyborgs in Freedom guarding the other side should prove a far more formidable sight."

"Alright, Norlene," sighed Marla, "your plan makes sense, but only if diplomacy fails."

"Then we'd all better be getting back to Nova before the Emperor arrives," said Lessa.

"Before we go," grinned Norlene, "I believe Gorda has a request."

"Dammit woman, are you going to tease me the rest of my life?"

"Yes."

"Ah well, forewarned is forearmed. Lady Norlene, it's the desire of my heart that we be a bonded pair. Will you accept me?"

"I will, Gorda. I've kept you waiting long enough. Lady Arlessa, only the High Priestess of my temple can seal this. Will you witness for us?"

"With great pleasure," smiled Lessa. "Norlene, are you set on this course? Will you hold yourself to this great warrior and be his companion in life, come what may?"

"I am indeed set on this course, Lady."

"Gorda, are you set on your course? To bind to a witch can be a hard life. Are you determined to be companion to the Black Witch of Legend?"

"I am set on that very course, Lady," grinned Gorda.

"Then, before these witnesses, I bless this union and declare it so."

There was a rousing cheer at that. Everyone came forward to congratulate them. As soon as things settled down a bit, Norlene took Gorda's arm and steered him towards the doorway. "Take me home, Lover," she grinned, "I hear the Emperor himself is coming to congratulate us."

————————●————————

AS SOON AS EVERYONE was back on Nova, Micha set to work. Once he was certain Nova's defenses were as strong as they could be, he had a short but private conference with Kella. She nodded, then ran to her speeder and took off.

No one asked what it was about, and Micha didn't say. Instead he called the crew together. They met at his farmhouse. They were all gathered around the long table and Edie beamed as she loaded that table with food and drink.

"Okay, people, the way things are looking we're in for some action. Here's what I have in mind. So far we're the only ones who know about Exile and Overlord. If things go badly here I say we retreat out to Exile and set up a rebel base there. Personally, I grew up a slave; I'll die before I face that life again. Anybody who wants out of this crew, this is your opportunity."

"Exile's not a bad spot," grinned Zartah. "We've got friends there."

"Micha, I promise you, no one on this crew is going to be enslaved," said Lessa. "I agree with your plan though."

"We're all in, Boss," said Zartah, "all of us."

"Are you all certain?" They were. "All right then, we need to make a few modifications to the ship. I want to change her name to something that should scare the hell out of an enemy. Let's call her Ravage.

"Rathbone, I want you to do everything in your power to make that ship the terror of the skies. I'll go talk to Commander Darks and his crew. I'm going to suggest they gather their families up and move them to Overlord."

"They won't go, Micha," grinned Jorge. "They're Novans now and the lads are Nova Crew Two. They won't leave any more than we will."

"That's good to know, Jorge, but I'll go bring them up to speed anyway. Now, let's eat then settle down for a short rest. Kella's folk say Loran should be here any day now."

———◉———

WHILE MICHA AND HIS crew plotted strategy, the Emperor approached Nova Prime. He was holding the engines back and he'd taken a wandering route to get here, but the planet was now in sight. During all his weeks of travel he had continued to rehearse his meeting with the witch. He only hoped she would see reason.

Emperor Loran

The aging speeder slowly approached Nova Prime. There was no official landing field so the pilot set the ship down near the largest building he could see; rightly guessing it was the temple. As the tall man descended to the ground he was met by a woman dressed in black robes. It wasn't Arlessa.

"Greetings, Emperor Loran, you've come a long way. Welcome to the temple of Nova Prime." Loran could sense her hatred and the power seething within her, her desire to destroy him completely. After his last encounter with Arlessa, he believed she could do it.

"Greetings, Lady of the Temple," he replied as he lowered himself to one knee as was the custom in this sector when one first addressed a Priestess of the Temple. "I've come alone, unarmed, and wish only to see my daughter and her companion. Will they receive me?"

"Follow me, you're expected."

She turned and walked toward the temple. He followed, somewhat bemused. If they knew who he was and that he was alone, why was he still alive? This must be Brenna's influence. Perhaps there was still a chance. Anything would be better than to spend eternity trapped inside his own offices.

Norlene led him into the inner chambers of the temple and announced him. "The Emperor Loran of the Galactic Empire seeks audience with Lady Arlessa and her companion, Brenna of Nova."

Lessa and Brenna were seated at a table laden with food and drink. Lessa gave a forced smile and spoke. "We will receive him. Will you sit and share food with us, Emperor?"

He looked somewhat startled. Loran had been studying the ways of the Borelians and knew that to share food and drink meant he was safe from attack. "Thank you, that is most gracious, considering the way our last meeting ended," he said, as he sat and took a bite from an apple.

"I'm quite curious, Loran," said Lessa. "Why have you come here, and why alone?"

"I came for two reasons. I arrived alone as anything else would have precipitated a war; a war neither of us wants. Will you hear me?"

"I will. You may speak freely at this table."

"Thank you. First, I came to make amends with Brenna. We were once very close, Brenna, and I miss those times deeply. Is there no chance for us to reconcile at all?"

"I see your time as Emperor has mellowed you, Father," replied Brenna. "In light of the past I don't see any way we could return to the way things were. However, there may be a way for us to build a future."

"You're right, daughter, I've done many evil things, but there was always a purpose."

"To gain greater power?"

"To end war and suffering, child," he sighed. "You often chastised me for my indifference to the plight of the masses. That wasn't true, but I dared not show weakness. If I had, the Board would have replaced me before I was ready."

"Brenna, how can you support and enrich the masses when all your resources are consumed by the military and their wars? The Galaxy is at peace now, Brenna. Once I convince the Borelians to come into the fold, all military can be scaled back, and resources channelled in new and more humanitarian directions."

"Convince the Borelians? So you plan to use diplomacy to bring us into the Empire? Your forces building up along the borders would indicate otherwise, Emperor," observed Lessa.

"It's a game, Arlessa; just a game," he replied. "We all know that if war was the method I wanted to use the Borelian Free States would already be defeated. All that saber rattling along the border was to keep the attention elsewhere while I came here alone."

"You present a convincing argument, Emperor, and I will admit the Viceroy and High Priestess Marla are open to discussions. Shall I arrange an audience for you?"

Loran bristled inwardly at her taunt, but showed no outward signs of it. He needed her and dared not offend her in any way. "Thank you, Arlessa; that would be most helpful. However, the second reason for my visit is to ask you for a favor, a different favor. I can set up diplomatic meetings; I have come to ask you for a healing."

Lessa was visibly taken aback. This was not at all what she had expected. "A healing? You ask me for a healing? Why?"

"I hoped it might help to heal the rift between us."

"What ails you that you wish to be healed?"

"A number of years ago a madman, a professional assassin began a vendetta against me. I had become ill and wasn't expected to remain alive and functional for long. If I was to survive to protect my family and see my dream of Galactic peace realized, I had to do something drastic. I had my body completely replaced with a mechanical one, well, mostly mechanical. My brain and soft organs are encased within a metal suit of armor.

"However, the genius who managed this for me was a traitor. He built something extra into my brain. With a remote control device, he could freeze me and implant suggestions into my mind. Upon being released from the stasis I would then proceed as though that suggestion was my own idea."

"I can see how that would be a problem," said Lessa, a smile playing at her lips. "So, how can I be of help?"

"I found and destroyed one of the remote devices, but there is another and I can't locate it. In the wrong hands this thing could destroy everything. Brenna said you're the greatest healer in the known worlds. Will you disable that circuit in my brain so I'm no longer vulnerable?"

"I have good news and bad for you, Emperor," said Lessa. Brenna struggled to hide her grin. "I find myself unwilling to perform the healing for you. That's the bad news. The good news is, the second remote has been found."

Loran was unable to hide both his surprise and his horror. "You see, Emperor, when he was last on Elliston Prime, my friend, Rathbone of Urn, picked up this little trinket for me." Lessa placed the remote on the table, well out of his reach. "He explained its uses to me, and I freely admit I have been tempted to test it out. However, as long as you play fair with the Borelian Free States, Emperor, this little trinket will remain safe within my inner office."

Even as Loran's shoulders slumped in apparent defeat, Ena and Micha eased away from the wall where they'd been eavesdropping. "Well, Ena?"

"He's lying, Micha. That man wants to destroy Nova, it is easy to see. Lessa has just signed our death warrants."

"Yes, she's had her fun, but now he'll come after us with everything he's got, and she'll never get close enough to use that toy on him."

"Micha, are you sure about this plan of yours?"

"It's the only way, Ena."

"Then you'd better get ready."

<hr />

THE NEXT MORNING THE Emperor's ship lifted off, headed for Borealis Prime. He planned to make a show of this, but as soon as he was safely back in his own Empire he'd bring the full force of the military down on Sector Nine. The complete fools, now that he knew where the damned controller was, he would blast Nova to oblivion from space. The witch would never get close enough to him to use the damned thing.

As soon as he cleared the atmosphere he changed course. The escort ship sent to accompany him had yet to arrive and he was pleased with that. This speeder could outrun any military ship in the area. Borealis Prime was the last place he would go. No, he would head straight back to the Empire. By the time the fools discovered what had happened it would be far too late to catch him. He opened up the engines to full burn.

Hours later, as he was making a near pass of an abandoned mining planet, he noticed a ship gaining on him at alarming speed. He adjusted course slightly and the pursuer followed. What could be fast enough to overtake him like this? What did that ship want? Then the ship opened fire.

Horrified, the Emperor of the Galaxy felt his ship shudder and the engines sputter. In a sudden rage he managed to spin the ship about and fire his own hidden energy weapon. He scored a direct hit and watched the screen as his enemy spiraled down towards the planet below.

However, his instruments told him he was going down too. At least he'd make a soft landing and perhaps find a way to repair his ship. His opponent wouldn't be so lucky.

Micha cursed like a maddened farmer as his ship hurtled towards the planet below. His plan had been to disable the emperor's ship then drag him back to Nova so Lessa could use the remote on him. That option was now lost; Loran had gotten in a lucky shot. He strapped a breather to his face and ejected as soon as he hit atmosphere. It was a long slow fall to the surface.

Before his feet touched the ground Micha saw his own ship explode and the Emperor make a soft landing. Still cursing, he managed to steer his chute to a place out of the Emperor's line of sight. As he rolled free of the tangled chute, Micha stopped cursing and went cold. This was a game of survival now, and the Emperor had the advantage.

Micha'd barely had time to set the distress beacon before he ejected. It would take a while for the crew to track him down, days perhaps, but they'd come. His task now was to stay alive and keep the Emperor on this abandoned planet.

He slipped into the scrub forest and started to make his way towards the Emperor's landing site. Micha knew this planet had been stripped for mining until the land was too poisonous to farm, so no one ever came here anymore. The entire landscape was tumbled and jumbled with the forests struggling to reclaim it.

Micha was on his own with no supplies and no weapons except his blaster. It was time to apply what little information and training Miriam had given the crew. It was all theory as there hadn't been time for a session in the field, but Micha felt that, with his upbringing on the farm added to it, his chances were good. Keeping the Emperor on the ground would be the trick. There was only one chance and he had to take it.

Loran managed a fairly soft landing. He was outside the ship inspecting the damage to his engines and formulating a plan to repair some of that damage when he saw movement out of the corner of his eye. His lightning reflexes worked well, and he battered aside his attacker.

Micha charged from his hiding place and fired his blaster. The Emperor battered him aside and he went flying. He picked himself up to see Loran holding his blaster.

With a smirk of delight, Loran scooped up the fallen weapon. As his opponent watched, he crushed it in his hand and tossed it aside. "The hound, well, well, well. So you didn't fall for my little subterfuge, eh? Too bad you missed, first with your ship and now with your blaster."

"I missed with the ship," groaned Micha, as he struggled to sit up, "but not with the blaster."

"What do you mean?"

"Look inside your ship."

Loran spun around and saw the truth. Micha hadn't fired at him, he'd shot the control panel. That ship would never rise again. With a snarl Loran turned to finish his enemy, but Micha was nowhere to be seen. "Run all you want, Hound," he roared. "You'll come to me in the end; I have food and water, you don't." The only answer he got was silence.

Only once the Emperor took a closer look did he realize how accurate Micha was with a blaster. He had fired twice; one shot destroyed the controls, the other the supply cabinet. The food was splattered and the water evaporated.

"I'm going to kill you, Hound," he bellowed, as he turned towards the spot where Micha had disappeared.

"You've got to catch me first, Robot," came the reply, as Micha stepped into view.

Loran leaped toward Micha with alarming speed. Micha fled into the scrub forest, but he was limping and Loran was gaining. The chase went on for a while then Loran stopped and shouted. "I will never tire, Hound, but you will. Sooner or later I will catch you and put an end to you forever."

"Talk's cheap, Robot."

Loran put on a burst of speed as they hit an open spot. Suddenly, just as he was reaching for Micha, his quarry dropped to the ground and he tripped over him. Loran fell headlong, arms flailing. When he regained his feet he was alone. There was no trace of Micha.

As Loran screamed out his frustration, Micha made his way silently back to Loran's ship. He was inside in a trice and ripped out the distress beacon. Grinning to himself he slipped back outside and into the forest once again. Now it was time to find shelter. Micha could see the storm clouds gathering.

———●———

"SOMETHING IS WRONG; I'm going after him." Edie was gathering up her weapons as she spoke, but Lessa laid a gentling hand on her arm.

"Edie, you and I both know how resourceful Micha is. I agree that something has happened, but I also get the sense that he is dealing with the situation."

"We're his crew; we should be out looking for him."

"We've been summoned by the High Priestess, Edie. We have to respond to that call."

"I don't," said Rathbone. "I'm not Borelian and I owe my allegiance to Micha. I'll go, Edie."

"I will go too," said Miriam. "I am of Exile and not Borelian. I owe Micha. But know nothing of a High Priestess."

Zartah stood, a huge grin on his face. "You take good care of Miriam, Rath. Bring the boss back in one piece."

"Zartah?" Lessa looked surprised.

"As First Man, I am sending all non-Borealian crew members to find our crew boss. The Borealians will answer the call. Rath, take Miriam and Jorge with you. Kella, you're not on the crew so I can't order you, but these folks don't know this part of space like you do."

"I'll go, Zartah. I owe Micha."

"Edie, you're looking a bit peaked, maybe you should stay behind while we answer Lady Marla's call," grinned Zartah.

A short time later the Ravage rose through the atmosphere and headed towards Borealis Prime. A lone Arcalian fighter dropped out of her hangar bay and hung back, searching for a trace of Micha's trail.

Rathbone was at the controls. "So, how is our stowaway doing?" he asked rather loudly.

"I'm just fine, Rath," laughed Edie, as she popped her head out of a gunner's turret.

"Wonderful. All right, Kella, we know the Emperor is a snake and we know he did not arrive on Borealis. He was in a speeder, so he probably made a run for his own borders. Micha would never allow him to make it, so we should search along that route. You know the most likely way, you take the controls."

"Aye, Boss," grinned Kella as she slid into the pilot's chair.

"Jorge, you keep checking on all crew frequencies, see if there is anything, any chatter at all. Miriam, I'll show you how to work the sensors and what you're looking for."

They went slowly and searched, but it was three days later before Miriam found the two wrecked ships on long range scanners. As they moved towards the planet Jorge caught the faint distress beacon Micha had launched as he was shot down. They found Micha's shattered ship and the wreckage of Emperor Loran's speeder the next day. There were no signs of either man.

"They were both here," said Miriam as she carefully studied the ground near the ship, "but it has rained hard and their tracks are washed away."

"Can you find them, Miriam?" asked Edie.

"I believe so," she replied. "Everyone remain here until I call on the comm unit." They watched as she began to move around the ship in an ever widening circle. Soon she was lost in the scrubby trees. The day was growing dark when she returned. "I have found their tracks, but they are a day or more old. Micha is hunting the Emperor, and the Emperor hunts him. We will pick up the trail at first light."

"Thanks be to the gods, he's alive," sighed Edie.

"This is your hunt, Miriam," grinned Rathbone. "You lead until we find them."

"Understood and agreed," she replied, pleased with herself at using the crew jargon properly.

The Reckoning

Emperor Loran sighed as he took inventory of his situation. That thrice cursed Hound had shot him down. He'd lost his temper then, but the Hound had eluded him, destroyed his distress beacon, his food and water, and then had managed to get him completely lost. Loran had spent a night huddled miserably under a few trees for shelter from the driving rain while the Hound had slept in a warm cave. He'd even had a fire. Loran had found it the next morning, but the fire was out and the Hound was gone.

His fall and several subsequent falls had severely damaged his skin and he had lost some blood. He had to be careful about that; he no longer had a lot of blood to spare. The Hound had even killed a small animal for food. Loran snarled his hatred for the man, yet he had to admire his resourcefulness. He could see why the witch chose him. Loran bemoaned the fact he had not had such a man to send against Rathbone; life might have been very different had it been so.

Ah well, there was no point belaboring that idea. He was in a tight situation and needed to think clearly. As much as it galled him, Loran realized he needed Micha to get off this planet and back to his own people. Maybe the merc could be bought. It was worth a try. First he had to find him, and that would not be easy.

Emperor Loran decided to find his way back to the downed ship at see if he could salvage anything useful that Micha had not already stolen. That would be a trick in itself. He had no idea which way to go. Loran had spent his entire life in an urban setting. He was poorly equipped to deal with his current situation and he knew it. Dammit all anyway; why couldn't they have crashed on a civilized planet?

Micha sighed with contentment as he finished the last of the small rodent he had killed. The cave he'd stumbled on was dry and his small fire was warm. Better yet, he'd seen the Emperor going the other way. He'd find him again in the morning. He drifted off to sleep with thoughts of Edie and the child she was carrying.

He was awake and on the move before dawn the next day. Micha grinned as he watched from hiding when the Emperor found his snug cave. He's left a clear trail for Loran to follow; he just hoped the man had the wit to follow it. Micha shook his head sadly as Loran struggled to find and follow the clear footprints in the fresh mud. The man was hopeless away from the cities.

All that day and the next Micha led the Emperor farther and farther away from the downed ships. He knew his crew would find them and then him; he just didn't want anyone else finding them first. Micha was leading Loran, constantly trying to find the proper terrain for an ambush. He had to find a way to weaken Loran.

Finally he found what he was looking for, a wide gorge. Micha left clear prints leading up to the edge he then carefully backed away in his own tracks. It took most of the day to find a narrow spot, but he found one. A running jump carried him across then he ran along the far side until he reached a point directly across from his decoy trail. Emperor Loran was there, shouting his name. Micha grinned with delight.

"What do you want?" he shouted back.

"I want to hire you, mercenary. Whatever the witch is paying you, I will double."

"Why should I trust you?"

"I honestly don't care if you live or die, boy. I just want to get back to my people. Think for a minute. If I die out here the entire galaxy will be plunged into war as others try to claim my throne, or to assert control over smaller portions of territory. I have stopped the wars. I can keep the peace, Micha. I can negotiate a deal with the Borelians and all wars will end; the galaxy will be at peace for the first time in history.

"Imagine a world where no one has to worry about soldiers invading, raping, pillaging and killing everyone in sight. Your own history is proof of the damage the wars can do. Do you want that for your children?"

"If you wanted to negotiate with the Borelians, why did you run?"

"I'm no fool, boy. They would have taken me prisoner and forced a treaty I could never live with. That would cause me to break the treaty and invade Sector Nine. That would be war and you know it. If I can negotiate from a position of power I can enforce a peaceful solution. That means no war, no unnecessary deaths. Think about it."

Micha's father had been a shrewd negotiator and he had cautioned his son. "When a man's argument makes the most sense, that's the time to trust him the least; always go with your instincts."

"All right, Emperor, what do you want with me?"

"I need you and that crew of yours to get me back to my own people. I also want you to bring my daughter home where I can protect her. Do this for me and I will make you rich beyond your wildest dreams.

"Micha, I know what you're doing. You're keeping me busy while your crew searches for you. They are quite resourceful. They will find us sooner or later. Think, Micha, why else would I have come into Sector Nine, risking my own life and everything I have worked for, if not to see my daughter? What do you say, Micha. Will you work for me?"

"It will cost you."

"I have already agreed to pay you well, Mercenary. I am fully prepared to do just that."

"Alright then, you'll probably want this," said Micha as he launched something high into the air towards the Emperor.

Loran caught the object easily. It was the remote control he fear the most. His eyes opened wide as he recognized what it was, and that it meant he had succeeded. He had turned the mercenary. "Thank you, Micha. Obviously you know what this is. This is a mighty gift indeed."

"So I guess they'll call me the Emperor's hound now."

"Oh, I will find a much nicer title for you than that," laughed Loran as he crushed the remote in his hand.

"All right, come on over, the ship's this way. It's a hard jump, but you can make it." Micha turned away and disappeared into the trees. Once out of sight he turned and crept back to where he could watch.

Loran looked dubious as he sized up the width of the chasm. He was unsure, but then he'd never truly tested his new abilities to their fullest. The hound had made that jump, surely he could. Slowly he backed off a few paces then took a running leap. With his heart in his mouth he sailed across the rift, landing slightly off balance at the edge.

Micha's eyes opened wide as he saw the power of that leap. Scrambling to his feet he rushed at the Emperor. As Loran struggled for balance Micha delivered a solid kick to his chest. With a scream of denial, the Emperor toppled backwards off the cliff and fell to the rocks far below. Micha lay down and peered over the edge. He swallowed hard as Loran struggled to his feet.

Micha watched as Loran struggled to his feet, blood oozing from several wounds and something else leaking from his shoulder joint. Loran tore away the leg of his pants and opened a section of his metal thigh. It contained a first aid kit, something he thought he'd never have to use. He swiftly sealed the wounds that bled, then began repairs on his hydraulic leaks. He tried an energy beam from the weapon embedded in his palm, but that was no longer functional.

He'd lost considerable fluid, and he limped as he moved away, vowing vengeance on Micha. Loran reached level ground and stopped to re-evaluate his injuries. He appeared to have survived rather well, but he needed to find the ship to replenish his fluids. "I know you're watching, Hound," he shouted. "Know this, I will kill you horribly. You had your chance to be the greatest hero in the galaxy, but you turned traitor. You're a fool, Hound. You had the remote, the only weapon that could have defeated me, yet you foolishly tossed it away."

"It wasn't real," shouted Micha. "It was a fake Rathbone made for me. He's still got the real one."

"You're lying," roared Loran, but Micha did not answer. He was running away. Darkness had fallen by the time Loran made his way out of the deep canyon. He spent another night, cold and miserable, out in the open.

Micha was in another small cave, working at the stones he'd gathered. Most were complete failures, but two had promise. Micha worked the stone carefully as Miriam had taught him. Morning found him ready; he had fashioned a crude spear. It was nothing that would impress his mentor, but it should serve the purpose. Micha had seen the Emperor's weakness. Loran was vulnerable now; Micha set his jaw and went hunting.

———◉———

"MICHA HAS GOOD SKILLS," smiled Miriam as she read the signs around the small cave. "He camped here, but he left in the morning before the other could find him. "He has been searching for good stone as well. This means he has no modern weapons. His tracks suggest he is injured, but not badly. The other hunts him, but does not realize Micha is leading him away from his ship. They went this way."

Later that day she stopped at the edge of the cliff, searched around. "Micha came here, left, and then returned again. Then he left a second time. He wanted to lead his pursuer to the edge, but the man did not fall; he jumped across. We must find a way around."

"How could anyone jump across that?" asked Edie. "Rathbone, you're the strongest cyborg; could you make that jump?"

"No, Edie, I don't believe I could. I don't know what O'Loran is now, but he's not human anymore. It would take a machine stronger than me to make that jump."

"We go this way," said Miriam, as she led them along the cliff edge. Eventually they found where Micha had crossed the chasm and followed him. It was late in the day as Miriam read the sign at this side of the cliff.

"Micha was here. He waited there while the other one jumped. As the enemy landed here, Micha knocked him over the edge."

Rathbone knelt and peered over the edge. He saw nothing so he pulled a small scope from his pocket and looked again. "I see dried blood and what looks like hydraulic fluid. Looks like Micha has managed to hurt him, but I can see where he's moved off. The Emperor is still alive."

"He won't be for long," said Edie.

"Oh? What makes you say that?" asked Rathbone.

"Micha tried to kill him," Edie replied. "Micha hates to leave a job half finished."

Suddenly Rathbone straightened up. "Skeeter," he muttered, as he reached for his comm unit. "Kella, Kella respond."

"Kella here."

"Kella, you and Jorge get that ship off the ground and don't come back until we call for you."

"Understood."

There was a sudden scream of engines in the distance as the Arcalian fighter lifted off and shot into space. "Kella to Rathbone."

"Here."

"We're in low orbit. What's up?"

"The Emperor is hostile and we have the only ship."

"Understood. Call when you need a pick up. Kella out."

"Micha went this way," said Miriam as she started away. She did not go too far before she found the cave where Micha had spent the night working on his weapons. Rathbone held the light for her while Miriam read the signs.

"He was here in the night, working stone," she said. "Micha has made weapons. See here, the stone chips, and here the torn branches? I believe her has made spears and is hunting the other now. We will pick up the trail in the morning."

"I'll take first watch," said Edie.

"We'll find him, Edie," Rathbone said gently. She gave him a weak smile, then turned away to begin the watch.

MICHA MOVED LIKE A stalking panther, his crude spear clutched in his hand. That spear had a stone tip, the second didn't and he hoped to get a clear shot with the first. Micha had reasoned out the Emperor's weakness. Loran had sealed the wounds that bled first, not the one that leaked hydraulic fluid. Why?

It had taken Micha a while to puzzle it out, but he did. The Emperor's new body might be a machine, but his brain and skin were not. For that brain to function it needed a constant source of blood. However, since there was not much human left, the blood supply would be a lot smaller than a normal man would have. Every drop would be precious. Micha had to make him bleed.

The day was well along before he found his quarry. As he suspected, the Emperor was hunting him too, but had lost the trail long since. The man was bent over, studying the ground. Dammit, he was learning fast. A few more days and the Emperor would be a competent tracker. Micha's window of opportunity was closing. As silent as possible he moved closer.

Micha had no illusions about his spear doing any real immediate damage. He fully expected it to shatter upon impact. Real damage was not the object of the game here, a bleeding wound that Loran could not reach to seal; that was the object of the game. One wound and then escape. The Emperor was limping, but Micha had no doubts the man could still outrun him.

In truth Micha wanted Loran to chase him; he just wanted to evade capture. At last he was well within range. Now if Loran would only oblige by turning to his right. It didn't seem likely so Micha threw a small stone to get the man's attention. As Loran whipped around to his right, Micha launched the spear.

The missile flew true and struck the Emperor between the shoulder blades, shattering upon impact. The razor sharp stone easily pierced the man's clothing and skin, ripping a wide gash along his back. Loran screamed in pain and rage as he whirled around to see Micha fleeing into the trees. He sprang after him, but Micha was able to elude him in the forest.

Cursing wildly, Loran stopped and sighed. "Damn that man to the nine hells," he muttered. "Did he really think to kill me with a stone spear? No, of course not; no matter what else he is, the hound is no fool. So why did he do that? He must have had a purpose?"

Suddenly Loran reached around to his back as best he could. His shirt was wet with blood, his blood. The thrice damned hound had cut him then forced him to run to increase the bleeding. A shiver of fear ran down Loran's spine. The hound knew his weakness. He had not needed the remote. Somehow he had to stop the bleeding. Lie down; pressing the cloth into his back would staunch the blood flow. This was not good.

As Loran lay with his back pressed tightly to a soft patch of ground he heard Micha call to him. "You haven't given up the chase already, have you, Loran? It's not like you to give up so easily."

The Emperor lay silent, barely breathing. He dared not allow his blood pressure to elevate and he dare not let the hound find him. It was nearly dark; perhaps he still had a chance. He had to find the remains of his ship, there would be a med kit and perhaps some weapons still functional. He had to evade the hound long enough to reach the ship. If only he could find it.

When Micha did not get a response to his taunting, he reasoned the Emperor had discovered the truth. It would be a different hunt now. Micha would no longer be the prey. He crawled into a tight thicket of brush to await the coming of the next day. With a bit of luck Loran would bleed out in the night. Exhausted, Micha fell into a deep sleep.

The sun was well up when he awakened. Cursing he crawled out of his hiding place, relieved himself, then began searching for edible roots and berries. He found a few and made a meager meal before setting out after the Emperor. It didn't take long to find where the robot had spent the night; there was blood and mud well packed down where he had lain.

Micha followed the trail, it was easy to find. He might have suspected a trap, but there were still a few drops of fresh blood in the tracks and it was obvious by the wandering the man was confused. The witch's hound was on the scent of prey. This day would see the end of the hunt.

Loran staggered and nearly fell. Confused he looked all around. He was looking for something; what was it? Something important, that was certain. There was something else he had to remember. Oh yes, hide from the hound. Why did he have to do that? He hadn't seen any sign of a dog anywhere. Wait, the hound was a man, a bad man. He needed to hide.

Loran staggered a few more steps into the huge clearing then stopped again. Wait, why should he hide? He was stronger than the man. Yes, he would kill the bad man. Now, what was it he was supposed to find? His fuzzy brain finally grasped the concept of sound nearby. He turned to see the bad man far away, banging two stones together. He would go kill that man then find what he was looking for, whatever it was. Limping badly he started toward Micha.

Micha saw him coming and rose to his feet, gripping his crude stone knife in his hand. He'd torn off a piece of his tunic to wrap around for a handle. Loran had seen him and was coming. One way or the other this would soon be over.

LESSA PACED NERVOUSLY while the others sat quietly, chatting among themselves. She was starting to lose her temper. First Micha disappeared, obviously going after the Emperor, then half the crew went to find him. There had been no word from them either. Worse, something had happened and they had been kept waiting for two days. The Black Witch was not happy.

Lady Marla hurried into the room with the Viceroy close behind her. "Lessa, I am so sorry to have kept you waiting so long. Please forgive me."

"It does not matter, Marla. You summoned me and I am here. I did not expect to be kept waiting like a supplicant begging an audience. Please tell me why I am here."

"It couldn't be helped, Lessa," sighed Lortax as he sank into a chair. The lines of worry were etched deeply into his face and she relented somewhat. "We're about to be overwhelmed at the borders. The thrice damned Arcalian King wouldn't move a ship until he met personally with Lady Marla."

"I think the poor boy has a crush on me," grinned Marla. "Anyway, I went, had dinner with the nice man, and now his considerable forces are at the front with the clans."

"We've still got a fair standoff, Lessa, but it won't last long. They're bringing in more ships every day and starting to edge forward. I think they're trying to provoke us into starting something. We fire a single shot and we're doomed. I know the kind of mass forces they can bring to bear."

"Lessa, where is Micha and the rest of your crew?" asked Marla.

"Yes, where is Micha," asked Lortax.

"We don't know," replied Lessa. "The Emperor made a run for it and Micha went after him in Kella's speeder. When we heard nothing Zartah sent several members of the crew to search for him."

"Zartah, you were called by the High Priestess and your Clan Chieftain," said Lortax as he rose to his feet. "Explain yourself, and it had better be good."

Zartah bristled at his tone and rose to go nose to nose with the chieftain. "As First Man it is my job to watch the Boss's back. When we didn't hear from him, I sent the non-Borelian crew members to look for him. The Borelians all answered the call."

"Where is Edie, Micha's mate?" asked Marla.

"She is with child," said Lesssa. "She was not feeling well so I told her to remain behind."

"Satisfied, Lortax?" asked Zartah.

"Not by half," growled Lortax, as he sat back down, "but there is little I can do about this. Dammit, Lessa, you know what is at stake here, and you let this get completely out of hand."

"I don't like your tone, Lortax," replied Lessa, her voice cold as deep space.

"All right, children," said Norlene as she rose to her feet. "Let's not fight amongst ourselves. There are plenty of enemies at the border for us to fight with. We all know what has to happen here so let's get on with it. We have reached the point where a clear head will be our best defense."

"Then you do it, Norlene," sighed Lessa, as she got her temper under control. "The rest of us are getting nowhere."

"As you wish," she replied with a twinkle in her eye. "We can do nothing here wringing our hands. The Emperor has betrayed us and now the situation can only be resolved at the border. Arlessa, take the Ravage and your crew; I'll travel with the Viceroy and Lady Marla. You take good care of Gorda for me; I want him back in one piece."

"What have you got in mind, Norlene?" asked Lortax.

"I propose a clear demonstration of the stupidity of attacking us," she replied. "When we arrive I intend to annoy Arlessa then turn her loose on the enemy. In point of fact, I intend to help her."

"Even the two of you cannot defeat the entire Empire," sighed Lortax.

"I'm wide open to alternative suggestions, Viceroy."

"I have none, Lady Norlene. The only other option is surrender. Perhaps that is the best course of action. If we surrender and allow ourselves to be absorbed into the Empire, millions of lives will be saved."

"I can't believe you'd even consider that, Lortax," said Lessa.

"I'm not, Lessa, I'm just desperate. If it comes to it the Clans will fight; you know that."

"Perhaps we should just head for the border and see what the situation is," said Norlene. "We might get lucky. Maybe Lessa and I can throw a scare into them."

"All right, Lady Norlene," sighed Lortax. "We've got nothing to lose at this point; let's go see if we can bluff them out."

<hr />

AS THE RAVAGE FOLLOWED the Viceroy's flagship toward the border, the Emperor was about to face him own doom. He was still struggling to think clearly. Why wasn't the bad man trying to run away, why was he just waiting? No matter, he would kill the bad man then go find whatever it was he needed to find.

As he reached his target the bad man moved. There was pain in his neck. He connected with the man and sent him sprawling, but he leaped to his feet and closed in. Loran was aware of something warm on his neck and his vision began to blur. Brenna! That's who he had to find. He had to find and protect Brenna.

He was struggling to move now, and the bad man struck again. Loran's consciousness began to fade. There was a man close by, perhaps he could help. "Please, help me," he managed slowly. "Please protect Brenna. I can't see..." he stopped moving, he stopped talking, and just stood there. A moment later his head left his shoulders.

Micha saw him coming, but the Emperor was moving quite slowly and was limping. He also seemed to be struggling to focus. Micha waited. As Loran reached for him, Micha struck with his stone knife, severing both the arteries and hydraulic tubing in the robot's neck. Loran managed to deal him a blow that sent him flying with cracked ribs, but he had done the damage. The last of the Emperor's blood spurted out of his neck mixed with hydraulic fluid.

The robot's speech was slurred, but Micha understood. He watched as the mighty machine stopped moving and stood still, slightly bent forward. A hard pass of the stone knife severed the head from the shoulders, but shattered in the process. No matter, it had done its job.

Of War and Peace

"He went this way," said Miriam as she followed Micha's tracks. "See here, there is more blood, but it is not Micha's."

"How can you know that?" asked Edie.

"It doesn't smell like him," replied Miriam. "It smells of machine fluids. It is Micha's quarry who bleeds."

"I didn't think he had blood anymore," mused Rathbone.

"He'd need enough to keep his brain functioning," said Edie.

"So Micha is trying to bleed him out," grinned Rathbone. "Remind me not to annoy that young man."

"This way," said Miriam, and she was off again. Soon she stopped and cast about. "Here, the prey lay down for the night; see the blood and fluid mixed with the mud. He was trying to stop the bleeding. Micha must have wounded him in a place he could not reach. This way."

A short while later she led them into a large clearing. Micha was there, sitting near the headless body of the robotic Emperor. Edie screamed and ran to him. He regained his feet in time to catch her in his arms.

"Easy girl, easy; you're killing me," gasped Micha.

"Oh, Micha, you're hurt. Where is it?"

"I've got a few scrapes all right, but he cracked my ribs. Breathing is a bit of a chore."

"Rath, I need my med kit. Get that ship down here now," barked Edie as she probed gently at Micha's ribs.

"Aye, Boss," grinned Rathbone as he reached for his comm. "Rathbone to Kella."

"Kella here."

"Lock onto my signal and come down here, we found the Boss and he's banged up a bit."

"Understood. Take her down fast, Jorge."

"Yes, Ma'am, going down fast." Like a stooping hawk the ship dropped through the atmosphere. She swooped in and landed softly within feet of the group on the ground. The hatch dropped open and Kella hit the ground, tossing Edie's med kit to her.

A few moments later Edie had Micha's ribs stabilized, his other wounds sealed, and had given him a shot of pain killers. She was holding him gently. "Oh my man, I should never have let you go without me."

"Edie, I got shot down. I'm happy you weren't there. This way I have you to patch me up. I don't suppose you have any ration bars with you? Those rodents I've been eating taste vile; I'd kill for some real food."

Rathbone passed him an opened bar and Micha sighed with delight as he bit off a chunk. "You have to be hungry for one of these to taste good," grinned Rathbone. "Boss, it seems like I owe you another one. You managed to do what I was unable to accomplish with years of trying. I can truly let Gen and Ari rest now."

"So, what happens now, Micha?" asked Kella. "All hell will break loose when he doesn't return."

"Then I guess he should return. He said he'd give me anything I want if I would take him back to his own people, and I promised to do just that."

"Micha? If we take the body back they'll know for certain he is dead," said Kella. "The whole galaxy will come unglued."

"Yep, that's the idea."

"You want a galaxy wide war? Micha?" Edie was astounded. She searched his eyes for some hint of what he had planned.

"Edie, trust me," sighed Micha as he placed his hand on her abdomen. "I promised to make a safe place for you and our friend here, and I mean to do just that."

"So we're going out to Exile?"

"Nope, you're going back to Nova, and I'm taking my metal friend there back to his people."

"Is that so?" said Edie, planting her fists on her hips. "You think you can just send me home to wait for you to come back or not."

"Edie..."

"Just what do you propose I use for a ship? Yours got shot down and you destroyed his. How am I supposed to get home?"

"She's got a point," said Kella, winking at Edie. "Now that Edie has mentioned it, you owe me a speeder, Mister. You broke the one I loaned you."

"Rath, help me here."

"Sure, Boss," grinned Rathbone, "I'll put that nasty robot on the ship for you, seeing as you're all banged up and all."

Micha just laughed and shook his head. "Edie, I just want you to be safe."

"Micha, my place is at your side. If our child is born on a battlefield we'll raise her to be a warrior. If she's born on a farm we'll teach her to farm. Either way, we do it all together, understand me?"

"Yes Ma'am, I hear and obey. Shut up, Rath." Everybody was laughing now. Rathbone passed the robot's body up to Jorge who stored it in the air lock. He tossed down a container for the head and that went aboard the fighter as well.

"All right, folks, let's get under way," said Micha as he painfully hauled himself into the fighter.

"Where to, Boss?" asked Jorge as the ship rose through the atmosphere and out into space.

"It's my guess everybody will be heading for the border by now," replied Micha. Let's go see if we can find them. Kella, I need you to contact your people. I want news of Loran's death to spread throughout the galaxy as fast as possible."

"Micha? Are you serious? You know what this will do."

"I know. Just do it."

"All right, as long as you know what you're doing, Micha," sighed Kella. "This is certainly going to be interesting."

"That will please my mate," smiled Miriam. "He likes things to be exciting."

———————⦿———————

"TRY TO RELAX, MY LOVE," said Brenna, as she laid her hand on Lessa's arm. There's nothing anyone can do until we get to the border. Norlene seems to have a plan."

"Yes she does, and I have a back-up plan. I don't like either one."

"Lessa?"

"Norlene wants us to put on a display of power to frighten the enemy. If we do that we will disturb the entire sector. Planets, even stars could be affected. Time itself will have strange ripples running through it. Things from other realms will bleed through into this one, dangerous things, bad things.

"If Norlene's plan fails, then my plan is to time shift the entire Borelian fleet one day into the future. That will give us a powerful advantage as we will be able to attack from behind for they will have scattered through the sector by then. I will then use all the power I can access. It may tear a hole in the fabric of reality as we understand it, but I will protect Nova, no matter the cost."

Lessa was just getting more agitated and Brenna sought for some way to distract her. "Lessa, I've always wondered; why is it witches only exist in Sector Nine, and only a few people at that? Can you tell me? Do you know?"

"That is a strange tale, my love," smiled Lessa, as she realized what Brenna was doing. She knew she had to calm down so she went along with the ploy. "A long time ago, when humans were first colonizing Sector Nine, a strange blue-orange star exploded. A wave of radiation swept out from the blast killing most humans in the sector, but some survived.

"The survivors had gained an affinity for energy; they found they could manipulate it to create or destroy almost anything they desired. In the early times most of those people destroyed themselves or each other, but not all.

"The ability was passed down through the generations. In those early days they could affect even the stars in their path, destroy planets, and more. The results of their learning to control the new abilities, and to teach their children that control, is witnessed by the odd configurations of stars and planets in this area of space."

"So, only those people directly descended from those survivors can work the magic."

"Yes. Most Borelians can to one small degree or another, but strong users are taken to the temples to be trained. Occasionally someone will be born with the ability to access the power as the original survivors did."

"Like you and Norlene."

"Yes, like us; oddly it is far more common in women. Brenna, we will not allow Nova to be enslaved again, but we could destroy much of the galaxy to prevent it and all space will be affected by what we do. I'm so afraid. Our only real hope is if Micha has caught Loran and is bring him back. I know we can negotiate a deal to keep our freedom, even if it is within the Empire."

"Then I hope we hear from him soon. Time is running out. We'll be at the front in a couple of days."

Brenna sank into a thoughtful silence and Lessa went back to her pacing.

THREE DAYS HAD PASSED and Micha's ribs were nearly healed. Lessa's enhancements were working fine; he would heal completely in a couple of days instead of a couple of months. Stretched out on the deck, staring at the bulkhead, he worked on the problem at hand.

"Micha?'

"Yes, Edie my love, I'm working on the problem."

"I thought you already had a plan."

"It could use a bit of refining."

"They all can," chuckled Jorge who was at the controls.

"Can you tell us about it?" asked Edie.

"It's a bit of a gamble, but I'm hoping to set off a few uprisings inside the Empire. If it starts to come apart, then the fleet will start to dissolve as different factions switch loyalty back to their own people."

"The Empire will tear itself apart and the whole galaxy will be at war," breathed Kella.

"Not quite," chuckled Rathbone. "I think I see where this is going. The Borelian Free States are already united and strong. As the empire falls apart, none will dare try to invade us. Sector Nine will be the strong man of the new world order. I like it."

"Yep, that's the plan," said Micha.

"What's your back-up plan, my love?" asked Edie.

"Make Lessa angry and point her at the enemy."

"Micha, do you really think she is powerful enough to destroy an entire fleet?"

"Yes, if we can get her close enough. We have to find her and the rest of the crew."

"Message coming in, Boss. It's from Zartah. They're on the Ravage and headed for the Border. It looks bad."

"Tell him we'll join up before he gets there. It looks like we're a day ahead of him."

"Aye, Boss." Jorge sent the coded message to the nearest relay beacon.

"It's a message from Micha, Lady," grinned Zartah. "They're going to meet up with us before we reach the border."

"That is good news indeed," sighed Lessa as she stopped pacing and dropped into the captain's chair. "Do they say anything about the Emperor?"

"They didn't say, Lady. I'll ask." Zartah sent his message and they waited finally an answer was relayed to them. "They have the Emperor with them." There was a collective sigh of relief at that. It was short lived.

"So Micha had to kill him," mused Gorda, slowly nodding his head as he worked his way through the logic of his conclusion.

"Why did you say that, Gorda?' asked Brenna.

"Micha is headed for the border, too; otherwise he would be much farther away. He knew we were going to Borealis Prime. If the Emperor was still alive, Micha would be headed the other way." The entire bridge fell silent as the logic of that statement sank in.

Lessa rose and exchanged places with Zartah. Once at the comms she contacted the Donar, Lortax's ship. She put the comms on bridge speaker so all could hear.

"Are you certain, Lessa?" asked Norlene.

"Not completely, but I know Micha and I believe Gorda's reasoning is sound."

"It will be; my man has a head for that sort of thing. So the Seer of Exile was right, the fate of the galaxy rested on Micha's shoulders and for whatever reason, he chose the path of war for us all. So be it; let us prepare. Tomorrow we will sight the enemy."

As Norlene signed off Lessa rose and left the bridge. "I must meditate," she said as she stepped through the door.

Zartah was gazing at Brenna. She had a sad look and he was concerned. "Are you all right, Brenna?"

"My father is dead, Zartah. I have known for years now that it had to happen, but I guess I have always hoped to prevent it and make him see reason. Now one of my best friends has killed him."

"If he did, the Boss must have had good reason."

"I know, Zartah, I know. Micha has a good reason for everything he does. Knowing the stakes here, I'm sure Micha had no other choice. I'm just a bit messed up with it all."

"Understood. If you need a few minutes alone, Brenna, the captain's quarters are empty right now."

"Thank you, Zartah. Perhaps I will take a few moments to let this all soak in." she rose and slowly left the bridge.

———◉———

NINE MEN IN IMPRESSIVE uniforms sat at a long conference table in the flagship of the Imperial Fleet. One man in plain clothes sat at the head of the table. He spoke first. "The Emperor commands that we continue to build up pressure along the border of Sector Nine, nothing more until he joins us here."

"Hoaka, we're all getting tired of your little charade," said one uniform. "No one has seen the Emperor for weeks; you've been running the show yourself. Now tell us the truth, is Emperor Loran still alive, or do you know?"

Hoaka's shoulders slumped. "I don't know," he sighed. "He should have joined us by now. I keep expecting his speeder to appear on screens at any moment. I warn you gentlemen, it is certain death to cross that man."

"We all know that," agreed another, "all too well. The question is what do we do if he doesn't return? Do we keep up the charade and attack Sector Nine?"

"We could keep on going," mused another. "Since Hoaka has been handling things quite well for weeks he might as well continue. If Loran returns then nothing has been lost. Should he not return then we still hold all the power and Hoaka is the Emperor, at least in name. The alternative is to have the whole damn thing fall apart and the galaxy dissolve into a thousand petty squabbles. What say you?"

"Hail Emperor Hoaka," grinned the first man to speak. Chuckling, the rest agreed.

"When Loran returns I will be the first one he kills," sighed Hoaka.

"Luck of the draw, Emperor," laughed one of the uniforms as they all rose from the table, "luck of the draw."

They filed out to return to their own ships, all except the captain of the flagship. "Is all in readiness, Captain?"

"Yes, Sir, everything is in place. Just speak the word and there will be eight new admirals in the fleet."

"Very good, my friend; we may just survive this thing yet."

A United Front

As the Donar, flanked by Freedom and the Ravage passed a gas giant on the edge of Arlen space, a fighter ship of Arcalian design swept in and vanished into the launch bay of the Ravage. Moments later Micha and his companion strode onto the bridge. Lessa flew into his arms and gave him a bear hug.

"Micha, I was starting to worry."

"Sorry, Lessa, I ran into a little trouble."

"Is my father dead, Micha?" Brenna had spoken softly, fearfully, and yet she already knew the answer. She just hadn't wanted to face it.

"I'm sorry, Brenna. I had to kill him; he gave me no other choice."

"I believe you, Micha. I do understand and I accept that it had to be done. I guess the man I knew as my father died a long time ago. Only the machine was left."

"Micha, tell us what happened," said Lessa.

Micha dropped into the captain's chair and sighed. "I caught up with him, but it took a while. Rath had mounted a one shot weapon on the speeder. The idea was to knock out his engines, but I didn't get a good hit; he still had some manoeuvrability and weapons. He shot me down.

"I managed to eject, but I was pretty high up. He came in after me, but the gravity took him and he crashed. I got out of the seat and made a reasonable landing then went looking for him. I'd sent out a beacon so I was sure the crew would find me sooner or later; I just had to keep him from getting away before they arrived.

"I managed to disable his ship, but he took exception to that and tried to hunt me down. Normally it would have been easy to evade him, but he busted me up a bit at the ship. My blaster was dead and I knew he was stronger, so I tried to stay out of reach.

"The thing is, a man should never talk to himself out loud. I got close enough to hear him making some plans, plans that involved the destruction of the Borelian Clans, the end of Nova and everybody on her, and the recapture of Brenna O'Loran and her mother.

"At one point he tried to hire me to kidnap Brenna and to kill you, Lessa. During that conversation I made him a promise. I swore to return him to his people. I intend to keep that promise."

"Boss, how did you manage to kill him without weapons? We know he was a lot stronger than we are," asked Zartah.

"I was able to manufacture weapons from stone, a skill your mate tried to teach me."

"You need lots of practice," giggled Miriam.

"I know they weren't anywhere near as good as you can make, Miriam," grinned Micha, "but they worked. Once we get back to Nova Prime I want you to teach me more."

"You sound like you have a plan, Micha. Care to share?" Lessa had a tiny smile on her face now. He would have something up his sleeve. She just hoped it would be good enough to convince the High Priestess and Viceroy.

"Lessa, the target here is to protect Nova and to keep her free of slavery, right?"

"That's right. That's our main target. The protection and preservation of the Borelian Free States is also a strong consideration."

"Will you trust me to get it done?"

"Dear friend, I have come to trust you and your abilities. I will trust you to get it done. Now we will have to convince Marla and Lortax. They're not going to be happy. You disobeyed a direct order from the High Priestess and the Clan Chieftain."

"Understood. You gave me these tattoos, Lessa; can you take them off me?"

"I can, Micha, but I'd rather not, at least not just yet. It's a big step to give up the protection of the clan. Don't be too hasty."

"Alright, Lessa, but I'm tired, hungry, and fed up with the politics. I want to get this finished and to go back to my farm."

"Then do it, Micha," said Lessa. "Take control of this situation and I'll back you to the hilt."

"Are you certain, Lessa?"

"Protect Nova, her freedom, and our families?"

"Above all else."

"Do it, old friend. I'm with you all the way."

"I'm in, Boss," grinned Zartah. The rest of the crew was quick to agree.

"All right," sighed Micha. "There's no going back, no way out, and nothing held back. We can do this, but if it goes sideways, there's no back-up."

"I'll be the back-up, Micha," said Lessa, her eyes hard and her face grim.

"Boss, Lortax is calling," said Jorge.

Micha's jaw hardened. "Give me ship to ship, open channel."

"Boss, we're close enough the whole fleet will hear everything. You sure you don't want a secure channel?"

"Dead sure, Jorge; ship to ship, open channel."

"Aye, Boss, open channel it is."

A moment later both Lortax and Marla appeared on the main screen. "Micha, where the nine hells have you been? Did you catch the Emperor? Is he with you? Will he honor his agreements?"

"In order, Chieftain," replied Micha, a hard edge to his voice, "I was shot down on an unknown planet while pursuing the Emperor." Micha had gone cold as deep space and Lortax involuntarily flinched. He didn't like the sound of this at all. "I caught up with the Emperor. His body is on this ship with me. No, he will not, nor did he ever intend to honor his agreements."

"My gods, Micha, you've destroyed any chance we had of peace," exclaimed Lortax.

"Peace, Chieftain?" Micha's voice was even colder. "You may have been born in a warm bed with servants to tend you, but I was born a slave. I can assure you, there is no peace to be had in slavery. I will go to my death and take my companion and unborn child into the mystery with me before I submit them to a life like I had.

"Run back to Borealis and hide if you want, but Nova will face the enemy head on. Jorge, set a course for the enemy flagship, full burn."

Stunned by Micha's accusation, Lortax did not reply. Norlene stepped in front of the screen. "Micha, wait. Give me time to get back aboard the Ravage. I'm a Novan all the way and my mate is on your crew."

"Understood, Lady Norlene. Waiting. Shall I send Gorda to pick you up?"

"Now hold on, dammit," said Lortax as he found his voice at last. "Micha of Nova, adopted of Nara Clan, as Chieftain of Nara and Viceroy of the Borelian Free States I now pronounce you Grand Marshall of all fighting forces and War Master for the Free States. The fleet awaits your orders, Grand Marshall."

"Viceroy?"

"You got us in and back out of Elliston Prime last year, Micha. I just hope you can do it again. My friend, I've got nothing to offer here. You make the play and the fleet will back you. We're all as good as dead anyway."

"Believe me; you were worse off with the Emperor still alive. He explained his plans for Sector Nine and for Nova Prime as he was trying to kill me."

"Do you want to come aboard the Donar?"

"The Ravage is my ship. Follow me. Jorge, is Lady Norlene aboard yet?"

"Aye, Boss, and the Freedom just pulled up on our wing."

"All right then, engage. The fleet can follow or not as they choose. I will lead no man or woman into battle that is unwilling."

"Aye, Boss, course and speed set and engaged."

As the Ravage approached the border where thousands of ships were facing each other Lortax sighed with relief. Not one single ship had withdrawn from the fleet. Whatever Micha was planning, everybody was staying for the show.

Throughout the entire fleet every man and woman knew this day could be their last. All chances of peace were gone and command of the fleet had been handed over to mercenary barely older than a boy. Worse yet, he was not known for his diplomacy.

———◉———

"THAT'S THE END OF IT, Hoaka," sighed the old Admiral, as they all sat around the table once again. "He didn't even try to code the message; he wanted us to hear it."

Hoaka just shook his head. "The Emperor is truly dead and we are facing a fleet commanded by that crazy merc. Ah well, surely with our superior numbers we can defeat them."

"We can," was the reply, "but what then?"

"We have to keep a lid on this," said another. "If word of Loran's death gets out the entire galaxy will erupt in rebellion."

"Not necessarily," said another. "We need someone to succeed him. I say we promote Hoaka to Emperor; he's been doing the job for weeks anyway."

"Now wait, ..." Hoaka got no further as a man burst into the room.

"Gentlemen, sorry to interrupt, but you need this information." He handed a reading tablet to Hoaka then withdrew.

"Well," sighed Hoaka as he leaned back in his chair and passed the tablet to the Admiral, "It appears I will not get to be Emperor after all."

"The latest breaking news," read the Admiral. "Another seven sectors of the galaxy have declared independence from the Empire. War has broken out on several fronts and the Imperial Fleet is nowhere to be found. Several ships of the Imperial Line have already defected to their home worlds and changed their colors to the newly independent state. The question on everybody's mind is where is the Emperor? It appears the rumors of his death are true.

"It goes on, but that's the gist of it, gentlemen. Somehow the word of Loran's death has reached the Hub Worlds and beyond. The damned media has better communication lines than we do."

"So, what do we do now?" asked another.

"That's up to Emperor Hoaka," said the Admiral.

"Oh, no..."

"Oh yes, Emperor."

Hoaka was a security man and one of the best. His trademark was the ability to assess a situation quickly and respond. "Very well, if that's the way you want it." He hit the summon button on his console and the Communications officer entered the room.

"Sir?"

"You will send a message fleet wide and also relay the information to the news media as quickly as possible. Emperor Loran is dead; Emperor Hoaka has succeeded him. Emperor Hoaka and the Imperial Fleet will deal with any and all uprisings immediately."

"Sir?"

"That's Sire," said the Admiral. "The Emperor has given you a command, Mister. Step lively!"

"Sir! Sire!" the man saluted and strode swiftly from the room.

"That should give us a bit of time to deal with this current situation," said Hoaka. "Now, Admiral, you are in command of the Imperial Fleet. Advise me."

The old Admiral nodded his head and smiled. He understood. Hoaka would play the Emperor for them, but they would make the big decisions. Hoaka would now tend mostly to his own security. A few moments later the Comms Officer returned. "Sire."

"Yes?"

"Messages sent as ordered, Sire. A new message has arrived." He passed the tablet to the new Emperor, but the Admiral reached for it. He saluted and stood quietly waiting.

"What does it say, Admiral?"

"It says the new flagship of the Borelian Free States will arrive shortly. The new War Master wants to confer. Should I send him our terms for surrender, Sire?"

Hoaka could see the glee in the old man's eye. The old fool wanted this battle. He would have to eliminate him soon, but he dare not do it now. "Indeed, Admiral; if nothing else it will shake his confidence a bit. Send the following to the new Grand Marshall.

"The Borelian Free States will be absorbed into the Empire and will pay allegiance to the Emperor. In return for this allegiance the Imperial Fleet will withdraw to attend to other matters. You have one day to accept our terms."

"That should do it," grinned the Admiral. "Now gentlemen, we need to make battle plans. There's no way in the nine hells that young upstart will surrender."

———◆———

THE MESSAGE WAS RECEIVED aboard the Ravage and handed to Micha. He passed it off to Lessa without a single word or any sign of emotion. The Crew settled themselves into combat mode; they'd seen him like this before and knew there would be action soon. "Looks like this could get exciting, Zartah," grinned Gorda.

"That's what I love about this crew," grinned Zartah, "there's always something exciting to do."

Their friendly banter took some of the tension out of the air. Norlene stepped in behind Micha and laid a gentle hand on his shoulder. "I know who you are, Micha. I have waited to see if this knowledge would come to you on your own, but we can wait no longer."

"Norlene, are you certain?" asked Lessa.

"Aren't you?"

"Yes, you're right. Now is the time. Micha, dear friend, there are two spirits living within you; we all know that. The Farmer and the Warrior seem to work well together; we weren't sure how far that could go, but now you need to access all of it. Will you allow Norlene to reveal to you who you truly are?"

"Ladies, there is no time for this," replied Micha.

"We can make the time," grinned Norlene, "Lessa will see to it."

"So, I'm about to get old again, am I," smiled Micha, relaxing at last.

"Just a bit," replied Norlene. "You relax in the captain's chair and have a short nap."

Micha started to reply, but her hand touched his temple and he was instantly asleep; asleep and dreaming.

Micha stood watching a battle unfold in a strange world. The people he stood near were human; at least they looked somewhat human. They were tall, slender, golden haired, and pale skinned for the most part but their ears and fingers were far too long to be truly human. He tried to speak to some of them but they ignored him. He could watch, but he could not interact.

The enemy was a completely alien looking race. Tall and broad with fierce looking fangs, great war clubs, and crude metal weapons; they were a frightening looking species.

The humanoids were vastly outnumbered but they fought fiercely. Their leader was an older man, his hair white and his face heavily lined, yet he was lethal in battle. Micha watched in awe as the old fellow directed his troops even while he tore into the enemy.

There were several magic users in the group as well, and Micha was awed at their power. They fought, and eventually overcame, the enemy wizards then turned their attention to the ground troops. The battle was soon over. Micha could see how, even though the leader had directed the battle, he had made certain his magic users were protected as they fought.

When the battle was obviously lost, the enemy had fled, but the old fellow lay dying. A female cradled his head in her arms, tears flowing down her cheeks. "Do not weep for me, Lila, my love, for even now I see the form I will take in the next life." He was looking right at Micha and smiling. "Above all else, live with honor; live free." He had spoken to both the woman and Micha. As he finished speaking he drew his last breath and Micha awakened.

Micha leaped to his feet and spun to face Norlene and Lessa. "What was that? What just happened? Was it real?"

"It was real, Micha," replied Norlene. "In the early times there was a great explosion and the magic of other realm bled into this one, and some of ours bled into theirs. Small hidden pathways remain that a strong witch can follow. Sometimes the spirit of one can reincarnate in another realm as well."

"Realm?"

"State of existence. State of being."

Micha nodded then shook his head to clear his thoughts. "Why did you show me this?"

"We did it so you would better understand yourself, and you needed to know another truth."

"Death is not the end."

"Exactly. Tell your crew what you saw." He did.

"So that's it," grinned Edie. "I always thought you were two people."

"Can you live with that, Edie my love."

"I've been doing quite well so far," she replied tartly, winking at Miriam. Keira giggle and poked Rathbone in the ribs.

"All right, enough of this," declared Micha as he turned back to the captain's chair. "I'm not finished with this realm yet. Jorge, where are we?"

"About two hours out from the front, Boss," replied Jorge. "What's the plan?"

"The plan, my friends, is to make the fools see reason. If that fails we go with the back-up plan."

"And that is?" asked Rathbone.

"We fight," he replied, his face hard as stone. "Our tactics are simple in this coming battle; if we have to face it. If it goes bad and we have to fight, the ladies Arlessa and Norlene will deal with the enemy. The rest of us will make sure they are kept alive to do their work. They fight, we protect.

"Get me Lortax, secure channel."

"Aye, Boss. Calling the Donar, secure channel. Donar, War Master Micha calling for the Viceroy." Micha just shook his head at Jorge who was grinning as he used Micha's fancy new title.

"Lortax here, Micha. We're almost there, have you got a plan."

"I do. The plan is to try talking sense into these people."

"You have a back-up in case that fails?"

"If that fails, Lady Arlessa and Lady Norlene will battle them and our task is to protect them while they do it. They'll be in the two Arcalian fighters backed up by the Ravage and the Freedom. Your task will be to keep as many as possible off us."

"Understood, Micha. Lady Marla wants you."

Marla stepped into view, her jaw set. "Micha, forgive me. I know all too well what our fate would be under the Empire's rule. I suggest you carry a lesser witch with you to help protect each of your warrior witches. I can still cast a fair protection spell and Meggan is quite strong as well. How about it, Micha, can you use two more volunteers?"

"Lady Marla, can you two withstand the gravitational shifts of a battle. I know the cyborgs can and so can the crew, but can you?"

"I believe we can, Micha, but if not; don't hold back."

"Agreed. Please come aboard. Jorge, inform the fleet that the Ravage is now the flagship and the High Priestess is coming aboard."

"Aye, Boss."

"I'm starting to pick up both fleets on long range scanners," said Murtah.

"All stop," said Micha.

"Aye, Boss, all stop."

"Once Lady Marla is aboard bring her here."

Marla soon appeared on the bridge with her assistant in tow. The young witch blushed shyly as she was introduced.

"All right," said Micha, "Lessa, Lady Norlene, pick your crews. Just leave me enough to fly this ship."

"I'll need Gorda to fly the ship, Micha," grinned Norlene, "and Marla for back-up."

"Very good," replied Micha. "Lessa, need a good pilot? I'm a bit of a gamer; I think I can handle it."

"She'll need a medic too," declared Edie.

Micha stepped to Edie and took her gently in his arms. "Edie, please, just this once, do this for me. Stay here with the crew." She gazed into his eyes for a long moment then lowered her gaze and nodded. He kissed her cheek and stepped away.

"Zartah, the ship is yours." As he spoke Micha made eye contact with Zartah and nodded slightly at Edie. Zartah nodded that he understood and Micha followed Lessa to the launch bay. Zartah started arranging his crew for battle.

"All right, people, here we go. Kiera, you, Rath, Murtah, and Ena are on weapons. Jorge, you're pilot, Brenna is comms, Edie, you and Miriam are in the Medic's bay just in case."

"Zartah, what was that look between you and Micha?"

"Why, Edie, I have no idea what you mean?"

"Talk to me, Zartah."

"All right, Edie the Relentless," he sighed. "If this all goes sideways, I'll take the Ravage out of the battle and head for Exile. You're carrying Micha's child too and she will be the first born child of a new Novan race. The child will grow up being loved, nurtured, protected, and taught by Nova Crew."

"Zartah..."

"Not this time, Edie. You have another life to think about besides your own now."

"So that's why Micha wanted to be Lessa's pilot?"

"He's the War Master, Edie. He can't leave the battle until it's over, you know that. If he did the rest of the fleet would fall apart. I have no choice here; please don't make this hard for me."

"Sweetie, you know he is right," said Brenna, as she gently laid her hand on Edie's arm.

"All right, Zartah," sighed Edie. "Come on Miriam, let's go get better acquainted." Miriam arose and followed Edie off the bridge.

The two Arcalian fighter ships slipped out of the Ravage's launch bay and moved slightly ahead. The entire fleet was aware that the War Master and the witches were now leading in the small fighter ships.

"Okay, this is your show now, Lessa," said Micha. "How is this going to work?"

"You do your thing, Micha and fly the ship. I'll work through the weapons ports. I'm not sure of the best way to make use of Meggan's talents. Meggan?"

"My speciality is protection spells," she replied shyly. "I believe I will be able to stop any energy beams and most of the missiles; at least I can try."

"Rathbone once told me that if you can't handle the tool, don't pick it up," said Lessa.

Stung, Meggan straightened up in her seat. "I can do it," she replied tartly. Lessa winked at Micha who grinned and turned away. Suddenly the comms squawked to life.

"Norlene to Arlessa."

"Go ahead."

"Gorda is flying the ship, I'm the new weapons system and Marla is shields, is that what you're doing?"

"Confirmed. Ready?"

"Understood and ready." Micha hit the engines and the ship leaped away towards the border. It was a short run. He glanced at the panel to see Gorda on his wing and the Ravage on the other. The Freedom was flying Gorda's wing. They were ready as they could be as they approached the standoff at the borders of Sector Nine; thousands of warships facing each other at the edge of an uninhabited star system.

———◆———

EMPEROR HOAKA STOOD on the bridge of his flagship, gazing at the masses of war ships lined up in space. Eventually he turned to the sensor array to see them all and he was pleased with what he saw. His forces outnumbered the Rebels by two to one. This should be an easy victory. Once Sector Nine had been brought to heel he would turn his attention to the rebels in the other sectors. He had greatly admired Emperor Loran and wanted to see his dream of Galactic peace come true.

Hoaka knew he would have to kill the admirals, of course. He had already placed his assassins on their ships. Once the battle was over he would give the command. Hoaka had always been a practical man. Through a series of chances he had been thrust from security chief to Emperor. He hadn't wanted it, but since there was no other option, he would do the job to the best of his ability. He was about to face his first test.

"Sire, there's two fighter ships approaching. They're calling for whoever is in command here."

"Put them on the forward screen."

"Aye, Sire; forward screen." The hard eyes face of a young man appeared. Hoaka recognized on of the mercs that had attacked R.I.M. headquarters and escaped the previous year.

———◉———

"THIS IS EMPEROR HOAKA, you may speak, Mercenary. What do you want?"

"Emperor? Well then, Emperor, I have a gift for you. I bring the dead body of your predecessor."

"Thank you, my people will confirm the identity. May I ask how he died?"

"I killed him."

"Indeed. In that case, Murderer, I assume you wish to surrender yourself to Imperial justice."

"You assume wrong," replied Micha. "My ship will now launch a coffin towards your ship. You may scan it or take it aboard to confirm the truth of its contents." As he spoke a small container was launched from the Ravage. It was taken aboard the flagship.

"Thank you, Mercenary. Now here are our terms for your surrender. Sector Nine will be absorbed into the Galactic Empire and will be governed by those I personally appoint. You, as the confessed murderer of the previous Emperor, will be tried, convicted, and executed for your crime. If these conditions are met, no one else needs to die today. You have one hour to discuss it among yourselves."

"There's no need," replied Micha. "Here are our terms for your safe withdrawal from Borelian space. "Leave now and never return. Do this and we will trade freely with the Empire and allow travel of its citizens back and forth across our borders. Refuse and die far from home.

"Word of Loran's death and visual evidence of it have already spread across the Empire. If you remain here to fight, your empire will fall apart beneath you. The only chance you have at all, Emperor, is to go home and tend to your own house. Think about it and give me your decision."

———◉———

DEEP IN THE BOWELS of the Emperor's flagship, two men in lab coats spoke to a uniformed officer. "This is so mangled," said one, "it is impossible to be certain from here. We'll need to take this back to the lab on Elliston."

"Then you'd better get going," replied the officer. "We're about to go into battle."

"What do you think?" one lab technician asked the other, as they closed the coffin and loaded it aboard a small ship. Can we rebuild this?"

"I believe we can," replied the other. "I have all the doctor's notes. Admit it, it will be fun to try." A moment later a small ship dropped out of the flagship and sped away towards the Hub worlds.

Decisions and Plans

Hoaka didn't wait; he didn't have to. He and the admirals had already made the decision before Micha arrived. There, in the fading light of a dying star, battle ships lined up against each other as far as scanners could reach. Literally millions of humans in thousands of spacecraft stood ready to fight. It would all come down to one man's decision. They did not have long to wait.

Even as Micha finished speaking a beam of energy lanced out from the Imperial flagship towards the small fighter that faced it. To the surprise of everyone, Micha's fighter did not explode; in fact it remained unharmed.

"Nicely done, Lady Meggan," grinned Micha. He had anticipated that move. He switched on the comms once again. "Emperor, am I to assume your attempt to kill me was your answer? Well, here's my response. Ladies, destroy that flagship."

At Micha's command strange beams of living energy lanced out from both fighters and sliced through the Imperial flagship like hot knives through butter. As one beam found the engines the great ship exploded.

A strange silence ruled for moments as the ship dissolved, escape pods and small fighters made their way to nearby ships, debris floated freely everywhere, and not a sound went over the comms on either side. Finally, Micha broke the spell. "All right, now who is the man in command of the Imperial fleet?"

There was silence for a few moments then an older man in a fancy uniform appeared on the screens. "That would be me, I am Admiral a..."

"Just give me your answer, will you leave or will you all die here?"

The Admiral glared at the screen for a long moment. It had been years since anyone had spoken to him in that tone. He didn't like it. With no thought for the lives of the people he commanded, or for the consequences of his actions, he spoke a single word. "Fire!"

If the Admiral had expected to obliterate the enemy with a single salvo he was horribly mistaken. If there was one thing Lortax was good at it was reading people. Even as the Admiral sucked in his breath to give the command Lortax spoke on fleet comms. "Evade and fire."

The entire star system went to hell in a heartbeat. Even as the Imperials opened fire their targets were in motion and returning fire. "Kill the command ships," bellowed Lortax, the Donar bucking and shifting beneath his feet as she moved against the Admiral's ship.

Lortax had to choose another target; the Novan Witches had already destroyed the Admiral's ship and he with it. It was far too late; the full battle was joined. Madness reigned everywhere and the destruction was terrible. As the day wore on the Imperials began to gain the upper hand by sheer force of numbers. Even the witches were beginning to tire and Micha could see the end. As he weaved his way among the larger ships, he reached for the comms.

"Micha to the Ravage and Freedom."

"Zartah here, Boss."

"Darks here."

"Commander Darks, you are now under Zartah's command. Zartah, get our people out of here. Plan three."

"Boss?"

"Do it. I'll catch up when I can."

"Understood. Plan three."

A moment later the Ravage abandoned the battle with the Freedom on her wing. It took them a while to fight their way out of the melee, but they eventually made it and vanished into the darkness of space.

EDIE NOTICED THE SHIP stop bucking beneath her. Grabbing Miriam's hand, she raced for the bridge. "Zartah, what...?"

"Edie..."

"You left him? You turned tail and ran? You..."

Edie was suddenly wrapped in Brenna's arms. "Hush now, Sweetie, hush now. There was no choice; Micha gave the order. Zartah didn't want to leave, but Micha made him do it."

"But where are they? They should be here with us..."

"Edie, sweet Edie, listen to me now. Lessa and Micha stayed back to make sure we could escape. Zartah, it's time to tell all. I too would like to know the full plan."

"All right, Brenna, we're clear so it is time. Jorge, ship to ship comms."

"Ship to ship comms, aye. Ravage to Freedom."

"Freedom here."

"Siemon, Zartah here, put this ship wide for your men."

"Done. We have new orders?"

"We do. All right people. Micha knew this could all go wrong, so he planned ahead for our survival, the survival of the enhanced and of the cyborgs. We are now going to carry out his plan. We will stop at Nova and gather our families, no one else. If the Empire comes they will not harm farmers, but the families of warriors may be different.

"For those of you who don't know, there is a single star out beyond the tip of the Galactic Arm. It has two habitable planets and they are somewhat inhabited. We are going to Exile as we already have allies there who will take us in. Those allies will need a bit of help and we will provide that for them.

"The few people who know of the existence of this place are now caught up in a battle that we are leaving behind. Micha didn't want to risk us any further. Don't mourn the Boss yet; he chose those Arcalian fighters for a reason. He will join us as soon as he can.

"Objections? Questions?"

"So, Micha protects his people to the last," said Commander Darks. "Orders received and understood, Zartah. There are no questions or objections. Darks out."

"I have an objection," said Edie.

"Edie, stop this now," said Zartah as he gently took her by the shoulders. "You are carrying Micha's child, the first who will be born with the enhancements. He knew that this could go wrong, but he wanted you and the child to survive. He wanted all of Lessa's enhanced people to survive and grow strong. He gave me this for you." He passed her a small device.

Edie looked at the recorder for a moment then touched the button and placed the device on a rail. Micha's image appeared in the air. "My beloved Edie, if you are seeing this, then things have not worked out as I hoped. I knew this could happen and so did Lessa.

"Edie, we may not survive this, but you and the others must. You are a new people and our child will be the first born of this new race. It will fall to you and Brenna to teach them to be loving and gentle, as well as strong and fierce. Lessa created us to be the protectors and defenders of the weak. It will be up to you, all of you, to make sure this new race of humans become worthy of her dream. I love you more than life itself, Edie. Be the gods willing, I will join you soon."

The image vanished and Edie collapsed in tears. Brenna gently held her until the storm of emotion passed, then she led Edie to her quarters and stayed with her. They cuddled up together just as they had done in the old days, each aching for the loss of a lover and praying for their return.

Back on the bridge all was subdued. They suddenly felt the magnitude of Lessa's dream and Micha's devotion to it, to them. They all wanted to go back and fight beside him, but they could not and they knew it. Silently, each vowed to live their lives bringing as much honor to that dream as possible. The trip to Nova was quite subdued. All thoughts were on the battle left behind.

———————◦———————

MICHA AND THE WITCHES fought frantically to cover Zartah's escape, yet they did not go with him. The future of the enhanced was on its way to safety, now they had to make certain there was no pursuit. They returned to the madness of the battle.

All semblance of order had long since been abandoned. If the Imperials had any illusion of their superior numbers easily carrying the day, they were soon abused of the notion. The Borealian Clans had a reputation as fierce and implacable fighters. That reputation was well deserved.

The Borelians attacked anything that looked or acted like a command ship. Soon the Imperials began to fall into disarray as no one wanted to be seen as directing the action. However, by the time several hours had passed, and hundreds of ships on both sides were destroyed; the sheer mass of Imperial ships began to carry the day.

Micha flexed his shoulders and continued to dodge his way through the insanity, issuing orders the whole time. No one on the Imperial side had any idea what was happening when the Ravage and Defender abandoned the field. They began to cheer as the Borelians started to regroup and pull back. The Imperials were between the fading star and their enemy. It had taken hours and countless lives to make it happen, but they were in position, or as close as possible.

"Can you do it Lessa, Norlene?" asked Micha.

"We can," came Norlene's reply, "but we will be quite useless for a few days after; if we survive."

"Make ready and tell me when to run," he ground out as he dodged another missile. "Lortax, fleet wide. On my mark, turn and run."

"Micha?"

"You'll know why when it happens. On my mark turn and run, full burn."

"All right, Micha. I don't know what you've got up your sleeve, but I hope it works."

"I hope some of us survive it," replied Micha. "Quickly now, spread the word."

"Understood."

"All right, Ladies, what do you need from me?"

"Get us as close as you can, Micha," replied Lessa. "Keep the ship as steady as possible. Are you ready, Meggan?"

"As ready as can be, Lady Arlessa. Let's do this. The temple will never be ruled from afar again."

"Now you're talking," grinned Lessa as she began to focus. As she allowed the rage to build within her, she felt Norlene reaching for the power. This could tear apart the very fabric of space in the Quadrant, but there was no other way.

The Imperial forces seemed confused as Micha and Gorda worked through the melee and out towards the old star. For a few moments, nothing followed or fired on them. It was the break that was needed. "Now, Micha," snarled Lessa in that deadly voice from a wrong place.

Micha grabbed the comms. "Now, Lortax, run!"

Lortax didn't wait for another signal, there was no need. He barked the order to the fleet, and like a flock of birds the Borelian fleet turned and fled at full burn. This move also caught the Imperials by surprise. Before they could recover, twin beams of raging fire energy leaped from the two lone fighter ships and streaked into the fading sun. They held there for a few moments then winked out, but they had done their done their work.

"Now, Micha," sighed Lessa as she sank to the deck.

He swung the ship around and opened up the engines. Both small ships bore down on the Imperial fleet at full burn. Momentarily stunned at the flight of the rebel fleet and the seeming attack by the two small ships, the Imperial fleet was slow to respond. A few ships fired on them, but they did not respond.

Suddenly the entire Imperial fleet was joining them in their flight. Too late. The suddenly revived star exploded, hurling debris and radiation in all directions. Fewer than a hundred ships survived that explosion.

Among the survivors Micha groaned as he picked himself off the deck and crawled back into the pilot's seat. A quick check of the instruments told him he had a small atmosphere leak, but otherwise the ship had managed to survive. Lady Meggan's shields had held with Lessa's help. He struggled to his feet, found the repair kit and patched the leak. Back in the seat he called for Gorda.

"Micha to Gorda, respond."

"Gorda here, Boss. We survived but Lady Marla is out cold and Norlene is looking a bit peaked. You okay?"

"Lessa and Meggan are sleeping it off. Ship seems to be in one piece. Let's find a quiet spot and regroup. My sensors are down, so if you've got any, you lead the way and I'll keep you on visual."

"Will do, Boss. I know just the place." Micha grinned as Gorda led him into the belly of a dead Imperial battle ship. They were well hidden from sight and could relax for a moment. "How's this?"

"Perfect, Gorda. What kind of shape are you in?"

"Fuel's nearly gone, but the hull is solid. I've still got some sensors and can repair the rest. Since Norlene was the weapons system all standard weapons are still fully functional and topped up."

"Good news at last," sighed Micha. "I had a small atmo leak, fuel is nearly depleted, but I think I can get the sensors back on line. How are you doing for radiation?"

"Lady Marla's shields held, Boss. You?"

"Clear so far as I can tell. I expect the whole system is an oven right now though. We'll have to be careful. Now, the first concern is fuel, I guess."

"Yeah, well, we're in the right neighbourhood for that," replied Gorda. "There has to be some on this wreck somewhere. I'll see if I can locate a supply."

"All right, but stay inside, Gorda. We don't want to suit up until the ladies are able to help shield us from the radiation."

"Understood."

Lessa groaned and pushed herself up on one elbow. "Did we survive?"

"We did, Lessa," grinned Micha. "We're a little beat up, but we're still in one piece."

"What's our status?"

"Both ships survived. Gorda's crew is in a little better shape than we are. We're both low on fuel and our sensors are off line. I have no idea what the radiation is doing out there."

"You see what you can do with the sensors while I see to Meggan," said Lessa as Meggan groaned, tried to sit up, and failed. Lessa reached out to help her up into a seat. "Welcome back, Meggan. That shield spell of yours is amazing."

"Thank you, Lady Arlessa," the girl smiled weakly.

"Rathbone, you're a treasure and a savior," grinned Micha as he pulled out the package of new parts for the sensor array. Seeing the two women looking at him with puzzled expressions, he went on. "Rath always stocks the ships with as many spare parts for vital systems as we can carry. The man likes to be prepared. Ah, there we go; sensors back on line."

"Gorda, I've got sensors back. Have you located any fuel?"

"Boss, it's better to be lucky than good. Somebody important must have been aboard this ship. I found a small cruiser with a full load of fuel. We can both top up if we can get outside to make the link."

"I'm showing a lot of radiation, Gorda. Don't go outside just yet."

"Understood."

"Ladies, we're nearly out of fuel and there is plenty of it to be had nearby. The problem here is the radiation levels. Is there any way you can shield me long enough for me to pirate a charge of fuel?"

"Not yet, Micha," sighed Meggan. "I can do it, but I need to rest."

"We all do, Meggan," said Lessa. "Micha, can we manage a sleep cycle before we try this?"

"I think we can manage."

"Boss, Norlene says they will need to rest and eat before we try going outside. I've got enough fuel for about ten hours before I power down."

"Understood. Let the ladies rest and eat; ten hours."

"Micha," Lessa said quietly. "How much fuel do we have?"

"Maybe ten hours," he replied, "if we're lucky."

"Wake me in eight, please."

"Aye, Boss," he grinned as he set the alarm system. It was taking a mad chance, but they all needed rest so no one stood the watch, everyone slept.

Nine hours later everyone was awake, but a long way from refreshed. They were all still exhausted from the battle and the power they had run. The women's hands trembled and their joints ached. Movement was difficult, and they were hungry.

Micha had been checking his ship and had even more bad news. "Our engines are done," he sighed. "We can maneuver a bit like we did to tuck in here, but if we open her up they'll fry. Rath is not going to be happy I lost his favorite ship.

"Micha to Gorda."

"Here Boss."

"My engines are nearly fried. We need a new plan and I think the ladies need more rest. That ship you found with the fuel; is it intact?"

"Looked like, Micha. What's the plan?"

"You pick us up then we lock up to that ship and board her. We can tow your ship behind and get the hell out of this system. Once we're clear we can rest, refuel and head out to join our people on Exile."

"Sounds like a plan to me, Boss. Locking up."

A few moments later they felt the soft bump as the two ships locked up. Once all were aboard Gorda's fighter he cut the crippled ship loose and headed for the cruiser Gorda had found. They locked up and crossed over into a luxury cruiser. There was plenty of room, sleeping quarters, and a fully stocked galley. Gorda fired up the engines and they roared to life. He grinned from ear to ear.

"Boss, this is an admiral's yacht."

"A what?"

"They all have one on their ship. An admiral doesn't come down in a shuttle; he arrives in a luxury yacht. That is what we've got."

"Like you said, Gorda, it's better to be lucky than good. Those sound like impressive engines."

"They are."

"Could we tow both fighters?"

"Probably could."

"All right, as soon as the ladies are rested up enough to shield us we'll attach both fighter to her sides and get out of this area. Once we're back in friendly space we'll trade this rig for some fuel and repairs.

"Ladies, eat hearty then rest. We'll take another sleep period then see what we can do to get ourselves out of here."

"Sounds good to me, Micha," sighed Meggan, as she snuggled deeper into a plush chair and closed her eyes.

"Cone on, girl," laughed Lessa, "the sleeping quarters are back here." She led the way and the rest of the women followed.

"I'll take first watch, Boss; you get some rest."

It was two days later before they were rested enough to get under way. The yacht hadn't been design for towing, so someone had to go outside and hook the two Arcalian ships onto the hull. Micha insisted he be the one to go. It took a lot longer to do than he'd thought and he was in bad shape by the time they got him back inside.

The whole system had been fried, including much of the Imperial fleet, even though the battle had been well outside the star's planetary range. All the witches were exhausted and struggling to keep the ship shielded. Gorda flew while they kept the radiation from cooking the entire ship. Micha lay groaning in a plush seat.

By the time they reached Arlen territory he was near death. Lessa did what she could, but her powers were depleted by the battle; she was barely keeping him alive. As soon as they touched down on a friendly planet, Norlene spoke a single word then stepped into another realm. Everyone except Lessa gasped as she disappeared.

"She's gone to rest," Lessa said wearily. "She'll return soon then we'll all go. We have to keep Micha alive until then."

"We will," said Marla, as she sat beside Micha and began to channel healing energy to him. Meggan joined her. Even as weakened as they were, they managed to keep him alive for another week until Norlene returned.

They were all gathered around Micha, the witches channeling healing energy to him and Gorda looking on sadly. In a flash of light, Norlene returned looking fully recovered. She kissed Gorda's cheek as she stepped past him and laid her hands over Micha's heart. He sighed deeply and relaxed as the wave of healing energy swept over him.

"Bring him," she said, as she rose and opened the magic portal once again. Norlene held the passageway open while the others carried Micha into that unseen realm. She stepped through and closed the gate behind them.

"Where are we?" asked Marla as she gazed around. "Oh, oh, this is the forbidden library, isn't it?"

"Yes," replied Norlene, "this is the library as it was/is in my time."

"Was/is?"

"Welcome to my world, Lady Marla. Wait here, I'll be right back." She stepped through a door and they could hear her speaking with someone outside. A short while later she returned with healing potions and other ingredients. She passed healing potions to the other three witches. She smiled with delight as she watched them visibly revive. Within an hour they felt as though they had just rested for a week.

Norlene passed a smaller potion to Gorda. "Drink up, my love; this'll put hair on your chest."

"We all know I need more of that," he grinned as he tossed down the drink. It was almost instant. He felt the wave of energy sweep through him and rose to his feet feeling better than he had in years. "I could sure start every day with a cup of that. Wow."

"Too much stimulant is bad for you, Dear," laughed Norlene. "Now, are you ladies feeling better? All right, Arlessa, you and I have a potion to prepare and you two watch carefully in case you ever need to do this again.

It took several hours, but they were going slow so Marla and Meggan could follow and remember. Norlene had given Micha a small draught of the healing potion and he was resting peacefully. When the main potion was ready Norlene stepped beside Micha and held out her hands. His body rose into the air and Lessa slipped a pail beneath him.

Lessa took over the levitation and Norlene began to pour out the mixture about two feet above Micha's sleeping form. As the liquid fell it turned to a clear mist that spread over and penetrated every inch of Micha's body. As the mist passed through Micha it turned a sickly greenish yellow and became a thick gooey liquid once again, dripping into the pail Lessa had placed to catch it.

When it was finished Norlene removed the pail of goo and set it aside. Lessa gently lowered Micha back to the pallet and he sighed deeply then opened his eyes. He stretched and yawned then sat up. "Man, I'm still tired, but I did get some sleep. How long was I out?"

"Close to three weeks all told, Boss," replied Gorda.

Micha looked closely at him, registering the concern and relief on his face. That look was on the other faces around him as well. "What happened?" he asked softly. "Last I remember was hooking the fighters to the yacht."

"Radiation sickness, Boss; you were outside way too long. We didn't think you were going to make it."

Micha slowly absorbed that bit of information then took in his surroundings. "Where are we?"

"You mean when/where are we," grinned Lessa, relief clear on her face as she suddenly hugged him tightly.

"Aw, Lessa, did I just age ten years again?" he asked, as he returned her embrace.

"You got younger, Micha," she replied, smiling through her tears. "We're in Norlene's library back in her time. Now that you're on the mend we can go home. We'll need to rest up for a few days once we get back, but we'll be all right." She stepped beside Norlene and Micha felt the air shimmer. The library vanished and a glowing corridor of light appeared.

"Let's go, family," grinned Norlene. They stepped through the portal and were back beside the ships on a spaceport platform.

A voice came over a loudspeaker system. "Nova Crew, your ships have been decontaminated, you are clear to disembark."

Micha traded the yacht for repairs on the engines and fuel for the fighters. As soon as they were ready they took off again. Two weeks later they arrived at the Arlen home world and contacted the governor.

The Arlen Alliance was in trouble; they were under attack.

"Micha, it is good to see you again, it's been months since the battle; we thought you didn't make it. Is the crew with you?"

"Small crew only, Governor," sighed Micha. "I sent most of them away just before the star exploded."

"Good to know," sighed Rathbone the Elder. "We lost a lot of ships in that battle, but you had no other choice. We were losing. Your warning was cutting it close, but a lot of us managed to limp away. Everybody went home to lick their wounds after that."

"So, who is attacking you?"

"The whole Galaxy has gone to hell, Micha, but that was your plan all along, wasn't it. Get them fighting among themselves and they'd leave us alone."

"Yeah, that was pretty much it. It nearly worked too, but nearly doesn't count. Millions of people died in that battle and I am the one who killed them. I truly wish there had been another way."

"Yes, well, there wasn't and we all know it. You did right, Micha. I've had far too much experience with Loran to trust that we'd survive under the Empire."

"So, who's attacking you?"

"The remnants of the Imperial Fleet. Some fool admiral who was on his way to join the big fleet when you blew it to the nine hells. He's declared himself Emperor and has managed to gain control of a sizable piece of the old Empire. He is determined to conquer Sector Nine."

"Well, how about it, Ladies?" asked Micha. "Are you up for another battle?"

"We're all rested and ready," said Marla grimly. "You were right all along, Micha. I remember what life was like when I wore that inhibitor, and I am ashamed that I nearly put an inhibitor on the entire sector. It is time I protected the people I swore to protect."

"Nova Temple is with you, Lady Marla," said Lessa. "We're ready to go."

"I'll have your ships serviced, then I'll lead you to the front. The Maccay have promised ships, but they'll be a while getting here."

Two days later they reached a pitched battle. In truth the Arlen's were holding their own, but once the witches entered the battle it didn't last long. They sliced up a few ships and the rest fled back towards the Hub; all but one. The self-declared Emperor would not surrender.

"Lessa, can you disable his weapons?"

"I think so, Micha," she replied.

"Do it," he said, reaching for the comms. "Lady Norlene, can you disable his engines?"

"I will, Micha." A few moments later the ship hung helpless in space. "All right, Governor, he's all yours."

"Micha, I do like your style," laughed Rathbone the Elder. "I'll call him."

"This is Governor Rathbone of the Arlen Alliance calling the second in command over there on the helpless ship."

"Captain Exor speaking; what are your terms of surrender?"

"Clap that idiot Admiral in the brig and get your people back to the hub. If you try anything else your ship will be destroyed."

"Understood and agreed. Do you want the Emperor as prisoner?"

"Just get him the hell out of my space."

"Understood. Sir, thank you for sparing our lives. We will stay out of Sector Nine in future."

"You're a smart man, Captain. All right, Micha, you can let him go."

"Let him go, Ladies." The witches released their grip on the ship and it turned towards the Hub at full burn.

Three days later the crew took their leave of the governor and headed for home.

— ⬤ —

EDIE WAS STARTING TO feel awkward as she made her way through the ship's passageways. She kept bumping her belly into things and the child always kicked hard when she did. She smiled as she felt another kick. "Relax, little Michella, relax. We will be at Exile soon and we can get some fresh air again."

It had been a long and sad flight from the battlefield to Nova. It had been even harder to explain to the Novans why only the crew's families were being evacuated and the rest were not. There had been no word at all from the battlefront. Edie refused to go into mourning and Brenna agreed with her. They had been through this before and firmly believed their mates would return.

"Edie, looks like we'll have you on solid ground soon," grinned Rathbone as she made her way onto the bridge.

"That's good news, Rath. I think my little friend wants to go out and play in the sun."

"You've got a few days yet," sang Keira. Edie laughed and sang back to her. Keira smiled at how well Edie had learned their singing-signing language.

"Zartah and Miriam are already on the surface," said Rathbone. "They're setting up with Miriam's people to make a place for us."

Suddenly the comms came to life. "Ravage, Ravage, get down here; we're under attack."

"Coming in, Zartah," replied Rath. "Leave the signal open. Jorge, take the helm; everybody else into the small fighters. Edie, stay with Jorge and man the sensors."

"I can work the guns too, Rath," she said as she move to position herself as the weapons station."

Down on the surface, Zartah and Miriam were fighting side by side with Kathan as they tried to hold off a large force of riders and hellhounds. Those were being supported by armed soldier/guardsmen from Overlord. The crew had arrived just as Orlem was being attacked.

Zartah had come in with guns blazing, scattering the attackers for a moment. He landed and Miriam leaped out just as a blast of energy disabled the ship. Zartah followed her out. Someone laid down covering fire from the cave mouth at the entrance to Orlem. They made a run for it.

"Zartah, good to see you again," shouted Kathan as he and his men fired at the attacking hellhounds, driving them back slightly.

"We were in the neighbourhood," replied Zartah as he joined Kathan. "I see you're still making friends with the locals."

"I don't think they like my politics," replied Kathan. "Nodran was quite upset that Lady Arlessa cured my addiction. His partners on Overlord weren't happy about Deela leaving either."

"Some people have no sense of humor," replied Zartah, as he reached for his comms. "Ravage, Ravage, get down here; we're under attack. Freedom, acknowledge."

"Freedom here, Zartah."

"Make sure nothing else lands or leaves this planet."

"Understood."

"I'm dry of charge," said Kathan as he tossed aside his blaster and began throwing stones at the hounds. It wasn't all that easy as there were arrows and some weapons fire aimed at the cave mouth as well.

"Here," said Zartah as he passed his blaster to Kathan. He picked up a large stone and hurled it at the enemy killing one hound instantly. "You know they have some heavier weapons and are swarming the crater from all sides."

"I know. Shoot them."

"You shoot them, you've got the blaster." At that point the Ravage began descent through the atmosphere being led by a half dozen small fighter ships. The small ships instantly went on the attack. The heavier weapons of the Ravage swiftly wiped out the cruder energy weapons of the attackers while the small fighters decimated the ranks of the hounds and hunters.

The people of Orlem had been defending themselves at the crater's rim as best they could and they gave a ragged cheer as the fighters swept the attacking forces from the rim, driving them deep into the forest. The Ravage landed, but the fighters continued to buzz around like angry bees until they were certain the attacking forces had been driven away.

Zartah and Miriam hunted through the community, rooting out and killing any hunters or hellhounds that had managed to penetrate the defenses. There were many. When it was finished, and Orlem secure, they found Kathan waiting with Wista to thank them.

"I remember Miriam and her mate," said the old woman.

"I remember Wista," replied Miriam.

"You have done a great service to Orlem. We are grateful."

"We have come to seek sanctuary," said Miriam. "Our people need a place of safety for a time, perhaps forever."

"You are welcome at Orlem; you may stay as long as you wish. We will share what we have."

"We are thankful for your hospitality," smiled Miriam.

"All right, people, land 'em; we've got permission to stay," Zartah said as he spoke into his comm unit. "Freedom, all clear up there?"

"Clear skies up here," replied Commander Darks. "Do we land?"

"Not yet. We need to secure a home here for you folks first."

"Understood." Siemon Darks sighed and smiled as he leaned back in the captain's chair.

"What?" asked his second in command.

"That crew, Dav," he replied. "Did you notice how they kept us out of the fighting because we've got our families on board?"

"I noticed. That would never have happened with the Company."

Down on the planet Zartah and Kathan were having a war council. The whole crew and several of the Muties were listening in. Commander Darks had come down to sit in as well.

"It's been pretty crazy, Zartah," sighed Kathan. "With the ship Micha gave us we have been able to keep them at bay, but a few weeks ago they located Orlem. They've been building weapons on Overlord and churning out the drugs here on Exile."

"Drugs?" asked Jorge. "Who do they sell them to?"

"They don't sell them; they use them to create and control the hunters and the hellhounds. There are very few real humans left in the compounds. They've also been sweeping the forests for humans and Muties they can convert to hunters."

"Why?" asked Jorge. "What's the whole point?"

"Slave labor for Overlord and for Exile, for one thing. They want total control on Exile for another."

"Micha wouldn't like that," said Edie.

"No, he wouldn't," agreed Zartah. "Is that why they attacked Orlem?"

"Yes. Orlem is a threat to them, or so they think. They tried to wipe us out about two weeks ago, but we managed to beat them back. This time they brought more weapons and more troops. They're bringing them in from the other compounds. All six compounds have banded together.

"I failed, Zartah. I wanted to keep Orlem safe and to find Deela to bring her here. I failed. They're still after her and me as well. Worse yet, my little ship is out of fuel. I can't even take her away to some isolated place to hide."

"Are you still breathing?" asked Edie.

"Of course."

"Then you're not finished. Zartah, you know what Micha would want us to do here."

"Yes I do, Edie. I also know he would want me to protect you and the child. We'll start tomorrow, first light."

"I do not understand," said Wista. "What are you going to do?"

"Micha does not allow slavery, Wista," smiled Edie. "He would want us to make it stop. He would want us to make Orlem safe from all this. He would destroy the slavers. Wista, we may have to stay here forever, and I will not raise my child a slave. We will make this madness stop."

"How can you make it stop?"

"Destroy the slavers," sighed Rathbone. "That's the easiest way." Keira nodded her agreement.

"All right, crew," said Zartah. "It's decided. They declared the war, so tomorrow we go to war."

"My men and I will join you," said Commander Darks.

"You need to stay on the Freedom to watch our backs and protect your families."

"There's enough civilians who can keep the Freedom in orbit," Darks grinned. "Zartah, there's nothing out here that's a threat to a ship like that and you know it. I appreciate that you're trying to keep us out of the fighting, but we're part of the crew too."

"Understood and accepted. First light we'll come at the nearest compound. We'll come in out of the rising sun. Make sure everyone understands; no retreat, no prisoners and no mercy."

"Understood, Boss," replied Darks, as he rose and headed for his small ship. "First light."

As the dawn began to break Edie was left to keep the Ravage secure while the others flew out. The compound was just waking up when the attack came. They made a strafing run, then landed. Kathan was amazed and the inhabitants of the compound were horrified at the speed and strength of these people.

The cyborgs moved with military precision as they cleared every building in the compound. Those who did not escape into the forest did not survive. The mercenaries cut down all in their path as they waded through the hunters and hellhounds. Within an hour there was a small group of human cowering in the central square, pleading for their lives while the buildings were burned to the ground and all signs of drug manufacture were destroyed.

The hard faced mercenary in charge simply pointed them to the forest and gave them a path to freedom. They could survive or not as they chose. Once the buildings were burned, the drugs destroyed, and energy weapons dismantled the walls were destroyed as well. The creatures of the forest would have easy access from now on.

Before the crew returned to Orlem at nightfall, a second compound had been destroyed. Two days later all six lay in ruins. Three small ships had tried to escape, but the Freedom had shot them down.

The next day the Ravage attacked Overlord. They set free as many slaves as possible and destroyed every plantation they could find. The professional guards who fought them were easily defeated and driven into the forests as well. Everywhere they went the message was the same. You are free to rebuild, but there will be no slavery.

By the end of a week the entire human society of two planets had been laid waste. It was time to rebuild. With the freed slaves now in control, Kathan was a man in demand. Everyone trusted and looked to him for leadership. Zartah had refueled his ship and he was constantly on the go.

The crew settled in to Orlem to wait for word about the war while Kathan ferried a number of freed slaves back to Exile to rebuild one of the compounds as a farming community. There would be no drug manufacture allowed either.

In the forest things were different and dangerous. Large numbers of hunters and hellhounds had escaped into the trees and were killing everything and everyone they could find. As their need for the drug increased, and no supply was available, the madness took them completely. Miriam led several hunting groups out to clear them away from Orlem. The rest would die from the madness of lack of the drug. In a month there would be no further threat from that quarter.

The days grew long and difficult for Edie as she grew heavier. Her time came and Micha had not returned. Edie bore her daughter in the care of Oggie, a Mutie healer, and Brenna who was more accustomed to binding wounds. Muties bear their children in the warm waters of Orlem if they can, and little Michella swam long before she walked.

The next day, after Edie had rested somewhat, everyone came to see and bless the child. It was another Mutie custom. The proud mother beamed as she showed off her baby to one and all. The last to come was Deela, leaning on Kathan's arm.

Deela gently touched the baby's forehead and suddenly lit up with a bright smile. He lives, Edie," she said. "He has returned from the shadows and is coming for you." She lightly stroked the child's cheek causing her to coo. "You are the first born of many, little one. You must help your mother all you can, for the children of the guardians will not have an easy life."

"Deela, what do you mean, returned from the shadows?"

"Your man took a burning wound, and long did he walk the shadow world between this ream and the next. Death could not claim him and he returns."

"Why didn't you tell me this before?"

"For long years I was held captive and not allowed to speak. When I was, I only spoke of darkness. Now I will only speak of light. Micha lives and is coming. Be happy, Edie."

Micha arrived three days later bringing Lady Marla with him. She wanted to see Kathan for herself. After a week of tearful reunions, celebrations, and telling of tales, Micha loaded his crew and family onto the Ravage and set course for Nova. It was time to get back to farming.

As the Ravage sped across the vast emptiness between Exile and Nova Prime, a farmer sat in the captain's chair, holding his baby daughter on his lap and smiling. The ancient warrior spirit within him slowly began to recede and allow him a measure of peace.

He had managed to survive and keep his people free from slavery. All was good in Micha's world for the moment. He smiled as he gazed at the Nova Sunburst mark on the child's shoulder. "They will all be born with it, Micha," said Lessa as she leaned over his shoulder. "Hold still now while I give you one just like it."

———⬤———

"WHAT IS IT, DEELA," asked Kathan, as he pulled her gently into his arms.

"She has marked them all now," she replied. "The time will come when that mark will be both loathed and revered, as will the people who wear it.

"Also the man of metal is being rebuilt, but he will not be the same."

"Should we find a way to warn Micha?"

"No," she smiled, "the Hound doesn't want to know his future. He told me so himself."

The End

About the Author:

Prudence MacLeod is a spiritual seeker, dog trainer, Reiki Master, interior designer, and personal trainer who has turned her hand to writing. She is an avid chess player and has recently become addicted to World of Warcraft.

In her own words, "I have roamed far and wide for over sixty years in this realm, and I have seen much; some I wish I had not, and a great deal that I would love to see again. Some days I feel like Bilbo Baggins, for I have been there and come back again. No, I haven't written a book about my wanderings, but much that I have experienced, observed, learned, surmised, or imagined, is woven into the tales I have written. I do hope you enjoy them."

Don't miss out!

Visit the website below and you can sign up to receive emails whenever Prudence MacLeod publishes a new book. There's no charge and no obligation.

https://books2read.com/r/B-A-ZKBBB-RCURC

BOOKS 2 READ

Connecting independent readers to independent writers.

Also by Prudence MacLeod

Watch for more at https://www.prudencemacleod.com/.

Telling a story is like knitting a sweater. Start with a ball of possibilities, pull out one small thread and begin. With luck and patience you will create something quite wonderful.

About the Author

On a far off windswept island Jennifer Crandall sits with her dogs and cats creating fantastic stories for all to enjoy. She publishes as JL Crandall, Prudence MacLeod, and Jenni Leigh.

Read more at https://www.prudencemacleod.com/.